Lauren

PUFFIN BOOKS

# THE NEW GOLDEN LAND

More than twenty-five years ago the poet and writer James Reeves compiled a wonderful treasury of stories and poems for parents to read with young children, and he named it *A Golden Land*. In it he combined favourite old stories like Aesop's 'Hare and Tortoise' and Andersen's 'The Constant Tin Soldier' with more recent tales from the best contemporary storytellers. Some were magical, some were more down to earth, but all were beautifully told and were the sort of stories that parent and child could share happily time after time, the kind that would linger in the memory long after the gates clanged shut on childhood.

But times and tastes keep changing, and the last twenty-five years have brought forward a wide range of talented new children's authors who deserve to be known and enjoyed with the best of the earlier writers: hence the need for this new version, carefully revised by Judith Elkin and called *The New Golden Land Anthology*. In it she has carefully preserved the best material from the old collection – for where else nowadays does one find the favourite old story of the Dutch boy who put his finger in the dyke to stop the flood, or the legend of Arthur sleeping among his warriors? – but she has included for the first time stories by Joan Aiken and Philippa Pearce and many other excellent writers who have made their mark since James Reeves compiled the first edition.

The result is a wonderfully fresh and lively collection of traditional tales and up-to-date stories, many of them comic. With finger plays and action rhymes for the very young, old- and new-fashioned nonsense from Edward Lear, Spike Milligan and Michael Rosen, riddles and tongue-twisters, folk tales and fantasies, ghost stories and school stories, this book is bound to appeal to something in every member of the family, not just the children, and to be the delight of many wet afternoons and dark winter evenings.

The book is newly illustrated with line drawings by Vanessa Julian-Ottie, with contributions from other well-known artists.

'Must be the best value ever in introducing children to a most enjoyable feast of stories and poems – old and new. This is most highly recommended' – *Books for Young Children*

# THE NEW
# GOLDEN LAND
## ANTHOLOGY

*Stories, Poems, Songs,*
*New and Old*

*Edited by Judith Elkin*

*Illustrated by Vanessa Julian-Ottie*
*and Others*

Puffin Books

PUFFIN BOOKS

Published by the Penguin Group
27 Wrights Lane, London w8 5tz, England
Viking Penguin Inc., 40 West 23rd Street, New York, New York 10010, USA
Penguin Books Australia Ltd, Ringwood, Victoria, Australia
Penguin Books Canada Ltd, 2801 John Street, Markham, Ontario, Canada l3r 1b4
Penguin Books (NZ) Ltd, 182–190 Wairau Road, Auckland 10, New Zealand

Penguin Books Ltd, Registered Offices: Harmondsworth, Middlesex, England

First published by Kestrel Books 1983
Published in Puffin Books 1984
3 5 7 9 10 8 6 4 2

*To the memory of*
JAMES REEVES

# Contents

Introduction                                                     13

LAZY TOK *by Mervyn Skipper*                                     17

LITTLE FAN (poem) *by James Reeves*                              22

'DID YOU EVER SEE A LASSIE'
  (song, Anon., with music)                                     24

THE RAT PRINCESS *by Norah Montgomerie*                          25

MY SISTER JANE (poem) *by Ted Hughes*                            28

THE YELLOW RIBBON *by Maria Leach*                               30

THE CONSTANT TIN SOLDIER *by Hans Andersen*                      32

'MOSES SUPPOSES HIS TOESES ARE ROSES'
  (poem, Anon.)                                                  38

THE HERO OF HAARLEM *by Mary Mapes Dodge*                        39

'SHE SELLS SEA-SHELLS ON THE SEA SHORE'
  (poem, Anon.)                                                  43

THE JUMBLIES (poem) *by Edward Lear*                             44

MRS SIMKIN'S BATHTUB *by Linda Allen*                            48

THE SMALL BROWN MOUSE *by Janet McNeill*                         53

QUESTIONS (poem) *by Raymond Wilson*                             62

THE GOLDEN TOUCH *by Honor Wyatt*                                63

THE STORY OF GIANT-KIPPERNOSE *by John Cunliffe*                 71

THE OLD WOMAN AND HER PIG (Anon.)                                80

PIG TALE *retold by Aidan Chambers*                             83

A GROWING TALE *by Norah Montgomerie*                            84

GROWING (poem) *by Max Fatchen*                                  86

GRUESOME (poem) by *Roger McGough* 87

'FROM WIBBLETON TO WOBBLETON' (poem, Anon.) 88

PAUL'S TALE by *Mary Norton* 89

'NOW I'LL TELL YOU A STORY' (poem, Anon.) 99

'FIVE LITTLE MONKEYS WALKED ALONG THE
SHORE' (poem, Anon.) 100

'OLD ROGER IS DEAD' (song, Anon., with music) 101

A THOUGHT (poem) by *A. A. Milne* 102

BIG SISTER AND LITTLE SISTER by *Charlotte Zolotow* 103

'PIGGY ON THE RAILWAY' (poem, Anon.) 106

FROM A RAILWAY CARRIAGE (poem) by *Robert Louis
Stevenson* 107

GIACCO AND HIS BEAN by *Florence Botsford* 108

THE LITTLE GIRL WHO GOT OUT OF BED THE
WRONG SIDE by *Ruth Ainsworth* 112

'THERE WERE TEN IN THE BED' (song, Anon.,
with music) 114

THE ALARM COCK by *Joan Aiken* 115

THE SNOOKS FAMILY by *Harcourt Williams* 125

'LAST ONE INTO BED' (poem) by *Michael Rosen* 127

THE HORRIBLE STORY by *Margaret Mahy* 130

NIGHT (poem) by *William Blake* 137

THE ADVENTURES OF ISABEL (poem) by *Ogden Nash* 138

'LITTLE ARABELLA MILLER' (song, Anon.,
with music) 140

'JELLY ON A PLATE' (poem, Anon.) 141

WHERE ARTHUR SLEEPS by *Gwyn Jones* 142

GRANNY (poem) by *Spike Milligan* 149

'OLD MOTHER TWITCHETT' (poem, Anon.) 149

'TWO LEGS SAT UPON THREE LEGS' (poem, Anon.) 150

'FOUR STIFF-STANDERS' (poem, Anon.) 151

I SAW A JOLLY HUNTER (poem) *by Charles Causley* 152

ROW, ROW, ROW YOUR BOAT (song, Anon., with music) 153

BOREDOM (poem) *by Eleanor Farjeon* 154

UNINVITED GHOSTS *by Penelope Lively* 155

A TEENY-WEENY TALE *by Norah Montgomerie* 161

THE DARK HOUSE (poem, Anon.) 163

BLIND ALLEY (poem) *by Eleanor Farjeon* 163

THE CORONATION MOB *by Jan Mark* 165

A FISHY TALE, OR HOW I JOINED THE MIXED MAGGOTS AND BOTTOM FEEDERS, *told to Gene Kemp by John Sweet* 176

THE SILVER FISH (poem) *by Shel Silverstein* 183

DADDY FELL INTO THE POND (poem) *by Alfred Noyes* 184

WELL BREAD (poem) *by Spike Milligan* 185

THE FOOL OF THE WORLD AND THE FLYING SHIP *by Arthur Ransome* 186

JUBA: A CHANT (poem, Anon.) 200

FIRST DAY AT SCHOOL (poem) *by Roger McGough* 201

BAD REPORT — GOOD MANNERS (poem) *by Spike Milligan* 202

SEND THREE AND FOURPENCE WE ARE GOING TO A DANCE *by Jan Mark* 203

'IF YOU DON'T PUT YOUR SHOES ON . . .' *by Michael Rosen* 212

WHAT DID YOU PUT IN YOUR POCKET? (poem) *by Beatrice Schenk de Regniers* 214

THE DINNER LADY WHO MADE MAGIC *by Dorothy Edwards* 219

TURTLE SOUP (poem) *by Lewis Carroll* 230

DEAR BREN *by Bernard Ashley*     231

SNAKE IN THE GRASS *by Helen Cresswell*     236

YOU TELL ME (poem) *by Michael Rosen*     245

FREDDIE, THE TOOTHBRUSH CHEAT
    *by Wendy Craig*     246

THE OWL AND THE PUSSY-CAT (poem)
    *by Edward Lear*     251

THE DUTCH CHEESE *by Walter de la Mare*     253

THE FAIRIES (poem) *by William Allingham*     262

CALICO PIE (poem) *by Edward Lear*     265

THE WELL OF THE WORLD'S END *by James Reeves*     268

THE WITCHES' CALL (poem) *by Clive Sansom*     276

IF ALL THE SEAS (poem, Anon.)     278

THE PARROT PIRATE PRINCESS *by Joan Aiken*     279

THE COW (poem) *by Ogden Nash*     291

THE CAMEL (poem) *by Ogden Nash*     292

HARE AND TORTOISE *by Aesop*     293

THE MONKEY AND THE CROCODILE *by Paul Galdone*     297

THE CROCODILE (poem) *by Lewis Carroll*     301

IF YOU SHOULD MEET A CROCODILE
    (poem, Anon.)     302

TWO OCTOPUSES *by Remy Charlip*     303

'ONE FINGER, ONE THUMB KEEP MOVING'
    (song, Anon., with music)     303

PETER HAMMERS WITH ONE HAMMER
    (song, Anon., with music)     304

I HAD A HIPPOPOTAMUS (poem) *by Patrick Barrington*     306

JOHNNY CROW'S GARDEN (poem) *by L. Leslie Brooke*     308

POOH AND PIGLET GO HUNTING *by A. A. Milne*     312

US TWO (poem) *by A. A. Milne*     317

NICHOLAS NYE (poem) *by Walter de la Mare*     319

COWS (poem) *by James Reeves*     321

THE CAT THAT WALKED BY HIMSELF
    *by Rudyard Kipling*     323

W (poem) *by James Reeves*     336

PRAYING LION *by Aidan Chambers*     337

'PETER PIPER PICKED A PECK OF PICKLED PEPPER'
    (poem, Anon.)     338

'BETTY BOTTER BOUGHT SOME BUTTER'
    (poem, Anon.)     339

TIKKI TIKKI TEMBO *by Arlene Mosel*     340

THESEUS AND THE MINOTAUR *by Charles Kingsley*     345

IT'S SPRING, IT'S SPRING (poem) *by Kit Wright*     352

A MORNING SONG (poem) *by Eleanor Farjeon*     354

TIM RABBIT *by Alison Uttley*     355

WRITTEN IN MARCH (poem) *by William Wordsworth*     360

SPELLS (poem) *by James Reeves*     362

OLD SHELLOVER (poem) *by Walter de la Mare*     363

GUESS *by Philippa Pearce*     364

THE WIND IN A FROLIC (poem) *by William Howitt*     372

THREE RAINDROPS *by Terry Jones*     375

*Index of Titles*     377

*Index of Authors*     379

*Index of First Lines of Verse*     381

*Index of Artists*     382

*The Stories and Poems Classified*     383

*Acknowledgements*     388

# Introduction

This is a new edition of the lovely big anthology of stories, poems, rhymes and songs, chosen by the writer and poet, James Reeves, 25 years ago and called *A Golden Land*. James Reeves was a perceptive editor who knew instinctively what would appeal to children. Over the years, the book established itself as a great favourite with children and also as a standard treasury for parents and storytellers.

Now, a quarter of a century later, we live in an electronic age where television, radio, video recorders, cassette recorders, computers, electronic games and microchip technology are part of a child's everyday experience. Yet there is still nothing that can really take the place of a book in terms of flexibility, ease of access and convenience. A book can be read almost anywhere: in the bath, in bed, up a tree, on a remote island. It can be read at the reader's individual pace and requires no additional equipment.

There is also no substitute for the direct impact of listening to and sharing stories with other people, whether they be parents, teachers, siblings or librarians. Storytelling can give an intimacy and directness which even the printed word does not always convey to the child. The joy of a story or poem shared is still something to be treasured.

Stories evoke response, recognition, identification and stimulation. They educate the emotions, they stretch the imagination and they develop a child's sense of humour, sense of fun, awareness of life. In his introduction to *A Golden Land*, James Reeves said, 'The regions to which language transports the adult are often dark and clouded. But to children the land of romance, is, or should be, a golden land. To a child, language makes familiar things permanent and unknown things near. He delights to discover a story or a poem which describes what he knows – his home, his pets, the world just outside his window; and curiosity about the world he cannot reach is awakened and fulfilled by stories of the unfamiliar.

'Books are of two kinds – those which are read to be forgotten, and those which are read to be remembered. Both kinds have their uses, but I have not here been concerned with the former kind. I have tried to find stories and poems and songs which children will want not only to hear and read, but to hear and read over and over again. The poems have been chosen for what has seemed to me some quality of language which will give pleasure long after the novelty has worn off. The stories are of three kinds – those which have delighted successive generations ever since they were written; those which were once known and have been unjustly forgotten; those which are new but have the qualities that make for lasting appeal.'

The last twenty-five years have seen an enormous growth in writing and publishing for children. In *The New Golden Land Anthology*, I have tried to reflect the wealth of this writing, whilst keeping faith with James Reeves's original aims. I have retained much of his original choice, particularly the stories, songs and poems which have not dated in any real sense. I have added to these, stories, poems, rhymes and songs by some of the many talented writers of the past 25 years: Philippa Pearce, Jan Mark, Joan Aiken, Bernard Ashley, Michael Rosen, Roger McGough, Spike Milligan. Some well-known children's writers have not written short tales and, as I have deliberately only selected stories which are complete in themselves, are not represented here.

I have tried to maintain a careful balance: between different types of stories, from reality to fantasy; between those items which should be read aloud and those intended for private reading; between the actual number of stories, poems and songs; between the serious and the light-hearted, so that children of different ages, abilities and interests might find something here for them. There are traditional tales and some present-day equivalents; the old much-loved nonsense of Edward Lear and Lewis Carroll and the more recent nonsense of Michael Rosen and Kit Wright; Greek legends, fantasy stories and stories with a contemporary setting; traditional rhymes and modern chants and songs.

As intended with the original edition, this is a book to be dipped into at random, so there is no logical or thematic arrangement. But I hope that wherever children begin in the book, they will quickly find something to please them. I also wanted the book to have lots of illustrations, so that it is worth looking at, a pleasure to the eye, as well as to the ear and the imagination. Vanessa Julian-Ottie has lavishly illustrated the collection, and there are also additional drawings by some of the very best of today's illustrators for children. I hope that there is something in this book for every member of the family, whether young or old, to share together or enjoy in private, to find afresh or to find anew the Golden Land.

JUDITH ELKIN

# Lazy Tok

Tok was born lazy. When she was a baby, everybody said what a good baby she was because she never cried, but really she was too lazy to cry. It was too much trouble. The older she grew the lazier she became, until she got so lazy that she was too tired to go and look for food for herself. One day she was sitting by the side of the river, too lazy to wonder where her next meal was coming from, when a Nipah Tree on the other side of the river spoke to her.

'Good evening, Tok,' he said. 'Would you like to know how to get your meals without having to work for them?'

Tok was too lazy to answer, but she nodded her head.

'Well, come over here and I'll tell you,' said the Nipah Tree.

'Oh, I'm much too weary to come over there. Couldn't you come over here?' yawned Tok.

'Very well,' said the Nipah Tree, and he bent over the river.

'Just tear off one of my branches,' he said.

'Oh, what a nuisance,' said Tok. 'Couldn't you shake one down yourself?'

So the Nipah Tree shook himself and down dropped one of his branches at Tok's feet.

'Good evening, Tok,' said the Nipah Branch. 'Would

17

you like to be able to get your meals without having to work for them?'

Tok was too lazy to answer, but she nodded her head.

'Well,' said the Nipah Branch, 'all you've got to do is to make a basket out of me.'

'Good gracious,' said Tok. 'What a bother. Couldn't you make yourself into a basket without my help?'

'Oh, very well,' said the Nipah Branch, and he made himself into a nice, neat, wide, fat basket.

'Good evening, Tok,' said the Basket. 'Would you like to be able to get your meals without having to work for them?'

Tok was too lazy to answer, but she nodded her head.

'Then pick me up and carry me to the edge of the road and leave me there.'

'Good gracious me,' said Tok, 'do you think I'm a slave? Couldn't you pick yourself up and go without bothering me?'

'Oh, very well,' said the Basket, and he picked himself up and went off and laid himself down by the side of the road.

He hadn't been waiting there long before a fat Chinaman came along.

'Shen mao tung shi!' said the Chinaman. 'Here's a fine basket somebody has dropped. It will just do for me to carry my goods home from market in.'

So he picked up the Basket and went off to market with it. He soon had it full of rice, potatoes, pumelos, durians, dried shrimps and other things too numerous to mention, and when it was full up he started off home with it.

After a while he felt hot and tired, so he put the Basket

under a tree and went off to sleep. As soon as the Basket saw that the Chinaman was fast asleep, up it jumped and ran away back to Lazy Tok.

'Here I am,' said the Basket. 'Here I am, full to the brim. You have only to empty me out, and you will have enough food to last you a week.'

'Dear, oh, dear!' said Lazy Tok. 'What a bother. Couldn't you empty yourself out?'

'Oh, very well,' said the Basket cheerfully, and he emptied himself into Lazy Tok's lap.

Next week, when Lazy Tok had eaten all the food, the Basket went off again and lay down on the grass by the side of the road. This time a Booloodoopy came along, and when he saw the Basket he thought it would be fine to carry his goods home from market; so he picked it up and took it off to the market. When it was full of pine-apples and pumelos and all sorts of things too numerous to mention, he started off home with it, but he hadn't gone far before he felt tired and hot and sat down on the side of the road to have a nap. As soon as he had fallen asleep, up jumped the Basket and ran home to Lazy Tok.

So every week the Basket got itself carried to the market and came back full of fruit and rice and all sorts of other nice things too numerous to mention; and Lazy Tok sat on the river bank and ate and ate and ate and got fatter and fatter and lazier and lazier, until she became so fat and so lazy that she simply couldn't feed herself.

'Here we are waiting to be eaten,' said the Fruit and the Shrimps and the other nice things one day.

'Oh, bother,' said Lazy Tok. 'Couldn't you feed me your-self, without giving me so much trouble?'

'We'll try,' said the Fruit and the Shrimps and the other
nice things; so after that they used to drop into her mouth
without giving her any unnecessary trouble.

So Lazy Tok grew fatter and FATTER and FATTER
and lazier and LAZIER and L A Z I E R, until one day the
Basket went off to lie down by the side of the road, just
when the fat Chinaman who had picked up the Basket the
first time came along.

'Twee!' he said angrily. 'There you are, you thieving
scoundrel!' and he picked up the Basket and took it to the
market to show all his friends what had been robbing them.
All his friends came round and looked at the Basket and
cried, 'That is the rascal that has been robbing us!'

So they took the Basket and filled it full of soldier ants,

lizards, hot-footed scorpions, bees, wasps, leeches and all sorts of other creeping, prickling, biting, stinging, tickling and itchy things far too unpleasant to mention; after which they let the Basket go.

Off ran the Basket with his load of bugs and beetles and centipedes and gnats and ran straight home to Lazy Tok.

'What have you got for me today?' asked Lazy Tok.

'You'd better get up and look,' said the Basket.

'Oh, dear me, no!' said Tok. 'I'm so tired, and I feel I couldn't stir a finger. Just empty yourself into my lap.'

So ... the Basket emptied the ants and beetles and other things too horrible to mention into Lazy Tok's lap.

Lazy Tok got up and ran and ran and ran, as she had never run in her life before. But the ants, beetles and scorpions ran after her, and the leeches and lizards crawled after her, and the wasps and bees flew after her; and they stung her and bit her and pricked her; and the harder she ran the harder they bit her. As far as I know, she may be running still, and she is thinner than ever.

MERVYN SKIPPER
*Illustrated by* COLIN MCNAUGHTON

# Little Fan

'I don't like the look of little Fan, mother,
  I don't like her looks a little bit.
Her face – well, it's not exactly different,
  But there's something wrong with it.

'She went down to the sea-shore yesterday,
  And she talked to somebody there.
Now she won't do anything but sit
  And comb out her yellowy hair.

'Her eyes are shiny and she sings, mother,
  Like nobody ever sang before.
Perhaps they gave her something queer to eat,
  Down by the rocks on the shore.

'Speak to me, speak, little Fan dear,
  Aren't you feeling very well?
Where have you been and what are you singing,
  And what's that seaweedy smell?

'Where did you get that shiny comb, love,
  And those pretty coral beads so red?
Yesterday you had two legs, I'm certain,
  But now there's something else instead.

'I don't like the looks of little Fan, mother,
  You'd best go and close the door.
Watch now, or she'll be gone for ever
  To the rocks by the brown sandy shore.'

JAMES REEVES
*Illustrated by* EDWARD ARDIZZONE

# 'Did you ever see a lassie'

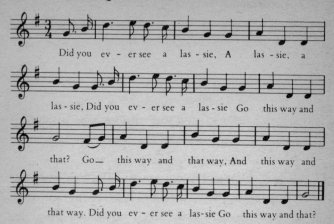

Did you ev – er see a las-sie, A las-sie, a las-sie, Did you ev – er see a las-sie Go this way and that? Go— this way and that way, And this way and that way. Did you ev – er see a las-sie Go this way and that?

[*Children form a ring. One child in the centre performs an action. Everyone imitates the action.*]

Did you ever see a lassie,
A lassie, a lassie,
Did you ever see a lassie
Go this way and that?

Go this way and that way,
And this way and that way.
Did you ever see a lassie
Go this way and that?

ANON.

*Illustrated by* SALLY KILROY

# The Rat Princess

Once upon a time there was a Rat Princess who lived with her mother, the Rat Queen, and her father, the Rat King. They all lived together in a ricefield.

The Rat King and the Rat Queen thought their daughter was the most beautiful rat in the whole world, and they would allow no one to play with her. When she grew up, they were determined she should marry the most powerful person on the earth or in the sky, for no one else would be good enough.

So they went to the Oldest and Wisest Rat and said, 'Tell us, who is the most powerful person in the world?'

The Oldest and Wisest Rat thought for a while and said, 'The Sun is the most powerful, for he makes the rice grow and ripen; yes, the Sun is the one.'

So the Rat King went to find the Sun. He climbed a mountain, ran along a rainbow and at last he came to the Sun.

'What do you want, little brother?' asked the Sun.

'I come to offer you the hand of my daughter, the Rat Princess, in marriage, for you are the most powerful in the whole world, O Sun, and no one else is good enough.'

'Ho! ho! ho!' laughed the Sun. 'You are kind, little brother, but if that is the case, the Princess is not for me. The Cloud is more powerful, for when he passes me I cannot shine.'

'Oh, indeed,' said the Rat King, 'then you'll not do.' And away he went, along the Sun's rays, till he came to the Cloud.

'What do you want, little brother?' sighed the Cloud.

'I come to offer you the hand of my daughter, the Rat Princess, in marriage, for you are the most powerful in the whole world, O Cloud, and no one else is good enough.'

'You are kind, little brother,' sighed the Cloud, 'but if that is the case, the Princess is not for me, for the Wind is far more powerful. When he blows, I must go wherever he sends me.'

'Oh, indeed,' said the Rat King, 'then you'll not do.'

Away he went till he came to the Wind's home at the very edge of the world.

'What do you want, little brother?' asked the Wind.

'I come to offer you the hand of my daughter, the Rat Princess, in marriage, for you are the most powerful in the whole world, O Wind, and no one else is good enough.'

'Ha! ha! ha!' laughed the Wind in a loud gusty roar. 'You are kind, little brother, but if that's the case, then the Princess is not for me. The Great Wall that man made is much stronger than I am. I cannot move him, no matter how hard I blow.'

'Oh, indeed,' said the Rat King, 'then you'll not do,' and away he went, back to earth and across the mountains till he came to the Great Wall of China.

'What do you want, little brother?' asked the Great Wall.

'I come to offer the hand of my daughter, the Rat ~~ess, in marriage, for you are the most powerful one~~ whole world, O Wall of China, and no one else ~~enough.'~~

'Ugh, ugh, ugh,' grumbled the Great Wall, 'you are very kind, but if that's the case, the Princess is not for me. I'm not the most powerful. The Grey Rat, who lives under me, is much stronger, for when he gnaws and gnaws at me, I crumble. And one of these days I shall fall down altogether!'

So, after searching the wide world for the most powerful person, the Rat King had to marry his beautiful daughter to an ordinary rat after all.

But the Princess did not mind, in fact she was very pleased, for *she* had wanted to marry the Grey Rat all the time.

NORAH MONTGOMERIE

## My Sister Jane

And I say nothing – no, not a word
About our Jane. Haven't you heard?
She's a bird, a bird, a bird, a bird.
Oh it never would do to let folks know
My sister's nothing but a great big crow.

Each day (we daren't send her to school)
She pulls on stockings of thick blue wool
To make her pin crow legs look right,
Then fits a wig of curls on tight,
And dark spectacles – a huge pair
To cover her very crowy stare.
Oh it never would do to let folks know
My sister's nothing but a great big crow.

When visitors come she sits upright
(With her wings and her tail tucked out of sight).
They think her queer but extremely polite.
Then when the visitors have gone
She whips out her wings and with her wig on
Whirls through the house at the height of your head –
Duck, duck, or she'll knock you dead.
Oh it never would do to let folks know
My sister's nothing but a great big crow.

At meals whatever she sees she'll stab it –
Because she's a crow and that's a crow habit.
My mother says 'Jane! Your manners! Please!'
Then she'll sit quietly on the cheese,
Or play the piano nicely by dancing on the keys –
Oh it never would do to let folks know
My sister's nothing but a great big crow.

TED HUGHES

*Illustrated by* JOHN DYKE *and* ROSS THOMPSON

# The Yellow Ribbon

Once there was a boy named John and a girl named Jane. John loved Jane very much. They lived next door to each other, and they went to nursery school together.

Every day John would carry Jane's books to school and every day Jane wore a yellow ribbon around her neck.

One day John said, 'Jane, why do you wear that yellow ribbon around your neck?'

'I can't tell,' said Jane, 'and anyway I don't feel like telling you.' But John kept asking, and finally Jane said perhaps she'd tell him later sometime.

The next year John and Jane were in the infant school. One day John asked again, 'Janey, why do you wear that yellow ribbon around your neck?'

'It's not really your affair, John; perhaps I'll tell you some-time . . . but not now,' said Jane.

Time went by; John still loved Jane and Jane loved John. And John carried Jane's books to school and Jane wore the yellow ribbon around her neck. They were in the junior school . . . then secondary school. And every once in a while John asked Jane why she wore the yellow ribbon, but Jane never told. 'We've been friends a long time, John, what difference does it make?' she said. And so time went by.

John and Jane went through secondary school together. John still loved Jane and Jane loved John. John carried Jane's books to school and Jane still wore the yellow ribbon around her neck. On the last day John said, 'Jane, we're leaving. Won't you *please* tell me why you wear that ribbon around your neck?'

'Oh, John,' said Jane, 'there's no point in telling you now . . . but some day I will.' And that day passed.

Time went by, and John still loved Jane and Jane loved John and Jane still wore that yellow ribbon around her neck.

One day, John and Jane became engaged.

'Why do you wear that yellow ribbon around your neck, Jane love?' said John, and finally Jane said perhaps she would tell him why on their wedding day.

But the wedding day came, and what with all the preparations for the wedding and the honeymoon, John just forgot to ask. But several days later, John asked Jane why she wore that yellow ribbon around her neck.

'Well, we are happily married and we love each other, so what difference does it make, John?' said Jane. So John let that pass, but he still *did* want to know.

Time went by. John loved Jane and Jane loved John. Lovely children were born to them, and they were so busy bringing them up that before they knew it, it was their golden wedding anniversary.

'Jane, why do you wear that yellow ribbon around your neck?' asked John once more. And Jane said, 'Since you have waited this long, you can wait a little longer. I'll tell you some day, John.'

Time went by. John loved Jane and Jane loved John. Finally, Jane was taken very ill and was dying. John bent on his knees by her bedside, and with sobs in his voice asked, 'Janey, *please* tell me: Why do you wear that yellow ribbon around your neck?'

'All right, John. You may untie it now,' said Jane.

So John did . . . AND JANE'S HEAD FELL OFF!

MARIA LEACH, *adapted by* VIRGINIA TASHJIAN

# The Constant Tin Soldier

There were once five and twenty tin soldiers, all brothers, for they had all been made out of one old tin spoon. They carried muskets in their arms, and held themselves very upright, and their uniforms were red and blue – very gay indeed. The first words they heard in this world, when the lid was taken off the box wherein they lay, were, 'Tin soldiers!' It was a little boy who made this exclamation, clapping his hands at the same time. They had been given to him because it was his birthday. He now set them out on the table.

The soldiers resembled each other to a hair. One only was rather different from the rest; he had but one leg, for he had been made last, when there was not quite enough tin left. He stood as firmly, however, upon his one leg as the others did upon their two; and this very tin soldier it is whose fortunes seem to us worthy of being told.

On the table where the tin soldiers were set out were several other playthings, but the most charming of them all was a pretty pasteboard castle. Through its little windows one could look into the rooms. In front of the castle stood some tiny trees, clustering round a little mirror intended to represent a lake. Some waxen swans swam in the lake and were reflected on its surface.

All this was very pretty, but prettiest of all was a little damsel standing in the open doorway of the castle. She, too, was cut out of pasteboard, but she had on a frock of the clearest muslin, a little sky-blue riband was flung across her shoulders like a scarf, and in the midst of this scarf was set a bright gold wing. The little lady stretched out both her arms, for she was a dancer, and raised one of her legs so high in the air that the tin soldier could not see it, and fancied she had, like him, only one leg.

'That would be just the wife for me,' thought he, 'but then she is of rather too high a rank. She lives in a castle, I have only a box. Besides, the box is not my own; there are all our five and twenty men in it; it is no place for her! However, there will be no harm in my making acquaintance with her,' and so he stationed himself behind a snuff-box that stood on the table. From this place he had a full view of the delicate little lady, who still remained standing on one leg, yet without losing her balance.

When evening came, all the other tin soldiers were put away into the box, and the people of the house went to bed. The playthings now began to play in their turn. They pretended to visit, to fight battles and give balls. The tin soldiers rattled in the box, for they wanted to play too, but the lid would not come off. The nut-crackers cut capers, and the slate-pencil played at buying and selling on the slate. There was such a racket that the canary-bird woke up and began to talk too; but he always talked in verse. The only two who did not move from their places were the little tin soldier and the beautiful dancer. She constantly remained in her graceful position, standing on the very tip of her toe, with outstretched arms; and, as for him, he stood just as firmly on his one leg, never for a single moment turning his eyes away from her.

Twelve o'clock struck. Crash! Open sprang the lid of the snuff-box, but there was no snuff inside it; no, out jumped a little black conjurer, in fact it was a Jack-in-the-box. 'Tin soldier!' said the conjurer, 'please keep your eyes to yourself!'

But the tin soldier pretended not to hear.

'Well, only wait till tomorrow!' said the conjurer.

When the morrow had come, and the children were out of bed, the tin soldier was placed on the window-ledge, and, whether the conjurer or the wind caused it, all at once the window flew open, and out fell the tin soldier, head foremost, from the third storey to the ground. A dreadful fall was that! His one leg turned over and over in the air, and at last he rested, poised on his soldier's cap, with his bayonet between the paving-stones.

The maid-servant and the little boy immediately came down to look for him; but although they very nearly trod on him they could not see him. If the tin soldier had but called out, 'Here I am!' they might easily have found him; but he thought it would not be becoming for him to cry out, as he was in uniform.

It now began to rain; every drop fell heavier than the last; there was a soaking shower. When it was over, two boys came by.

'Look,' said one, 'here is a tin soldier; he shall have a sail for once in his life.'

So they made a boat out of an old newspaper, and put the tin soldier into it. Away he sailed down the gutter, both the boys running along by the side and clapping their

hands. The paper boat rocked to and fro, and every now
and then veered round so quickly that the tin soldier became
quite giddy; still he moved not a muscle, looked straight
before him, and held his bayonet tightly clasped.

All at once the boat sailed under a long gutter-board.
He found it as dark here as at home in his own box.

'Where shall I get to next?' thought he. 'Yes, to be sure,
it is all that conjurer's doing! Ah, if the little maiden were
but sailing with me in the boat I would not mind it being
twice as dark!'

Just then a great water-rat that lived under the gutter-
board darted out from its nest.

'Have you a passport?' asked the rat. 'Where is your passport?'

But the tin soldier was silent, and held his weapon with
a still firmer grasp. The boat sailed on, and the rat followed.

Oh! how furiously he showed his teeth, and cried out to sticks and straws: 'Stop him, stop him! he has not paid the toll; he has not shown his passport!' But the stream grew stronger and stronger. The tin soldier could already catch a glimpse of the bright daylight before the boat came from under the tunnel, but at the same time he heard a roaring noise, at which the boldest heart might well have trembled. Where the tunnel ended, the water of the gutter fell into a great canal. This was as dangerous for the tin soldier as sailing down a mighty waterfall would be for us.

He was now so close to the fall that he could no longer stand upright. The boat darted forwards, the poor tin soldier held himself as still and immovable as possible; no one could accuse him of having even blinked. The boat span round and round three, nay, four times, and was filled with water to the brim; it must sink.

The tin soldier stood up to his neck in water; deeper and deeper sank the boat, softer and softer grew the paper; the water went over the soldier's head. He thought of the pretty little dancer whom he should never see again, and these words ran in his ears:

> Wild adventure, mortal danger,
> Be thy portion, valiant stranger!

The paper now tore asunder, the tin soldier fell through the rent; but at that moment he was swallowed up by a large fish. Oh, how dark it was! worse even than under the gutter-board, and so narrow too! But the tin soldier was as constant as ever; there he lay, at full length, still shouldering his arms.

The fish turned and twisted about, and made the strangest movements. At last he became quite still; a flash of lightning, as it were, darted through him. The daylight shone brightly, and someone exclaimed, 'Tin soldier!' The fish had been caught, taken to the market, sold and brought home into the kitchen, where the servant-girl was cutting him up with a large knife. She seized the tin soldier by the middle with two of her fingers, and took him into the next room, where everyone was eager to see the wonderful man who had travelled in the maw of a fish. Our little warrior, however, was by no means proud.

They set him on the table, and there – no, how could anything so extraordinary happen in this world? – the tin soldier was in the very room in which he had been before. He saw the same children, the same playthings on the table – among them the beautiful castle with the pretty little dancing maiden, who was still standing upon one leg, while she held the other high in the air; she too was constant. It quite affected the tin soldier; he could have found it in his heart to weep tin tears, but such weakness would have been unbecoming in a soldier. He looked at her and she looked at him, but neither spoke a word.

And now one of the little boys took the soldier and threw him without ceremony into the stove. He did not give any reason for so doing, but no doubt the conjurer in the snuff-box must have had a hand in it.

The tin soldier now stood in a blaze of red light. He felt extremely hot. Whether this heat was the result of the actual fire or of the flames of love within him he knew not. He looked upon the little damsel, she looked upon him, and he felt that he was melting; but, constant as ever,

37

he still stood shouldering his arms. A door opened, the wind seized the dancer, and, like a sylph, she flew straightway into the stove, to the tin soldier; they both flamed up into a blaze, and were gone. The soldier was melted and dripped down among the ashes, and when the maid cleaned out the fireplace the next day she found his remains in the shape of a little tin heart; of the dancer all that was left was the gold wing, and that was burnt black as coal.

HANS ANDERSEN
*Illustrated by* ANTONY MAITLAND

## 'Moses supposes his toeses are roses'

Moses supposes his toeses are roses,
But Moses supposes erroneously;
For nobody's toeses are posies of roses
As Moses supposes his toeses to be.

ANON.

# The Hero of Haarlem

Many years ago there lived in Haarlem, one of the principal cities of Holland, a sunny-haired boy of gentle disposition. His father was a *sluicer*, that is, a man whose business it was to open the sluices, or large oaken gates that are placed at regular distances across the entrances of the canals, to regulate the amount of water that shall flow into them.

The sluicer raises the gates more or less according to the quantity of water required, and closes them carefully at night, in order to avoid all possible danger of an over-supply running into the canal, or the water would soon overflow it and inundate the surrounding country. As a great portion of Holland is lower than the level of the sea, the waters are kept from flooding the land only by means of strong dikes, or barriers, and by means of these sluices, which are often strained to the utmost by the pressure of the rising tides. Even the little children in Holland know that constant watchfulness is required to keep the rivers and ocean from overwhelming the country, and that a moment's neglect of the sluicer's duty may bring ruin and death to all.

One lovely afternoon, when the boy was about eight years old, he obtained his parents' consent to carry some cakes to a blind man who lived out in the country, on the other side of the dike. The little fellow started on his errand with a light heart, and having spent an hour with his grateful old friend, he bade him farewell and started on his homeward walk.

Trudging stoutly along by the canal, he noticed how the autumn rains had swollen the waters. Even while humming his careless, childish song, he thought of his father's brave old gates and felt glad of their strength, for, thought he, 'if *they* gave way, where would father and mother be? These pretty fields would be all covered with the angry waters – father always calls them the *angry* waters; I suppose he thinks they are mad at him for keeping them out so long.' And with these thoughts just flitting across his brain, the boy stooped to pick the pretty blue flowers that grew along his way. Sometimes he stopped to throw some feathery seed-ball in the air and watch it as it floated away; sometimes he listened to the stealthy rustling of a rabbit, speeding through the grass, but oftener he smiled as he recalled the happy light he had seen arise on the weary, listening face of his blind old friend.

Suddenly the boy looked around him in dismay. He had not noticed that the sun was setting: now he saw that his long shadow on the grass had vanished. It was growing dark, he was still some distance from home, and in a lonely ravine, where even the blue flowers had turned grey. He quickened his footsteps; and with a beating heart recalled many a nursery tale of children lost in dreary forests. Just as he was bracing himself for a run, he was startled by the sound of trickling water. Whence did it come? He looked up and saw a small hole in the dike through which a tiny stream was flowing. Any child in Holland will shudder at the thought of a *leak in the dike*! The boy understood the danger at a glance. That little hole, if the water were allowed to trickle through, would soon be a large one, and a terrible inundation would be the result.

Quick as a flash, he saw his duty. Throwing away his flowers, the boy clambered up the heights until he reached the hole. His chubby little finger was thrust in, almost before he knew it. The flowing was stopped! 'Ah!' he thought, with a chuckle of boyish delight, 'the angry waters must stay back now! Haarlem shall not be drowned while *I* am here!'

This was all very well at first, but the night was falling rapidly; chill mists filled the air. The boy began to tremble with cold and dread. He shouted loudly; he screamed, 'Come here! come here!' but no one came. The cold grew more

intense, a numbness, commencing in the tired little finger, crept over his whole hand and arm, and soon his whole body was filled with pain. He shouted again, 'Will no one come? Mother! Mother!' Alas, his mother, good, practical soul, had already locked the doors, and had fully resolved to scold him on the morrow for spending the night with blind Jansen without her permission. He tried to whistle, perhaps some straggling boy might heed the signal; but his teeth chattered so, it was impossible. Then he called on God for help; and the answer came, through a holy resolution – 'I will stay here till morning.'

The midnight moon looked down upon that small solitary form, sitting upon a stone, half-way up the dike. His head was bent, but he was not asleep, for every now and then one restless hand rubbed feebly the outstretched arm that seemed fastened to the dike – and often the pale, tearful face turned quickly at some real or fancied sound.

How can we know the sufferings of that long and fearful watch – what falterings of purpose, what childish terrors came over the boy as he thought of the warm little bed at home, of his parents, his brothers and sisters, then looked into the cold, dreary night! If he drew away that tiny finger, the angry waters, grown angrier still, would rush forth, and never stop until they had swept over the town. No, he would hold it there till daylight – if he lived! He was not very sure of living. What did this strange buzzing mean? And then the knives that seemed pricking and piercing him from head to foot? He was not sure now that he could draw his finger away, even if he wished to.

At daybreak a clergyman, returning from the bedside of a sick parishioner, thought he heard groans as he walked along on the top of the dike. Bending, he saw, far down the side, a child apparently writhing with pain.

'In the name of wonder, boy,' he exclaimed, 'what are you doing there?'

'I am keeping the water from running out,' was the simple answer. 'Tell them to come quick.'

It is needless to add that they did come quickly and that the dike was repaired before further damage occurred. As for the boy who saved Haarlem, he was taken home and soon recovered his strength. Ever since that time, the people of Holland have remembered him as one of the heroes of their country.

MARY MAPES DODGE

## 'She sells sea-shells on the sea shore'

She sells sea-shells on the sea shore;
The shells that she sells are sea-shells I'm sure.
So if she sells sea-shells on the sea shore,
I'm sure that the shells are sea-shore shells.

ANON.

# The Jumblies

## I

They went to sea in a Sieve, they did,
   In a Sieve they went to sea:
In spite of all their friends could say,
On a winter's morn, on a stormy day,
   In a Sieve they went to sea!
And when the Sieve turned round and round,
And every one cried, 'You'll all be drowned!'
They called aloud, 'Our Sieve ain't big,
But we don't care a button! we don't care a fig!
   In a Sieve we'll go to sea!'
     *Far and few, far and few,*
       *Are the lands where the Jumblies live;*
      *Their heads are green, and their hands are blue,*
       *And they went to sea in a Sieve.*

## II

They sailed away in a Sieve, they did,
  In a Sieve they sailed so fast,
With only a beautiful pea-green veil
Tied with a riband by way of a sail,
  To a small tobacco-pipe mast;
And every one said, who saw them go,
'O won't they be soon upset, you know!
For the sky is dark, and the voyage is long,
And happen what may, it's extremely wrong
  In a Sieve to sail so fast!'
    *Far and few, far and few,*
      *Are the lands where the Jumblies live;*
      *Their heads are green, and their hands are blue,*
      *And they went to sea in a Sieve.*

## III

The water it soon came in, it did,
  The water it soon came in;
So to keep them dry, they wrapped their feet
In a pinky paper all folded neat,
  And they fastened it down with a pin.
And they passed the night in a crockery-jar,
And each of them said, 'How wise we are!
Though the sky be dark, and the voyage be long,
Yet we never can think we were rash or wrong,
  While round in our Sieve we spin!'
    *Far and few, far and few,*
      *Are the lands where the Jumblies live;*
      *Their heads are green, and their hands are blue,*
      *And they went to sea in a Sieve.*

### IV

And all night long they sailed away;
   And when the sun went down,
They whistled and warbled a moony song
To the echoing sound of a coppery gong,
   In the shade of the mountains brown.
'O Timballo! How happy we are,
When we live in a sieve and a crockery-jar,
And all night long in the moonlight pale,
We sail away with a pea-green sail,
   In the shade of the mountains brown!'
     *Far and few, far and few,*
      *Are the lands where the Jumblies live;*
      *Their heads are green, and their hands are blue,*
      *And they went to sea in a Sieve.*

### V

They sailed to the Western Sea, they did,
   To a land all covered with trees,
And they bought an Owl, and a useful Cart,
And a pound of Rice, and a Cranberry Tart,
   And a hive of silvery Bees.
And they bought a Pig, and some green Jack-daws,
And a lovely Monkey with lollipop paws,
And forty bottles of Ring-Bo-Ree,
   And no end of Stilton Cheese.
     *Far and few, far and few,*
      *Are the lands where the Jumblies live;*
      *Their heads are green, and their hands are blue,*
      *And they went to sea in a Sieve.*

## VI

And in twenty years they all came back,
  In twenty years or more,
And every one said, 'How tall they've grown!
For they've been to the Lakes, and the Terrible Zone,
  And the hills of the Chankly Bore';
And they drank their health, and gave them a feast
Of dumplings made of beautiful yeast;
And every one said, 'If we only live,
We too will go to sea in a Sieve, –
  To the hills of the Chankly Bore!'
    *Far and few, far and few,*
      *Are the lands where the Jumblies live;*
      *Their heads are green, and their hands are blue,*
        *And they went to sea in a Sieve.*

*Written and illustrated by* EDWARD LEAR

# Mrs Simkin's Bathtub

'Are you aware,' said Mr Simkin to Mrs Simkin one morning, 'that the bathtub's half-way down the stairs?'

'How very inconvenient,' said Mrs Simkin, going to have a look. 'How long has it been there?'

'I have no idea,' said Mr Simkin. 'It was in the bathroom when I went to bed last night, and now it's here, so it must have moved when we were asleep.'

'Well, we shall just have to make the best of it,' said Mrs Simkin. 'Will you bath first or shall I?'

'I will,' said Mr Simkin bravely.

He stepped into the bathtub. It wobbled a bit at first, but it soon settled down. Mrs Simkin fetched soap and towels, shampoo and bath salts, and arranged them nicely on the stairs.

'There,' she said, 'it doesn't look too bad now, and if I polish the taps and scrub the feet it should look quite smart. I'm sure none of the neighbours has a bathtub on the stairs.'

Mr Simkin said she was probably right.

After a day or two they hardly noticed that the bathtub was there at all. It didn't really inconvenience them to squeeze past it when they wanted to go upstairs, and the landing smelt so pleasantly of bath oil that Mrs Simkin began to feel quite happy about it.

She invited the lady next door to have a look, but the lady next door said that she didn't approve of these modern ideas and, anyhow, she had never been one to give herself airs.

One morning Mr Simkin went to have his bath. 'My dear!' he cried. 'Come and see! The bathtub's gone!'

'Gone!' cried Mrs Simkin, leaping out of bed. 'Gone where?'

'I don't know,' said Mr Simkin, 'but it isn't on the stairs.'

'Perhaps it's back in the bathroom,' said Mrs Simkin. They went to have a look but it wasn't there.

'We shall have to buy another one,' said Mr Simkin as they went down to breakfast. The bathtub was in the kitchen.

'You know, my dear,' said Mr Simkin a few minutes later, 'this is a much better place for a bathtub than half-way down the stairs. I quite like having breakfast in the bath.'

'Yes,' said Mrs Simkin, 'I like it here, too. The bath towels match the saucepans, and think of all the soup I shall be able to make when we have a large dinner-party.'

'That's a very good point,' agreed Mr Simkin. 'I can't think why everybody doesn't want a bathtub in their kitchen.'

One day Mr and Mrs Simkin went downstairs to find that the bathtub had moved again. It was in the living-room, sitting snugly before the fire.

'Oh, I don't think I like it there,' said Mrs Simkin, looking at it with her head on one side.

'Neither do I,' said Mr Simkin, 'although it will be very pleasant bathing in front of the fire.'

'I don't suppose it will stay there very long,' whispered

Mrs Simkin. 'Once a bathtub has started to roam, it never knows when to stop.'

She was quite right. The following morning the bathtub was underneath the sideboard, which was rather difficult for bathing, but they managed somehow. Two or three days later they found the bathtub in the basement with spiders in it.

On the day that Mrs Simkin was forty-two years old they couldn't find the bathtub anywhere.

'What shall I do?' cried Mrs Simkin, 'I wanted to use that lovely bubble-bath that you gave me for my birthday.'

'So did I,' said Mr Simkin.

The lady next door came round.

'Happy birthday,' she said. 'Did you know that your bathtub was on the front lawn?'

They all went to have a look.

There was a horse drinking out of it.

'Go away,' said Mrs Simkin to the horse. 'How dare you drink my bathwater, you greedy creature?' and she stepped recklessly into the bathtub.

The lady next door said she didn't know what the world was coming to and she went home and locked herself indoors.

As the bubbles floated down the street, lots of people came to see what was going on. They saw Mrs Simkin sitting in the bathtub. They were very interested. They leaned on the fence and watched. They asked if they could come again.

As the days went by, Mrs Simkin began to think that the bathtub would stay on the front lawn for ever, but one morning when there was rather a chilly wind about they found the bathtub in the greenhouse. The people in the street were very disappointed. They got up a petition asking Mr Simkin to bring it back.

'My dear,' said Mr Simkin a few days later, 'do you happen to know where the bathtub is today?'

'No, Stanley,' said Mrs Simkin, 'but today's Tuesday. It's quite often in the garage on Tuesdays.'

'It isn't there today,' said Mr Simkin.

'Have you tried the verandah?' suggested Mrs Simkin. 'It hasn't been there for some time.'

'I've looked everywhere,' said Mr Simkin. 'It isn't in the house and it isn't in the garden.'

Mrs Simkin was busy with something else. 'I do hope it hasn't gone next door,' she sighed. 'The lady next door has no sympathy with that kind of thing.'

Mr Simkin went to inquire. The lady next door said that she wouldn't allow anyone else's bathtub in her house, and that she was of the opinion that people ought to be able to control their bathtubs. Mr Simkin went home.

Mr Robinson from across the street rang up. 'I know it's none of my business,' he said, 'but I thought you'd like to know that your bathtub's sitting up on the roof of your house.'

Mrs Simkin thanked him for the information. Mr Simkin went to take his bath. He said there was a marvellous view from up there. Mrs Simkin climbed up. All the people cheered. She thought it was rather nice, but she had no head for heights. Perhaps it was time to ring the plumber.

The plumber said that wandering bathtubs weren't really in his line of business and why didn't they get in touch with the Department of the Environment?

Mrs Simkin said she wasn't going to all that trouble. She would soon get used to bathing on the roof. So they left the bathtub where it was. And that's where it liked to be best of all.

The people in the street had a meeting in Mr Simkin's greenhouse. They decided to have their bathtubs on their roofs as well. All except the lady next door. She preferred to take a shower.

LINDA ALLEN

# The Small Brown Mouse

You might not think that smells would travel round the corners in a mousehole, but you would be wrong. The small brown mouse knows at exactly what angle in the hole to sit so that all smells from the room beyond are reflected to him, accurately and deliciously. He is safe there, with the roof of the mousehole just above his head, and the sides of it sitting snugly to his shoulders, so that nothing can jump at him suddenly from any direction, and he can see the light from the room shining up the tunnel which generations of his family have polished with their furry flanks. Whichever of his ancestors it was who had been the architect for the mousehole, he had known his business well, and each evening the small brown mouse takes up his position, and his quivering nose-tip explores all the smells that reach him.

In the winter evenings the most exciting of the smells are of cocoa and digestive biscuits. And when he smells those the small brown mouse knows that soon there will be a stir in the room, chairs will be pushed back, someone will say, 'Come on, puss – time you were out,' doors will open and shut again, feet will sound on the stairs, light feet first, then heavier feet, and at last the room will be left in the quiet dark, but for the glimmer from what is left of the fire.

This is the moment that the mouse has been waiting for. He comes out of the mousehole and across the floor like the flicker of a shadow, and he has his supper from the crumbs on the carpet, and he is thankful that digestive biscuits are so very brittle, and that the family make so many crumbs.

One evening in the middle of winter, the small brown mouse was sitting just round his particular angle in the mousehole, waiting for his supper. It was cold and frosty outside, and he was hungry, and he hoped the biscuits had been rather more brittle than usual, and the family more careless. He waited and he waited, growing hungrier and hungrier, but also more and more puzzled. For mixed up with the smells of cocoa and digestive biscuits he smelt other, unfamiliar smells, which greatly puzzled even so wise a mouse as he. There was cigarette smoke, of course, and the smell of the fire, and he rather thought someone had been sucking peppermints. But there was a very unusual smell – unusual, that is, for a drawing-room – a fresh keen outdoor smell, a smell that didn't belong to a house at all, and there were other sweeter smells that were foreign to him, and most exciting.

The small feet had gone up to bed a long time ago. The other, heavier feet should have been on their way, but still the light burned and there came the continued sound of voices. What with hunger and curiosity, the small brown mouse crept another inch towards the room – and then crept an inch back again, for the cat was still there, the silent presence that turned your legs to water and made your heart sick, the dreadful and inescapable cat.

The mouse was beginning to think he should go back

up the mousehole and take his supper off the piece of cheese-
rind he had stored there, in case of emergencies, when at
last he heard the familiar sounds that he had been waiting
for. Chairs scraped across the floor, the cat was called, the
front door opened and closed again, the light was extinguished and feet – slow, tired feet – went up the stairs.

The small brown mouse came out of the mousehole and
looked around him. And he forgot all about the digestive
biscuits, but sat back on his little haunches, and with bright
unwinking eyes he stared his fill.

It was a tree, a tall strong tree, set in a tub at the further
end of the room. That was the outdoor smell, though what
a tree was doing inside the house the mouse did not know.
But he breathed in the sharp sweet smell of its branches,
and it reminded him of the wood where, in the sunny
summertime, he had sometimes wandered. But this tree was
different from all other trees. Its dark green branches were
hung and spattered from tip to toe. It burned and glittered
and sparkled. It was alive with bright colours that were
not fruit nor blossom. And at the top was a figure, half
child, half bird, and he knew that it was an angel.

Forgetting how hungry he was, the mouse crept forward
to investigate this unexpected tree. He climbed carefully
over the tub and up among the branches, nosing around
backward and forward, smelling and feeling and looking
at all the things that he found there. There was a bottle
of French perfume, and though it was tightly wrapped and
stoppered, his nose discovered it, and it made him feel very
romantic and sentimental, so that he nearly ran away home
up the mousehole to tell his wife about it right away. But
a little higher up there was a cigar, and although there was

only a breath of it coming through its silvery case, it was enough to make our mouse feel bold and manly, so that he went higher up still, examining everything as he went.

There were boxes of chocolates and trumpets, balls and oranges, candles, wisps of tinsel, cotton-wool snow, tiny shining birds that dipped on the branches as his small weight came on to them, and flaunted bright glittering tails. There were books and boxes of handkerchiefs, and many other things which baffled the mouse completely, so strange and unusual they were. But what he most admired were the large bright balls, red and blue, green and gold, in which, by the light of the fire, he could see his own reflection looking out at him – a warlike red mouse in the red ball, a romantic blue mouse, a mermaid mouse of cool translucent green. Best of all was an amber ball which reflected a tawny

benevolent lion of a mouse, a mouse as truly golden as the cheese that mice dream about when they are happiest.

Soon he had been all over the tree, except for the highest branches, where there was little foothold, and where even his feather weight might find little enough support. It was only then that he remembered how hungry he was, and he went down to the carpet again, and ate up the crumbs of the digestive biscuits, and as he chewed he never took his eyes off the splendid tree.

His supper gave him courage, and he decided that after all he would attempt the last perilous inches to the top, where on the slender stem the angel was poised.

So up he went again, scrambling and sliding, and he paused only to look just once more at his golden self, reflected in the amber glass ball. And at last there was only a slim six inches between him and the small white feet of the angel.

But just at the base of the final pinnacle was something that the mouse had not seen in his first excursion, something as small as himself, something in fact very like himself – three chocolate mice. They lay side by side on the very last branch, just beneath the angel, and our mouse looked at them, first with curiosity and then with pity, for they were clumsy things compared with his own exquisite shape. Their ears were no more than humps on either side of their thick heads; their eyes were just spots of white sugar on the chocolate – set on unevenly at that; there wasn't a whisker between them; and their tails were poor things of limp string that hung down behind them. Our mouse looked back at his own elegant tapered tail that kept the balance of his body, and he looked again at the dangling bits of string, and he felt rather ashamed. But he also felt extremely interested, for the smell of chocolate had reached him so suddenly and so magnificently that he almost lost his balance and fell from his precarious perch.

It was like the smell of cocoa, of course, but so much better, so much richer, that there was really little comparison. The shock of its sweetness paralysed him for a moment, and then he came a little closer, delaying – just for the pure pleasure of delaying – the lovely moment when his tongue should slide up the shining sides of the first mouse.

'No,' said the angel suddenly – so suddenly that the small brown mouse once more had difficulty in keeping his footing – 'No. Not now – not yet – not for you.'

She wasn't scolding, she was just telling him, and she smiled at him as she spoke so that the mouse was at once ashamed of himself. 'Yes, ma'am,' he said, and because the chocolate mice still smelt so overpoweringly beautiful – so much so that he could not keep his whiskers from vibrating – he came down off the tree, where the smell of them was mixed up with a lot of other smells, and he finished up a few crumbs of biscuit that he had previously overlooked.

He should then have gone back into the safety of his mousehole, but he could not bring himself to leave the enchanted tree, and all night he sat in front of the fire, watching it.

Even when the last flicker of the fire had burned itself out, and the coals sighed and fell together in white ash on the hearth, the mouse still sat on, for of course a mouse can see in the dark, and this mouse had never seen anything like this before. He forgot his wife who was waiting for him, he forgot to count the hours striking on the big clock in the hall, he forgot everything except the tree. That was why, when morning had come, he was still there when the mistress of the house opened the door – and the cat walked in! Before he knew it the great cat was coming softly and steadily across the hearth towards him, and the mouse knew that he was lost indeed.

The cat sat down placidly, a few feet away, and made no spring. The mouse watched him, sick with fear, unable to move. He wished the cat would be quick and spring, and make a finish to it.

'Hallo, nipper,' said the great animal, and the mouse saw his strong white pointed teeth as he spoke, 'don't be in a hurry to move. You needn't mind me.'

And still he didn't spring.

'I'm not going to chase you,' the cat said. And for some reason that he could not explain the mouse believed the cat, just as he had believed the angel.

'Why not?' he asked, trying to keep the wobble out of his voice.

'I don't know exactly,' the cat replied, blinking a mild yellow eye, 'but it's a thing we always do at this time of year. Traditional, you know.'

The mouse didn't know, but a warm gratitude made it impossible for him to speak.

'Mind you,' the cat went on, 'I shall chase you tomorrow, and every other day that I get the chance. Like as not I shall catch you too. But not today.' And he busied himself licking the pads of his great paws, keeping the claws politely hooded.

The mouse believed this too. He knew that the cat would

indeed chase him tomorrow and every other day, but he also knew that after this it would always be different. He would be able to run away from the cat now, because he knew that the cat was just another animal, as he himself was an animal – a much stronger animal of course, but just an animal: not a horror that turned your legs to water and made your heart sick. Oh yes, he could run away from the cat now. Out of sheer bravado he crept across the few feet that lay between the cat and himself, and he leaned for a small daring moment against the cat's side, and felt the warmth and power of his great body. That would be something to tell his wife about when he got home.

Then the house began to stir, there were laughter and voices, people came and went, the cat was called for his breakfast – and the small brown mouse, who was by this time so excited that he hardly knew what he was doing, instead of running to his mousehole and safety, streaked for the tree, and lay hidden among its branches and saw all that was going on.

There was plenty to see. Visitors arrived all day long. They greeted each other, and laughed, and opened parcels, and kissed, and sang. And in the evening they drew the curtains across the windows, and they lighted the candles on the tree.

This was something so alarming that the mouse, between the striking of one match and the next, fled up the tree where there were no candles, and found himself lying once again beside his chocolate cousins.

When all the candles were lit, the parcels were untied from the tree, and handed down into small excited hands, and the mouse, from his point of vantage, looked down on the children's upturned faces. Then it was the turn for the grown-up people to receive their parcels, and at last each pair of hands was filled.

There was nothing left on the tree now, except the angel and the candles and the bright balls – oh, and the chocolate mice. 'I'd forgotten about these,' someone said, and a hand reached up and up, among the branches.

There was no hope for it – he would be discovered. But just as the fingers fumbled for the chocolate mice, the angel's golden wing tilted ever so slightly, and the small brown mouse was safely sheltered behind it. There he lay, hidden and safe, until the party was over, until people had said goodbye, until the door had opened many times and shut again, until the candles were blown out and the light extinguished, and until the last of the feet had once more gone up the stairs and the house was quiet.

Suddenly it seemed rather sad. Even the tree looked a little sad. The mouse thought of all the hands that had gone home full of treasures, and he felt sad, too – sad, and also tremendously tired.

'I'll go now,' he said to the angel, 'and thank you, ma'am, for helping me.'

And he got slowly down off the tree – he was stiff with lying so long in one position – and he crossed the room to the mousehole. Just before he went home he turned to the tree, for one last look.

'You are sad,' the angel said. 'What is the matter?'

He found it difficult to explain. 'You said, "Not yet – not now",' he faltered, 'but the party is over.'

Just then the amber ball slid off the twig that held it,

softly down from one branch to another, gently to the ground, and it rolled to his feet and stopped there.

The mouse looked up at the angel questioningly. 'For me?' And the angel smiled and nodded.

You might not think that a bright ball from a Christmas tree would travel round the corners in a mousehole. But you would be wrong.

JANET MCNEILL
*Illustrated by* FAITH JAQUES

# Questions

I often wonder why, oh why,
All grown-ups say to me:
'When you are old and six foot high,
What do you want to be?'

I sometimes wonder what they'd say
If I should ask them all
What *they* would like to be, if they
Were six years old and small.

RAYMOND WILSON

# The Golden Touch

Long ago, when the world was younger than it is now, people believed that there was not one god, but many. They believed that everything had its own special god to look after it. Some were important, like the God of Love and the God of the Harvest; others, who were less important, were half human and half animal, with horns and pointed ears. These haunted the forests, fields and streams and were known as satyrs.

Many stories are told about the gods and satyrs. This story of the golden touch is one of them:

Once, in the country of Greece, there lived a king called Midas. Midas was the richest man on earth. He collected money as you or I might collect stamps or little glass animals, not because it was useful but because he liked to look at it and play with it. Midas would spend many hours every day with the big chests in which he kept his money, dipping his hands in among the coins. In those days money was made of gold, so that when Midas let it fall through his fingers it glittered in the light. Midas thought that the yellow of gold was the best of all, better than the red of roses, than the blue of the sky, than the green of grass. He thought he loved gold more than anything else in life. But he was to find out that other things were more precious to him, as you shall hear.

One day the king was walking in the forest near his palace, thinking. He was thinking how he could be even richer than he was already. Perhaps he could sell some of the corn from his fields? Perhaps he could make a law saying that all the people he ruled over must give him money? Then suddenly he heard the sound of snoring. It seemed to come from a field of grapes – a vineyard – on the edge of the forest. Midas went towards it and there, sure enough, fast asleep with a grape-vine trailing over his face, was a very old satyr called Silenus. Midas knew Silenus. He lived with Bacchus, the God of Wine, and Bacchus loved him well. The king shook the satyr's shoulder.

'Wake up, Silenus! What are you doing here?'

Silenus opened his eyes and yawned. 'Oh, it's you, Midas! I'm lost.'

'I'm not surprised!' the king told him. 'You are a very long way from home.'

'I know. But I've had such a lovely day wandering in the vineyards eating grapes! I've eaten thousands and thousands of grapes.'

'Very greedy of you!' said Midas sternly.

Silenus grinned and put his hands on his stomach. 'M'm! Grapes are tasty! Wine is made from grapes and wine is the best thing in the world. Bacchus taught me that.'

Midas shook his head. He knew, of course, that it was not wine but gold that was the best thing in the world. But he did not say so. He said:

'Come, I will take you home, Silenus. And as you are so tired you may travel on my back.'

Bacchus lived on a mountain called Olympus, way up above the clouds that covered its top, in a cave as big as a palace. He was overjoyed to see Silenus again and very grateful to Midas for his trouble.

'What would you like as a reward?' he asked the king. 'Wish for anything you like and it shall be yours.'

Midas could hardly believe his good luck. Here at last was a way to become rich beyond his dreams.

'I wish,' he said, 'that everything I touch may turn to gold.'

Bacchus looked a little sad. 'Are you sure that's really what you want?'

Midas said he was quite sure, and Bacchus sighed. 'Very well it shall be as you ask. But I wish you had made a better choice, for I fear the Golden Touch will bring you sorrow.'

But Midas felt only joy as he went away through the misty clouds and down the mountainside. As soon as he came to the woods at the foot of Olympus he decided to try his new power. Could it really be true that whatever he touched would turn to gold? He broke a twig from a small oak tree. And – he could scarcely believe it – it was gold, with golden leaves and a little golden acorn. Enchanted, the king picked up a stone from the ground. And it was a golden stone. Then he walked through a field of corn and every blade he touched stood stiff and golden, flashing in the sun. Back in his Palace garden, Midas picked an apple from a branch to make a golden apple. A little lizard basking on the wall became a golden model of a lizard, and the king thought how it would make a pretty toy for his little daughter.

Still full of happiness Midas entered his Palace, turning the pillars and doorways to gold as he went. And then, feeling hungry after so much excitement, he called for his dinner. His servants brought in a table covered with crisp bread, roast meat, chicken, cakes and fruit. And it was then that the first dreadful thing happened. The king put out his hand to take the bread and ... horror! the bread was as hard as a brick and as hard as – gold. Trembling with fear he put a piece of meat in his mouth, and his teeth bit on metal. He lifted a glass of wine to his lips, and liquid metal poured into his mouth and nearly choked him. He spat it out in disgust and rose from the table. He knew that not all the food in the world could stop his hunger now, nor all the wine and water quench his thirst. He would sleep and forget his terror. On his way up the wide golden stairway the king paused to look from a window over the evening landscape. In the west the sun was setting in a blaze of golden light, casting its glitter on a distant river and on the tops of the trees. Midas turned sadly away. The brilliance of gold no longer seemed beautiful. His heart felt heavy within him. He thought, 'Perhaps my heart too is turning to gold.'

But there was worse to come. For when Midas lay down to sleep his head was on a pillow of solid gold, while a heavy golden counterpane pressed down on his body. He could not sleep a wink but lay listening to the owl in the woods and the sweet song of the nightingale, thinking how much happier were these creatures of nature than he, the richest man in the world.

Dawn glimmered in the room. And the king heard footsteps. By his bed stood a little girl who smiled at him.

'Good morning, Father!'

The king greeted her joyfully. 'Good morning, my

daughter!' For the first time in many hours he was happy, for even food and sleep were not so precious to him as his own child. He remembered the golden lizard in the garden, and he said to her,

'Go to the wall that surrounds our garden, and there in the shade of an olive tree you will find a toy I brought for you yesterday!'

The child ran excitedly to do his bidding, and Midas dressed himself. He knew even before he touched his clothes that he would be wearing a heavy golden tunic that day and that the cloak he threw over his shoulders would be shining and stiff. When he was ready his daughter came running back with the lizard in her hand.

'Oh Father, isn't it pretty! It looks so real, except, of course that it's made of gold, so it isn't alive. Thank you! thank you!'

With sudden dread the king saw that she was running to kiss him. He cried out in terror.

'Stop! Don't touch me!'

But it was too late. King Midas held in his arms a little golden girl, as lifeless as a statue.

This was more than he could bear. He knew beyond any doubt that he never wanted to see gold again if only that little statue, with her graceful golden limbs and hair of finest golden thread, could become flesh and blood again.

There was only one thing to be done. He must go to Bacchus and ask to be forgiven for making such a foolish wish. Then perhaps the god would have pity on him and take away the golden touch.

On his way up the mountain to Bacchus's cave, Midas could hardly bear to brush against the corn and trees as

he passed, so sickened had he become by the very sight of gold. He found Bacchus and Silenus having a late breakfast of grapes and wine. When the god heard why Midas had come he smiled.

'Ah! So you have enough gold at last, Midas!'

'Too much!' cried the king. 'I know I have been greedy and silly, but I have been cruelly punished. And now I have only one wish – that you will take the golden touch from me.'

Thoughtfully Bacchus helped himself to another grape and ate it while Midas watched him anxiously. At last the god nodded.

'Very well. I will take my terrible gift away from you. I think you have learned for good that gold is of little worth. But if you want to wash the golden touch from your skin, you must go to the river called Patroclus, which you can see from your Palace, and bathe in its waters . . .'

Bacchus had hardly finished speaking before the king was setting off down the mountainside. When he reached the river he was breathless, for he had run all the way. In a moment he had laid his golden clothes on the bank and had plunged into the cool water. As he did so he noticed that the river became cloudy with golden dust. When he came out he put his hand on his tunic which lay there, stiff as a statue. And to his joy the stuff turned to linen under his fingers. Hurriedly he put it on, then his cloak of finest wool.

'There you are, Father!' The voice was his daughter's. She did not know that she had been turned to gold, but thought she had slept and had an evil dream, in which she stood, unable to move, staring in front of her. It was such a silly dream that she did not even speak of it. And now here she was by the river, holding a lizard in her palm. 'Look, Father, it isn't gold after all, it's alive! Look at its lovely skin, green and gold and blue. I think he's prettier than if he were all gold.'

'I think so too,' said the king. And he stroked his daughter's silky hair. 'And now,' he went on, 'shall we go back to the Palace? I happen to be very hungry!'

So they went home. And for the rest of his life King Midas never forgot that food and rest were more precious than gold, and that his child was the most precious thing in his life.

But from that day on, the river called Patroclus rolled over golden sands and carried gold-dust to the sea. And whenever Midas walked beside it he was reminded of the foolish wish which had nearly taken all happiness from him.

HONOR WYATT

# The Story of Giant Kippernose

Once there was a giant called Kippernose. He lived on a lonely farm in the mountains. He was not fierce. Indeed he was as kind and as gentle as a giant could be. He liked children, and was fond of animals. He was good at telling stories. His favourite foods were ice-cream, cakes, lollipops and sausages. He would help anyone, large or small. And yet he had no friends. When he went to the town to do his shopping, everyone ran away from him. Busy streets emptied in a trice. Everyone ran home, bolted their doors and closed all their windows, even on hot summer days.

Kippernose shouted,

'Don't run away! I'll not hurt you! Please don't run away, I like little people. I've only come to do my shopping. Please come out. I'll tell you a good story about a dragon and a mermaid.'

But it was no use. The town stayed silent and empty; the doors and windows stayed firmly closed. Poor Kippernose wanted so much to have someone to talk to. He felt so lonely that he often sat down in the town square and cried his heart out. You would think someone would take pity on him, but no one ever did. He simply couldn't understand it. He even tried going to another town, far across the mountains, but just the same thing happened.

'Has all the world gone mad?' said Kippernose to himself, and took his solitary way home.

The truth was that the people were not afraid of Kippernose, and they had not gone mad, either. The truth *was* . . . that Kippernose had not had a single bath in a hundred years, or more! The poor fellow carried such a stink wherever he went that everyone with a nose on his face ran for cover at the first whiff. Oh, how that giant reeked! Pooh, you could smell him a mile away, and worst of all on hot days. People buried their noses in flowers and lavender-bags, but still the stench crept in. The wives cried shame and shame upon him, and swore that his stink turned their milk sour, and their butter rancid. What made matters worse, he never washed his hair or his whiskers, either. Smelly whiskers bristled all over his chin, and little creatures crept amongst them. His greasy hair fell down his back. He never used a comb. He never brushed his teeth. *And*, quite often, he went to bed with his boots on.

When he was a boy, Kippernose was always clean and smart, his mother saw to that. Long long ago, his good mother had gone off to live in far Cathay, and he had forgotten all she had told him about keeping clean and tidy, and changing his socks once a week. It was a lucky thing when his socks wore out, because that was the only time he would change them. He had no notion of the sight and smell he was. He never looked in a mirror. His smell had grown up with him, and he didn't notice it at all. His mind was deep among tales of dragons and wizards, for people in stories were his only friends. If only someone could have told him about his smell, in a nice way, all would have been well. The people grumbled enough amongst them-selves. Mrs Dobson, of Ivy Cottage, was one of them. Friday was market day, and ironing day too, and every Friday night she would bang her iron angrily, and say to quiet Mr Dobson by the fireside,

'That giant's a scandal. It's every market day we have the sickening stench of him, and the whole pantry turned sour and rotten, too. Can't you men do something about it? You sit there and warm your toes, and nod off to sleep, while the world's going to ruin . . .'

'But, Bessie, my dear,' mild Mr Dobson answered, 'what can we do? You cannot expect anyone to go up to an enormous giant and say, "I say, old chap, you smell most dreadfully" – now can you? Besides, no one could get near enough to him: the smell would drive them away.'

'You could send him a letter,' said Mrs Dobson.

'But he cannot read. He never went to school. Even as a boy, Kippernose was too big to get through the school door, my old grandfather used to say.'

'Well, the government should do something about it,' said Mrs Dobson, banging on. 'If that Queen of ours came out of her palace and took a sniff of our Kippernose, *she'd* do something quickly enough, I'll bet.'

But it was not the Queen, or the government, or Mr Dobson, who solved the problem in the end. It was a creature so small that no one could see it.

One Friday in the middle of winter, a cold day of ice and fog, Kippernose went to town to do his shopping as usual. He felt so unhappy that he didn't even bother to call out and ask the people to stay to talk to him. He just walked gloomily into the market-place.

'It's no good,' he said to himself, 'they'll never be friends with me. They don't seem to think a giant has feelings like anyone else, I might just as well be . . .'

'Hoi! Look where you're going!' an angry voice shouted up from the foggy street. 'Oh, I say, oh, help!' Then there was a great crash, and there were apples rolling everywhere. Then a babble of voices gathered round Kippernose.

'The clumsy great oaf – look, he's knocked Jim Surtees's apple-cart over. Did you ever see such a mess? Tramping about, not looking where he's going, with his head in the sky.'

Amongst all this angry noise stood Kippernose, with an enormous smile spreading across his big face. The smile grew to a grin.

'*They're not running away.* They're *not running away*,' said Kippernose, in a joyous whisper. Then he bent down, right down, and got down on his knees to bring his face near to the people.

'Why aren't you running away from me?' he said, softly,

so as not to frighten them. 'Why aren't you running away as you always do? Please tell me, I beg of you.'

Jim Surtees was so angry that he had no fear of Kippernose, and he climbed upon his overturned apple-cart, and shouted up at him,

'Why, you great fool, it's because we cannot *smell* you.'

'Smell?' said Kippernose, puzzled.

'Yes; smell, stink, pong, stench; call it what you like,' said Jim.

'But I don't smell,' said Kippernose.

'Oh, yes you do!' all the people shouted together.

'You stink,' shouted Jim. 'You stink to the very heavens. That's why everyone runs away from you. It's too much for us — we just *have* to run away.'

'Why can't you smell me today?' said Kippernose.

'Because we've all caught a cold in the head for the first time in our lives, and our noses are stuffed up and runny, and we cannot smell anything, that's why,' said Jim. 'Some merchant came from England, selling ribbons, and gave us his germs as well. So we cannot smell you today, but next week we'll be better, and then see how we'll run.'

'But what can I do?' said Kippernose, looking so sad that even Jim felt sorry for him. 'I'm so lonely, with no one to talk to.'

'Well, you could take a bath,' said Jim.

'And you could wash your whiskers,' said Mrs Dobson. '. . . And your hair,' she added.

'*And* you could wash your clothes,' said Mr Dobson.

'*And* change your socks,' said Mrs Fox, eyeing his feet.

Distant memories stirred in Kippernose's head. 'Yes. Oh . . . yes. Mother did say something about all that, once, long ago; but I didn't take much notice. Do I really smell as bad as all that? Do I really?'

'Oh yes, you certainly do,' said Mrs Dobson. 'You smell a good deal worse than you can imagine. You turned my cheese green last week, *and* made Mrs Hill's baby cry for two hours without stopping when she left a window open by mistake. Oh, yes, you smell badly, Kippernose, as badly as anything could smell in this world.'

'If I do all you say, if I get all neat and clean, will you stop running away and be friends?' said Kippernose.

'Of course we will,' said Jim Surtees. 'We have nothing against giants. They can be useful if only they'll look where they're putting their feet, and they do say the giants were the best story-tellers in the old days.'

'Just you wait and see,' shouted Kippernose. As soon as he had filled his shopping basket, he walked purposefully off towards the hills. In his basket were one hundred and twenty bars of soap, and fifty bottles of bubble-bath!

That night Kippernose was busy as never before. Fires roared, and hot water gurgled in all the pipes of his house. There was such a steaming, and a splashing, and a gasping, and a bubbling, and a lathering, and a singing, and a laughing, as had not been heard in Kippernose's house for a hundred years. A smell of soap and bubble-bath drifted out upon the air, and even as far away as the town, people caught a whiff of it.

'What's that lovely smell?' said Mrs Dobson to her husband. 'There's a beautifully clean and scented smell that makes me think of a summer garden, even though it is the middle of winter.'

Then there was a bonfire of dirty old clothes in a field near Kippernose's farm, and a snip-snipping of hair and whiskers. Then there was a great rummaging in drawers and cupboards, and a shaking and airing of fresh clothes. The whole of that week, Kippernose was busy, so busy that he almost forgot to sleep and eat.

When Friday came round again, the people of the town saw an astonishing sight. Dressed in a neat Sunday suit, clean and clipped, shining in the wintry sun, and smelling of soap and sweet lavender, Kippernose strode towards them. He was a new Kippernose. The people crowded round him, and Jim Surtees shouted,

'Is it really you, Kippernose?'

'It certainly is,' said Kippernose, beaming joyously.

'Then you're welcome amongst us,' said Jim. 'You smell

as sweetly as a flower, indeed you do, and I never thought you'd do it. Three cheers for good old Kippernose! Hip. Hip.'

And the crowd cheered,

'Hooray! Hooray! Hooray!'

Kippernose was never short of friends after that. He was so good and kind that all the people loved him, and he became the happiest giant in all the world.

Ever afterwards, if any children would not go in the bath, or wash, or brush their teeth, or have their hair cut ... then their mothers would tell them the story of Giant Kippernose.

JOHN CUNLIFFE
*Illustrated by* FRITZ WEGNER

# The Old Woman and Her Pig

An old woman was sweeping her house, and she found a little crooked sixpence. 'What,' said she, 'shall I do with this little sixpence? I will go to market, and buy a little pig.'

As she was coming home, she came to a stile; but the piggy wouldn't go over the stile.

She went a little further, and she met a dog. So she said to him: 'Dog! dog! bite pig; piggy won't get over the stile; and I shan't get home tonight.' But the dog wouldn't.

She went a little further, and she met a stick. So she said: 'Stick! stick! beat dog! dog won't bite pig; piggy won't get over the stile; and I shan't get home tonight.' But the stick wouldn't.

She went a little further, and she met a fire. So she said: 'Fire! fire! burn stick; stick won't beat dog; dog won't bite pig; piggy won't get over the stile; and I shan't get home tonight.' But the fire wouldn't.

She went a little further, and she met some water. So she said 'Water! water! quench fire; fire won't burn stick; stick won't beat dog; dog won't bite pig; piggy won't get over the stile; and I shan't get home tonight.' But the water wouldn't.

She went a little further, and she met an ox. She said: 'Ox! ox! drink water; water won't quench fire; fire won't burn stick; stick won't beat dog; dog won't bite pig; piggy won't get over the stile; and I shan't get home tonight.' But the ox wouldn't.

She went a little further, and she met a butcher. So she said: 'Butcher! butcher! kill ox; ox won't drink water; water won't quench fire; fire won't burn stick; stick won't beat dog; dog won't bite pig; piggy won't get over the stile; and I shan't get home tonight.' But the butcher wouldn't.

She went a little further, and she met a rope. So she said: 'Rope! rope! hang butcher; butcher won't kill ox; ox won't drink water; water won't quench fire; fire won't burn stick; stick won't beat dog; dog won't bite pig; piggy won't get over the stile; and I shan't get home tonight.' But the rope wouldn't.

She went a little further, and she met a rat. So she said: 'Rat! rat! gnaw rope; rope won't hang butcher; butcher won't kill ox; ox won't drink water; water won't quench fire; fire won't burn stick; stick won't beat dog; dog won't bite pig; piggy won't get over the stile; and I shan't get home tonight.' But the rat wouldn't.

She went a little further, and she met a cat. So she said: 'Cat! cat! kill rat; rat won't gnaw rope; rope won't hang butcher; butcher won't kill ox; ox won't drink water; water won't quench fire; fire won't burn stick; stick won't beat dog; dog won't bite pig; piggy won't get over the stile; and I shan't get home tonight.' But the cat said to her: 'If you will go to yonder cow, and fetch me a saucer of milk, I will kill the rat.' So away went the old woman to the cow.

But the cow said to her: 'If you will go to yonder hay-stack, and fetch me a handful of hay, I'll give you the milk.' So away went the old woman to the hay-stack; and she brought the hay to the cow.

As soon as the cow had eaten the hay, she gave the old woman the milk; and away she went with it in a saucer to the cat.

As soon as the cat had lapped up the milk, the cat began to kill the rat; the rat began to gnaw the rope; the rope began to hang the butcher; the butcher began to kill the ox; the ox began to drink the water; the water began to quench the fire; the fire began to burn the stick; the stick began to beat the dog; the dog began to bite the pig; the little pig in a fright jumped over the stile; and so the old woman got home that night.

ANON.

# Pig Tale

A little boy went to stay with relatives in the country for his holiday. The relatives lived on a farm and the boy enjoyed himself no end, seeing things he'd never seen before.

When he got back home, he told his mother all about it. But one thing had impressed him very much, and that was a pig with its young ones.

'What did the pig do?' his mother asked.

'Oh, the little ones chased it,' said the boy, 'and when they caught it they knocked it down on its back and started pulling the buttons off its waistcoat.'

*Retold by* AIDAN CHAMBERS

# A Growing Tale

There was once a tiny boy called Tim. He was much smaller than his sister Sally and smaller than his brother Billy. He was the smallest person in the house, except the kitten and the canary, and you can't count them.

Tim was so tiny he could only just walk, he could only just talk and he only had one candle on his birthday cake. So you can guess how small he was. He couldn't wash himself, he couldn't dress himself and he couldn't blow his own nose. His mother had to do almost everything for him. She gave him a tiny chair to sit on, and a tiny bed to sleep in every night.

He didn't know his right foot from his left foot. He didn't know what was red and what was blue. He couldn't say what one and one makes. He was much too small to count. He was very good at shouting, at banging and at bawling. He was very good at throwing, at grabbing and at crawling. Tim was so very tiny he could walk beneath the table and never bump his head!

But he wished and he wished he could see over the fences, and turn door-handles all by himself.

He grew and he grew until he was two, he grew and he grew until he was three, and he grew and he grew and then he was FOUR. And when he was four, Tim was a Great Big Boy. He had four candles on his birthday cake.

He could see over fences and what was on tables. He could turn door-handles all by himself. He was MUCH too big for his tiny little chair, he was much too big for his tiny little cot, so he slept in a real bed of his very own. He could wash himself, dress himself and blow his nose on a great big pocket handkerchief. He put his left shoe on his left foot, his right shoe on his right foot, and he tied both the laces in a very tidy bow. He knew what was red and what was blue, so he didn't bother bawling and he didn't bother crawling. He was much too big for that!

Tim was so BIG, he went to the Nursery School. But he was still much smaller than his sister Sally, and he was still much smaller than his brother Billy. For they had grown too!

NORAH MONTGOMERIE

# Growing

When I grow up I'll be so kind,
Not yelling 'Now' or 'Do you MIND!'
　　Or making what is called a scene,
　　Like 'So you're back' or 'Where've you BEEN?'
Or 'Goodness, child, what is it NOW?'
　　Or saying 'STOP . . . that awful row,'
　　Or 'There's a time and place to eat'
　　And 'Wipe your nose' or 'Wipe your feet.'
I'll just let people go their way
And have an extra hour for play.
　　No angry shouting 'NOW what's wrong?'
　　It's just that growing takes so long.

MAX FATCHEN

# Gruesome

I was sitting in the sitting room
toying with some toys
when from a door marked: 'GRUESOME'
There came a GRUESOME noise.

Cautiously I opened it
and there to my surprise
a little GRUE lay sitting
with tears in its eyes

'Oh little GRUE please tell me
what is it ails thee so?'
'Well I'm so small,' he sobbed,
'GRUESSES don't want to know'

'Exercises are the answer,
Each morning you must DO SOME'
He thanked me, smiled,
and do you know what?
The very next day he . . .

ROGER MCGOUGH

## 'From Wibbleton to Wobbleton'

From Wibbleton to Wobbleton is fifteen miles,
From Wobbleton to Wibbleton is fifteen miles,
From Wibbleton to Wobbleton,
From Wobbleton to Wibbleton,
From Wibbleton to Wobbleton is fifteen miles.

ANON.

*Illustrated by* RAYMOND BRIGGS

# Paul's Tale

' "Ho! Ho!" said the King, slapping his fat thighs. "Methinks this youth shows promise." But at that moment the Court Magician stepped forward ... What is the matter, Paul? Don't you like this story?'

'Yes, I like it.'

'Then lie quiet, dear, and listen.'

'It was just a sort of stalk of a feather pushing itself up through the eiderdown.'

'Well, don't help it, dear, it's destructive. Where were we?' Aunt Isobel's short-sighted eyes searched down the page of the book; she looked comfortable and pink, rocking there in the firelight ... *stepped forward ... You see the Court Magician knew that the witch had taken the magic music-box, and that Colin* ... Paul, you aren't listening!'

'Yes, I am. I can hear.'

'Of course you can't hear – right under the bedclothes. What are you doing, dear?'

'I'm seeing what a hot-water bottle feels like.'

'Don't you know what a hot-water bottle feels like?'

'I know what it feels like to me. I don't know what it feels like to itself.'

'Well, shall I go on or not?'

'Yes, go on,' said Paul. He emerged from the bedclothes, his hair ruffled.

Aunt Isobel looked at him curiously. He was her godson; he had a bad feverish cold; his mother had gone to London. 'Does it tire you, dear, to be read to?' she said at last.

'No. But I like told stories better than read stories.'

Aunt Isobel got up and put some more coal on the fire. Then she looked at the clock. She sighed. 'Well, dear,' she said brightly, as she sat down once more on the rocking-chair. 'What sort of story would you like?' She unfolded her knitting.

'I'd like a real story.'

'How do you mean, dear?' Aunt Isobel began to cast on. The cord of her pince-nez, anchored to her bosom, rose and fell in gentle undulations.

Paul flung round on his back, staring at the ceiling. 'You know,' he said, 'quite real – so you know it must have happened.'

'Shall I tell you about Grace Darling?'

'No, tell me about a little man.'

'What sort of a little man?'

'A little man just as high –' Paul's eyes searched the room '– as that candlestick on the mantelshelf, but without the candle.'

'But that's a very small candlestick. It's only about six inches.'

'Well, about that big.'

Aunt Isobel began knitting a few stitches. She was disappointed about the fairy story. She had been reading with so much expression, making a deep voice for the king, and a wicked oily voice for the Court Magician, and a fine cheerful boyish voice for Colin, the swineherd. A little man – what could she say about a little man? 'Ah!' she ex-

claimed suddenly, and laid down her knitting, smiling at
Paul. 'Little men . . . of course . . .

'Well,' said Aunt Isobel, drawing in her breath. 'Once
upon a time, there was a little, tiny man, and he was no
bigger than that candlestick – there on the mantelshelf.'

Paul settled down, his cheek on his crook'd arm, his eyes
on Aunt Isobel's face. The firelight flickered softly on the
walls and ceiling.

'He was the sweetest little man you ever saw, and he
wore a little red jerkin and a dear little cap made out of
a foxglove. His boots . . .'

'He didn't have any,' said Paul.

Aunt Isobel looked startled. 'Yes,' she exclaimed. 'He had
boots – little, pointed –'

'He didn't have any clothes,' contradicted Paul. 'He was
bare.'

Aunt Isobel looked perturbed. 'But he would have been
cold,' she pointed out.

'He had thick skin,' explained Paul. 'Like a twig.'

'Like a twig?'

'Yes. You know that sort of wrinkly, nubbly skin on
a twig.'

Aunt Isobel knitted in silence for a second or two. She
didn't like the little naked man nearly as much as the little
clothed man: she was trying to get used to him. After a
while she went on.

'He lived in a bluebell wood, among the roots of a dear
old tree. He had a dear little house, tunnelled out of the
soft, loamy earth, with a bright blue front door.'

'Why didn't he live in it?' asked Paul.

'He did live in it, dear,' explained Aunt Isobel patiently.

'I thought he lived in the potting-shed.'

'In the potting-shed?'

'Well, perhaps he had two houses. Some people do. I wish I'd seen the one with the blue front door.'

'Did you see the one in the potting-shed?' asked Aunt Isobel, after a moment's silence.

'Not inside. Right inside. I'm too big. I just sort of saw into it with a flashlight.'

'And what was it like?' asked Aunt Isobel, in spite of herself.

'Well, it was clean – in a potting-shed sort of way. He'd made the furniture himself. The floor was just earth, but he'd trodden it down so that it was hard. It took him years.'

'Well, dear, you seem to know more about this little man than I do.'

Paul snuggled his head more comfortably against his elbow. He half closed his eyes. 'Go on,' he said dreamily.

Aunt Isobel glanced at him hesitatingly. How beautiful he looked, she thought, lying there in the firelight with one curled hand lying lightly on the counterpane. 'Well,' she went on, 'this little man had a little pipe made of straw.' She paused, rather pleased with this idea. 'A little hollow straw, through which he played jiggity little tunes. And to which he danced.' She hesitated. 'Among the bluebells,' she added. Really this was quite a pretty story. She knitted hard for a few seconds, breathing heavily, before the next bit would come, 'Now,' she continued brightly, in a changed, higher and more conversational voice, 'up in the tree, there lived a fairy.'

'In the tree?' asked Paul, incredulously.

'Yes,' said Aunt Isobel, 'in the tree.'

Paul raised his head. 'Do you know that for certain?'

'Well, Paul,' began Aunt Isobel. Then she added playfully, 'Well, I suppose I do.'

'Go on,' said Paul.

'Well, this fairy . . .'

Paul raised his head again. 'Couldn't you go on about the little man?'

'But, dear, we've done the little man – how he lived in the roots, and played a pipe, and all that.'

'You didn't say about his hands and feet.'

'His hands and feet!'

'How sort of big his hands and feet looked, and how he could scuttle along. Like a rat,' Paul added.

'Like a rat!' exclaimed Aunt Isobel.

'And his voice. You didn't say anything about his voice.'

'What sort of a voice,' Aunt Isobel looked almost scared, 'did he have?'

'A croaky sort of voice. Like a frog. And he says "Will 'ee" and "Do 'ee".'

'Willy and Dooey . . .' repeated Aunt Isobel.

'Instead of "Will you" and "Do you". You know.'

'Has he – got a Sussex accent?'

'Sort of. He isn't used to talking. He is the last one. He's been all alone, for years and years.'

'Did he –' Aunt Isobel swallowed. 'Did he tell you that?'

'Yes. He had an aunt and she died about fifteen years ago. But even when she was alive, he never spoke to her.'

'Why?' asked Aunt Isobel.

'He didn't like her,' said Paul.

There was silence. Paul stared dreamily into the fire. Aunt Isobel sat as if turned to stone, her hands idle in her lap.

After a while, she cleared her throat.

'When did you first see this little man, Paul?'

'Oh, ages and ages ago. When did you?'

'I – Where did you find him?'

'Under the chicken house.'

'Did you – did you speak to him?'

Paul made a little snort. 'No. I just popped a tin over him.'

'You caught him!'

'Yes. There was an old, rusty chicken-food tin near. I just popped it over him.' Paul laughed. 'He scrabbled away inside. Then I popped an old kitchen plate that was there on top of the tin.'

Aunt Isobel sat staring at Paul. 'What – what did you do with him then?'

'I put him in a cake-tin, and made holes in the lid. I gave him a bit of bread and milk.'

'Didn't he – say anything?'

'Well, he was sort of croaking.'

'And then?'

'Well, I sort of forgot I had him.'

'You forgot!'

'I went fishing, you see. Then it was bedtime. And next day I didn't remember him. Then when I went to look for him, he was lying curled up at the bottom of the tin. He'd gone all soft. He just hung over my finger. All soft.'

Aunt Isobel's eyes protruded dully.

'What did you do then?'

'I gave him some cherry cordial in a fountain-pen filler.'

'That revived him?'

'Yes, that's when he began to talk. And he told me all about his aunt and everything. I harnessed him up, then, with a bit of string.'

'Oh, Paul,' exclaimed Aunt Isobel, 'how cruel.'

'Well, he'd have got away. It didn't hurt him. Then I tamed him.'

'How did you tame him?'

'Oh, how do you tame anything. With food mostly. Chips of gelatine and raw sago he liked best. Cheese, he liked. I'd take him out and let him go down rabbit holes and things, on the string. Then he would come back and tell me what was going on. I put him down all kinds of holes in trees and things.'

'Whatever for?'

'Just to know what was going on. I have all kinds of uses for him.'

'Why,' stammered Aunt Isobel, half rising from her chair, 'you haven't still got him, have you?'

Paul sat up on his elbows. 'Yes. I've got him. I'm going to keep him till I go to school. I'll need him at school like anything.'

'But it isn't – You wouldn't be allowed –' Aunt Isobel suddenly became extremely grave. 'Where is he now?'

'In the cake-tin.'

'Where is the cake-tin?'

'Over there. In the toy cupboard.'

Aunt Isobel looked fearfully across the shadowed room. She stood up. 'I am going to put the light on, and I shall take that cake-tin out into the garden.'

'It's raining,' Paul reminded her.

'I can't help that,' said Aunt Isobel. 'It is wrong and wicked to keep a little thing like that shut up in a cake-tin. I shall take it out on to the back porch and open the lid.'

'He can hear you,' said Paul.

'I don't care if he can hear me.' Aunt Isobel walked towards the door. 'I'm thinking of his good, as much as of anyone else's.' She switched on the light. 'Now, which was the cupboard?'

'That one, near the fireplace.'

The door was ajar. Timidly Aunt Isobel pulled it open with one finger. There stood the cake-tin amid a medley of torn cardboard, playing cards, pieces of jig-saw puzzle and an open paint box.

'What a mess, Paul!'

Nervously Aunt Isobel stared at the cake-tin and, falsely

innocent, the British Royal Family stared back at her, painted brightly on a background of Allied flags. The holes in the lid were narrow and wedge-shaped, made, no doubt, by the big blade of the best cutting-out scissors. Aunt Isobel drew in her breath sharply. 'If you weren't ill, I'd make you do this. I'd make you carry the tin out and watch you open the lid –' She hesitated as if unnerved by the stillness of the rain-darkened room and the sinister quiet within the cake-tin.

Then, bravely, she put out a hand. Paul watched her, absorbed, as she stretched forward the other one and, very gingerly, picked up the cake-tin. His eyes were dark and deep. He saw the lid was not quite on. He saw the corner, in contact with that ample bosom, rise. He saw the sharp edge catch the cord of Aunt Isobel's pince-nez and, fearing for her rimless glasses, he sat up in bed.

Aunt Isobel felt the tension, the pressure of the pince-nez on the bridge of her nose. A pull it was, a little steady pull as if a small dark claw, as wrinkled as a twig, had caught the hanging cord . . .

'Look out!' cried Paul.

Loudly she shrieked and dropped the box. It bounced away and then lay still, gaping emptily on its side. In the horrid hush, they heard the measured planking of the lid as it trundled off beneath the bed.

Paul broke the silence with a croupy cough.

'Did you see him?' he asked, hoarse but interested.

'No,' stammered Aunt Isobel, almost with a sob. 'I didn't. I didn't see him.'

'But you nearly did.'

Aunt Isobel sat down limply in the upholstered chair. Her hand wavered vaguely round her brow and her cheeks looked white and pendulous, as if deflated. 'Yes,' she muttered, shivering slightly, 'Heaven help me – I nearly did.'

Paul gazed at her a moment longer. 'That's what I mean,' he said.

'What?' asked Aunt Isobel weakly, but as if she did not really care.

Paul lay down again. Gently, sleepily, he pressed his face into the pillow.

'About stories. Being real . . .'

MARY NORTON

# 'Now I'll tell you a story'

Now I'll tell you a story, and this story is new,
So you listen carefully, and do as I do.


This is Tom Thumb – and this is his house;
[*Hold up thumb, then make a roof shape with two forefingers.*]
These are his windows, and this is Squeaky, his mouse.
[*Make 'spectacles', then hold up one finger for the mouse.*]
One morning very early the sun began to shine;
[*Indicate the sunshine with arms held high, then gradually
    lowered.*]
Squeaky mouse sat up in bed and counted up to nine.
[*Wriggle the 'mouse' finger and point to nine fingers in turn.*]
Then Squeaky made a jump – right on to Tom Thumb's
    bed;
[*Jump the 'mouse' finger on to the other hand.*]
She quickly ran right up his arm and sat upon his head.
[*Run the finger right up the arm and on to the head.*]
Squeaky pulled his hair, and Squeaky pulled his nose,
[*Pretend to pull hair and nose.*]
Until Tom Thumb jumped out of bed
And put on all his clothes.
[*Run thumb and forefinger down the 'Tom' thumb to indicate
    dressing.*]
Then they sat down to breakfast
[*Mime the actions.*]
And ate some crusty bread,
And when that was all quite finished
Little Tom Thumb said,
'Now I'll tell you a story, and this story is new . . .' etc.

ANON.

## 'Five little monkeys walked along the shore'

Five little monkeys walked along the shore;
One went a-sailing,
Then there were four.
Four little monkeys climbed up a tree;
One of them tumbled down,
Then there were three.
Three little monkeys found a pot of glue;
One got stuck in it,
Then there were two.
Two little monkeys found a currant bun;
One ran away with it,
Then there was one.
One little monkey cried all afternoon,
So they put him in an aeroplane
And sent him to the moon.

ANON.

# 'Old Roger is dead'

Old Rog-er is dead and he lies in his grave,

lies in his grave, lies in his grave. Old Rog-er is dead and he

lies in his grave, heigh - ho, lies in his grave.

Old Roger is dead and he lies in his grave,
Lies in his grave, lies in his grave.
Old Roger is dead and he lies in his grave,
Heigh ho, lies in his grave.

*Other verses:*

They planted an apple tree over his head, etc.

The apples grew ripe and they all tumbled down, etc.

There came an old woman a-picking them up, etc.

Old Roger got up and he gave her a poke, etc.

This made the old woman go hippety-hop, etc.

[*One child lies in the centre of the ring of children who
    walk round as they sing.*
*For apple trees, raise arms above the head.*
*For apples tumbling, drop fingers with a wriggling movement.*
*One child then pretends to pick up the apples and put them in
    her apron.*
*Roger gets up and pokes her.*
*The old woman hops all round the ring.*]

ANON.

Old Rog-er is dead and he lies in his grave,

lies in his grave, lies in his grave. Old Rog-er is dead and he
lies in his grave, heigh-ho, lies in his grave.

ANON.

# A thought

If I were John and John were Me,
Then he'd be six and I'd be three.
If John were Me and I were John,
I shouldn't have these trousers on.

A. A. MILNE

# *Big Sister and Little Sister*

Once there was a big sister and a little sister. The big sister always took care. Even when she was skipping, she took care that her little sister stayed on the path. When she rode her bicycle, she gave her little sister a ride. When she was walking to school, she took the little sister's hand and helped her across the road. When they were playing in the fields, she made sure little sister didn't get lost. When they were sewing, she made sure little sister's needle was threaded and that little sister held the scissors the right way. Big sister took care of everything, and little sister thought there was nothing big sister couldn't do. Little sister would sometimes cry, but big sister always made her stop. First she'd put her arm around her, then she'd hold out her handkerchief and say, 'Here, blow.' Big sister knew everything.

'Don't do it like that,' she'd say. 'Do it this way.'

And little sister did. Nothing could bother big sister. She knew too much.

But one day little sister wanted to be alone. She was tired of big sister saying,

'Sit here.'

'Go there.'

'Do it this way.'

'Come along.'

And while big sister was getting lemonade and biscuits for

them, little sister slipped away, out of the house, out of the garden, down the road and into the meadows where daisies and grass hid her. Very soon she heard big sister calling, calling and calling her. But she didn't answer. She heard big sister's voice getting louder when she was close and fainter when she went the other way, calling, calling. Little sister leaned back in the daisies. She thought about the lemonade and the biscuits. She thought about the book big sister had promised to read to her. She thought about big sister saying,

'Sit here.'

'Go there.'

'Do it this way.'

'Come along.'

No one told little sister anything now. The daisies bent back and forth in the sun. A big bee bumbled by. The weeds scratched her bare legs. But she didn't move. She heard her big sister's voice coming back. It came closer and closer and closer. And suddenly big sister was so near, little sister could have touched her. But big sister sat down in the daisies. She stopped calling. And she began to cry. She cried and cried just the way little sister often did. When the little sister cried, the big one comforted her. But there was no one to put an arm around big sister. No one took out a handkerchief and said, 'Here, blow.' Big sister just sat there crying all alone.

Little sister stood up, but big sister didn't even see her, she was crying so much. Little sister went over and put her arm around big sister. She took out her handkerchief and said kindly, 'Here, blow.' Big sister did. Then the little sister hugged her.

'Where have you been?' big sister asked.

'Never mind,' said little sister. 'Let's go home and have some lemonade.'

And from that day on little sister and big sister both took care of each other because little sister had learned from big sister and now they both knew how.

CHARLOTTE ZOLOTOW

# 'Piggy on the railway'

Piggy on the railway,
Picking up stones;
Along came an engine
And broke poor Piggy's bones.

'Oh!' said Piggy,
'That's not fair.'
'Oh!' said the engine driver,
'I don't care!'

ANON.

*Illustrated by* RAYMOND BRIGGS

# From a Railway Carriage

Faster than fairies, faster than witches,
Bridges and houses, hedges and ditches,
And charging along like troops in a battle,
All through the meadows the horses and cattle:
All of the sights of the hill and the plain
Fly as thick as driving rain;
And ever again, in the wink of an eye,
Painted stations whistle by.

Here is a child who clambers and scrambles,
All by himself and gathering brambles;
Here is a tramp who stands and gazes;
And there is the green for stringing the daisies!
Here is a cart run away in the road,
Lumping along with man and load;
And here is a mill, and there is a river;
Each a glimpse and gone for ever!

ROBERT LOUIS STEVENSON

# Giacco and His Bean

Once upon a time there was a little boy named Giacco who had no father or mother. The only food he had was a cup of beans. Each day he ate a bean, until finally there was only one left. So he put this bean into his pocket and walked until night. He saw a little house under a mulberry tree. Giacco knocked at the door. An old man came out and asked what he wanted.

'I have no father or mother,' said Giacco. 'And I have no food except this one bean.'

'Poor boy,' said the kind old man. He gave Giacco four mulberries to eat and let him sleep by the fire. During the night the bean rolled out of Giacco's pocket and the cat ate it up. When Giacco awoke, he cried, 'Kind old man, your cat has eaten my bean. What shall I do?'

'You may take the cat,' said the kind old man. 'I do not want to keep such a wicked animal.'

So Giacco took the cat and walked all day until he came to a little house under a walnut tree. He knocked at the door. An old man came out and asked what he wanted.

'I have no father or mother,' said Giacco. 'And I have only this cat that ate the bean.'

'*Too* bad!' said the kind old man. He gave Giacco three walnuts to eat and let him sleep in the dog kennel. During the night the dog ate up the cat, and when Giacco awoke, he cried, 'Kind old man, your dog has eaten my cat!'

'You may take the dog,' said the kind old man. 'I do not want to keep such a mean brute.'

So Giacco took the dog and walked all day until he came to a little house under a fig tree. He knocked at the door. An old man came out and asked what he wanted.

'I have no father or mother,' said Giacco. 'I have only this dog that ate the cat that ate the bean.'

'How very sad!' said the kind old man, and gave Giacco two figs to eat and let him sleep in the pigsty.

That night the pig ate up the dog, and when Giacco awoke he cried, 'Kind old man, your pig has eaten up my dog!'

'You may take the pig,' said the kind old man. 'I do not care to keep such a disgusting creature.'

So Giacco took the pig and walked all day until he came to a little house under a chestnut tree. He knocked at the door. An old man came out and asked what he wanted.

'I have no father or mother and only this pig that ate the dog that ate the cat that ate the bean,' said Giacco.

'How pitiful!' said the kind old man, and gave Giacco one chestnut to eat and let him sleep in the stable. During the night the horse ate up the pig, and when Giacco awoke he cried, 'Kind old man, your horse has eaten up my pig!'

'You may take the horse,' said the kind old man. 'I do not want to keep such a worthless beast.' So Giacco rode away on the horse.

He rode all day until he came to a castle. He knocked at the gate and a voice cried, 'Who is there?'

'It is Giacco. I have no father or mother and I have only this horse that ate the pig that ate the dog that ate the cat that ate the bean.'

'Ha! Ha! Ha!' laughed the Soldier. 'I will tell the King.'

'Ha! Ha! Ho! Ho!' laughed the King. 'Whoever heard of

a bean that ate the cat that ate the dog that ate the pig that ate the horse.'

'Excuse me, Your Majesty, it is just the other way around,' said Giacco. 'It was the horse that ate the pig that ate the dog that ate the cat that ate the bean.'

'Ha! Ha! Ho! Ho!' laughed the King. 'My mistake! Of course, it was the bean that ate the horse; no, I mean the horse that ate the bean; no, I mean – Ha! Ha! Ho! Ho!' laughed the King, and the knights began to laugh, and the ladies began to laugh, and the maids began to laugh, and the cooks began to laugh, and the bells began to ring, and the birds began to sing, and all the people in the kingdom laughed and sang, and the King came to the gate and said,

'Giacco, if you will tell me every day about the bean that ate the horse; I mean the horse that ate the bean; no, I mean the horse that ate the pig that ate the dog that ate the cat that ate the bean – Ha! Ha! Ha! Ha! Ho! Ho! Ho! Ho! you shall sit on the throne beside me!'

So Giacco put on a golden crown and sat upon the throne, and every day he told about the horse that ate the pig that ate the dog that ate the cat that ate the bean, and everybody laughed and sang and lived happily ever after.

FLORENCE BOTSFORD

# The Little Girl Who
# Got Out of
# Bed the Wrong Side

There was once a little girl who got out of bed on the wrong side. Oh, how cross she was! Cross as two sticks! She made a terrible fuss getting dressed. She put her tights on back to front and she complained that her jersey was tickly. She put her feet into the wrong shoes.

When she came down to breakfast, things were even worse. Her porridge was too hot. The milk was too cold. And her banana had black specks in it.

'I shan't eat my horrid breakfast,' said the little girl.

The kitten hid under the sofa and the puppy went into the brush cupboard and closed his eyes and pretended he wasn't there. The little girl was rather sorry, because she liked playing with the kitten and the puppy.

Everyone in the house left her alone and hoped she would soon feel better.

During the morning, her mother was busy making the Christmas puddings. When she had the mixture ready in her big mixing bowl, it looked delicious and smelt even more delicious. She asked the little girl if she would like to give the puddings a stir and have a wish.

'You'd better wish to be a happy girl,' said her mother.

The little girl took the tall wooden spoon and stirred round and round, and as she stirred she *did* wish to be a happy girl. The wish came true even before she had licked the spoon. The kitten came out from under the sofa, and the puppy came out of the brush cupboard, and they had a lovely game all over the house.

When lunch-time came, the little girl ate all her first course, which was fish fingers, and all her pudding, which was apple crumble. Afterwards, she went upstairs for her nap and the kitten and the puppy had their naps, too. When she woke up, she was very careful to get out of her bed on the *right* side.

RUTH AINSWORTH

# 'There were ten in the bed'

There were ten in the bed,
And the little one said:
'Roll over! Roll over!'
So they all rolled over,
And one fell out.

There were *nine* in the bed, etc.

There were *eight* in the bed, etc.

There was one in the bed,
And the little one said:
'Roll over, roll over!'
So he rolled over and fell right out.

ANON.

# The Alarm Cock

Once there was a shop with a sign over the door that said,
VINE, WOLF AND PARROTT, HELPERS.

If you opened the door and went in, you saw the Vine right
away, for it grew out of the floor and up the walls of the
little shop, so the whole room was lined with leaves, and
clusters of flowers hung from the ceiling. Beautiful orange
trumpet-shaped flowers they were, and the Vine was covered
with them all the year round.

The next thing you saw was Wolf. He was a real wolf,
big and grey, with a handsome ruff round his neck, and he
sat on the counter looking thoughtful and wise, with his long
chin sunk on his shaggy grey chest.

And the last thing you saw was old Mr Parrott, who was
not a bird but a grey-haired old man, generally at work in
some corner of the shop, pruning the Vine, or twining a
new shoot so that it would grow comfortably up the wall.

Another sign, over the counter, said,

NO FEE UNLESS SATISFIED.

PAYMENT IN KIND ACCEPTED.

WE HELP YOU WITH ALL YOUR PROBLEMS.

And it was true, there were not many problems that the
firm of Vine, Wolf and Parrott could not solve.

For instance, one day a man came in to complain, 'My
dog sits up on the roof all day. Even at night he won't

come down. What's the use of a dog who's never in the house and won't even come for a walk? Is something wrong with him?'

'Does he bark or howl?' asked Wolf.

'No, just sits watching the clouds and the birds.'

'Wolf had better go and talk to him,' said old Mr Parrott. 'What is your address?'

'Eighty-four Smith Street.'

So old Mr Parrott got out his bicycle and a ladder, and cycled along to Number Eighty-four Smith Street, with the ladder on his shoulder and Wolf sitting on one end of it, and he held the foot of the ladder while Wolf climbed up on to the roof to talk to the dog, and soon found out that he was annoyed because his master never watched greyhound racing on television, and so he had gone on a roof-strike, but would agree to come down if he might sometimes be allowed to watch his favourite TV programme.

A man came in to say, 'My car has caught a cold. It keeps sneezing. What should I do?'

'Get it a warmer bonnet. And put socks on its tyres. And give it a basinful of this Car Cough Mixture night and morning.'

A girl came in to say, 'My record player has slowed down. Instead of the record going round thirty-three times and a half every minute, it goes round once every thirty-three and a half minutes. What can I do about it?'

'You can slow down too,' said old Mr Parrott, after consulting his partners. 'Swallow this slow-down pill and then you'll be able to hear the music just as well as before.'

The girl swallowed the pill, and it slowed her down so much that it took her half an hour to walk to the door of the shop, and she hasn't reached home yet.

An old lady who lived just along the street, Mrs Heyhoe, came in with her little granddaughter. Mrs Heyhoe was called Anna, so was her granddaughter, and there were exactly seventy years between them. One was seven, the other seventy-seven. And they both looked the same; fair hair, bright blue eyes, straight noses, rather short, very cheerful.

'What can I do for you, Mrs Heyhoe, ma'am?' said old Mr Parrott, while little Anna patted Wolf, who wagged his tail.

'I can't get to sleep, Mr Parrott. I haven't slept a wink these three weeks.'

'Dear me,' said Mr Parrott. 'That's serious, that is. What you need is a nutmeg-scented fan. Buy a fan, soak it in nutmeg essence, fan yourself a hundred times, and that should do the trick.'

'Shall I pay you now?' said old Mrs Heyhoe.

'No, no,' he said, pointing to the sign, 'not until you are satisfied.'

So old Mrs Heyhoe went down the road to a fan shop, where she and little Anna chose a very pretty fan, lace, painted all over with roses.

They ground up a hundred nutmegs in the mincer and made a strong nutmeg tea. They sprinkled the fan with nutmeg tea three times an hour for three days, and then at bedtime old Mrs Heyhoe fanned herself a hundred times. Then little Anna fanned her a hundred times. Then she fanned herself again. Little Anna went to sleep, but her grandmother stayed wide awake all night until the sun came in the kitchen window and turned all the teacloths pink.

She thought of all sorts of useful things during the night: where she had put her glasses, a way to use up all her old stockings by stuffing cushions with them, and five new ideas for puddings, but she went back to Mr Parrott, and said,

'The nutmeg fan didn't work.'

'Dear me,' he said. 'It's not often that one of our suggestions doesn't work. Then you had better try playing the flute for half an hour, last thing before you go to bed, with your feet in a big bowl of honey.'

Mrs Heyhoe tried that. She already had a flute that her son, Anna's father, had played when he was a boy. And she kept bees, so she had plenty of honey.

But her next-door neighbour came to the back door, knocking, just when Mrs Heyhoe had got her feet into the honey, to say that Anna's father had called up on her telephone, and was wishful to speak to his mum, who hadn't got a phone.

So that was a nuisance, and it took Mrs Heyhoe quite a long time to get the honey from between her toes, and even so some got spilt on the kitchen floor, and after all, her son only wanted to know if little Anna was behaving herself.

'Which I am, aren't I, Granny?' said little Anna.

'Beautifully, my dearie.'

Then they found that the flute had fallen into the honey.

And that night again Mrs Heyhoe didn't sleep a wink.

'Really,' said old Mr Parrott, when she went back to him next day. 'I don't know that we've ever had a more awkward case. You had better try sniffing at a clove orange, while at the same time imagining that you are inside a teapot.'

So Mrs Heyhoe and Anna bought a whole lot of cloves and made two clove oranges (one for little Anna to take to her mother when she went home). They stuck the cloves all over the oranges, so tight together that you couldn't get a pin between them.

Mrs Heyhoe's kitchen smelt delicious, with the oranges, and the cloves, and the honey, and the nutmeg fan, which they had put up over the fireplace.

At bedtime Mrs Heyhoe shut her eyes and sniffed one of the oranges, and imagined that she was inside a teapot.

But next morning she went back to Vine, Wolf and Parrott.

'It didn't work,' she told Mr Parrott. 'That was the dirtiest teapot I've ever been inside. I had to spend the whole night scrubbing to get it clean. Never had a wink of sleep the whole night long.'

'Humph,' said old Mr Parrott. 'This certainly is a serious case.'

He consulted again with his partners.

'If we could find out *why* Mrs Heyhoe can't get to sleep,' said the Vine in her soft voice, 'we might be able to suggest the cure for her trouble.'

When the Vine spoke, her voice came out through all of her trumpet-shaped orange flowers.

'*Why* can't you get to sleep, ma'am?' asked old Mr Parrott.

'Because I'm so worried about waking up in time,' said old Mrs Heyhoe.

'Then,' said the Vine, 'what she needs is an alarm cock.'

'What's that?' said little Anna.

'A rooster alarm clock. You've heard of a cuckoo clock? A rooster clock is just the same. Only, instead of going Cuckoo, it goes Cock-a-doodle-doo, and wakes you up.'

'Well,' said old Mrs Heyhoe, 'we had better get one.'

So she and little Anna walked all over the town, going to each clock shop in turn. But nowhere could they find a rooster alarm clock. They could find owl clocks and pigeon clocks, nightingale clocks and ostrich clocks, peacock clocks, lark, duck and chick clocks, moorcock, blackcock and wood-cock clocks, but not a single shop had a plain cock clock.

'I wonder,' said little Anna presently, 'if just an ordinary rooster wouldn't do as well, like the one Daddy has at home?'

'But where should we find a rooster in the town?' said her granny.

'Well,' said little Anna, 'as we walk along, I'm sure I can sometimes hear a rooster going Cock-a-doodle-doo.'

'It would be a funny thing if you could,' said her granny, 'right in the middle of the town.' But she began to listen, she listened and she listened, and by and by she thought she could hear a rooster somewhere going Cock-a-doodle-doo.

'It seems to be loudest in this street,' said little Anna.

They were in Smith Street.

They walked north, and the crowing got fainter. So then they walked west along Jones Street, and it grew louder. Then it grew fainter, so they walked south along Brown Street, till it grew louder. Then it grew fainter, so they walked east along Robinson Street.

'Now we're back where we began, in Smith Street,' said little Anna.

'It's a puzzle,' said old Mrs Heyhoe.

'*I* believe the rooster's up above,' said little Anna.

They looked up. They had been walking round a big building which took up a whole city block. The building was fifty storeys high – so high that, as it was a misty day, the top was out of sight in the clouds.

'*I* think we'll have to go up,' said little Anna.

So they walked through the main entrance of the building, and went up. They went up in a lift, and at each floor they stepped out and asked the people there,

'Do you know of a rooster living on this floor?'

Nobody knew of a rooster – not on the fifth floor, nor the tenth, nor the twentieth, nor the twenty-fifth, nor the thirtieth, nor the fortieth.

At last they reached the fiftieth floor and stepped out through a little door on to the roof, right above the clouds.

And there on the roof was a tiny cottage, with an old man sitting in the doorway peeling potatoes, and beside the door in the sunshine, sitting on an upside-down basket, was a beautiful glossy red rooster, with black and green feathers in his wings, and a black, blue and green tail, and black legs, and a red cockscomb.

Little Anna ran to the cottage door.

'Oh, please,' she said to the old man, busy peeling his potatoes, 'could we buy your rooster?'

'Cock-a-doodle-doo!' shouted the rooster indignantly. 'Nobody's going to buy me!'

'No indeed!' said the old man. 'How would I be able to wake in the mornings without my rooster?'

'Besides,' said the rooster, 'I'm happy up here above the clouds. I wouldn't *dream* of living down below where it's all misty and grey. Up here the sun shines all day and the moon shines all night.'

Little Anna and her granny looked at each other sadly.

'They are right, you know,' said old Mrs Heyhoe. 'Why should the old man lose his rooster? And why should the rooster live below the clouds if he doesn't want to?'

But little Anna thought again and said to the old man, 'I suppose we couldn't *rent* your rooster, just for a week or two, till my granny gets into the habit of sleeping again?'

And she said to the rooster, 'The sun does shine down there sometimes. And Granny makes very good mashed potato.'

'Why, if you put it like that,' said the old man, whose name was Mr Welladay, 'that doesn't sound such a bad idea. In fact it sounds like a very *good* idea. I've been feeling rather tired lately; I could do with a few weeks' sleep.'

'Well,' said the rooster, whose name was Enrico, 'since you put it that way, that doesn't sound like a bad idea at all. In fact it would be very pleasant to get down out of the hot sun for a week or two.'

'What sort of rent would you like?' asked old Mrs Heyhoe.

'How about a nice chocolate cake?' asked old Mr Welladay.

So they went home, back down the lift, back along the street, with Enrico sitting on little Anna's shoulder. And Mrs Heyhoe at once baked a nice big chocolate cake, and little Anna took it back to Mr Welladay, who just had time to eat it before he fell fast asleep.

That evening, after they had all had supper – Enrico had cornflakes and milk, so did little Anna – old Mrs Heyhoe, too, fell fast asleep in her armchair, and slept there the whole night through, very peacefully, until Enrico woke her at seven next morning, shouting,

'Cock-a-doodle-doo! It's time to wake up and make my breakfast.'

Every night for seven nights, old Mrs Heyhoe slept soundly. And every morning for seven mornings, Enrico woke her in the same way. On the eighth morning, he woke her by shouting,

'Cock-a-doodle-doo! It's time to get up and put little Anna on the train to go home!'

'Oh, thank goodness you woke me,' said old Mrs Heyhoe. 'I've been worrying about getting Anna on to that train this month past.'

'Is *that* why you couldn't sleep while I've been staying with you, Granny?' said little Anna.

'Of course it is!' said old Mrs Heyhoe.

So they walked to the station, and little Anna got on to the train, with her bag of clothes, and a sandwich, and an apple, and the clove orange for her mother, and she blew a kiss and waved and called out, 'Goodbye, Granny! Thank you for the lovely visit!'

Then old Mrs Heyhoe went along to Vine, Wolf and Parrott, to thank them for their help. She had made another chocolate cake to pay them, as Mr Welladay had enjoyed his so much. Mr Parrott shared it with Wolf, as the Vine did not eat cake.

And then Mrs Heyhoe took Enrico back to old Mr Welladay, who had enjoyed his long sleep so much that he said,

'You are welcome to borrow my rooster again whenever your granddaughter comes to visit. If Enrico agrees, of course.'

'Certainly I agree,' said Enrico. 'Mrs Heyhoe makes the best mashed potato I ever tasted. And little Anna polished my comb every night. Whenever her granddaughter is here on a visit, I'll be glad to oblige Mrs Heyhoe.'

'And I'll be glad to have you,' said Mrs Heyhoe.

So that is what they did.

JOAN AIKEN *Illustrated by* JAN PIEŃKOWSKI

# The Snooks Family

One night Mr and Mrs Snooks were going to bed as usual. It so happened that Mrs Snooks got into bed first, and she said to her husband, 'Please, Mr Snooks, would you blow the candle out?' And Mr Snooks replied, 'Certainly, Mrs Snooks.' Whereupon he picked up the candlestick and began to blow, but unfortunately he could only blow by putting his under lip over his upper lip, which meant that his breath went up to the ceiling instead of blowing out the candle flame.

And he puffed and he puffed and he puffed, but he could not blow it out.

So Mrs Snooks said, 'I will do it, my dear,' and she got out of bed and took the candlestick from her husband and began to blow. But unfortunately she could only blow by putting her upper lip over her under lip, so that all her breath went down on to the floor. And she puffed and she puffed, but she could not blow the candle out.

So Mrs Snooks called their son John. John put on his sky-blue dressing-gown and slipped his feet into his primrose-coloured slippers and came down into his parents' bedroom.

'John, dear,' said Mrs Snooks, 'will you please blow out the candle for us?' And John said, 'Certainly, Mummy.'

But unfortunately John could only blow out of the right corner of his mouth, so that all his breath hit the wall of the room instead of the candle.

And he puffed and he puffed and he puffed, but he could not blow out the candle.

So they all called for his sister, little Ann. And little Ann put on her scarlet dressing-gown and slipped on her pink slippers and came down to her parents' bedroom.

'Ann, dear,' said Mr Snooks, 'will you please blow the candle out for us?' And Ann said, 'Certainly, Daddy.'

But unfortunately Ann could only blow out of the left side of her mouth, so that all her breath hit the wall instead of the candle.

And she puffed and she puffed and she puffed, but she could not blow out the candle.

It was just then that they heard in the street below a heavy steady tread coming along the pavement. Mr Snooks threw open the window and they all craned their heads out. They saw a policeman coming slowly towards the house.

'Oh, Mr Policeman,' said Mrs Snooks, 'will you come up and blow out our candle? We do so want to go to bed.'

'Certainly, Madam,' replied the policeman, and he entered and climbed the stairs – blump, blump, blump. He came into the bedroom where Mr Snooks, Mrs Snooks, John Snooks and little Ann Snooks were all standing round the candle which they could *not* blow out.

The policeman then picked up the candlestick in a very dignified manner and, putting his mouth into the usual shape for blowing, puffed out the candle at the first puff. Just like this – PUFF!

Then the Snooks family all said, 'Thank you, Mr Police-man.' And the policeman said, 'Don't mention it,' and turned to go down the stairs again.

'Just a moment, Policeman,' said Mr Snooks. 'You mustn't

go down the stairs in the dark. You might fall.' And taking a box of matches, he LIT THE CANDLE AGAIN!

Mr Snooks went down the stairs with the policeman and saw him out of the door. His footsteps went blump, blump, blump along the quiet street.

John Snooks and little Ann Snooks went back to bed. Mr and Mrs Snooks got into bed again. There was silence for a moment.

'Mr Snooks,' said Mrs Snooks, 'would you blow out the candle?'

Mr Snooks got out of bed. 'Certainly, Mrs Snooks,' he said . . .

And so on *ad infinitum*.

HARCOURT WILLIAMS

# 'Last one into bed'

'Last one into bed
has to switch out the light.'
It's just the same every night.
There's a race.
I'm ripping off my trousers and shirt –
he's kicking off his shoes and socks.

127

'My sleeve's stuck.'
'This button's too big for its button-hole.'
'Have you hidden my pyjamas?'
'Keep your hands off mine.'
If you win
you get where it's safe
before the darkness comes –
but if you lose
if you're last
you know what you've got coming up is
the journey from the light switch
to your bed.
It's the Longest Journey in the World.

'You're last tonight,' my brother says.
And he's right.
There is nowhere so dark
as that room in the moment
after I've switched out the light.

There is nowhere so full of dangerous things –
things that love dark places –
things that breathe only when you breathe
and hold their breath when I hold mine.
So I have to say:
'I'm not scared.'
That face, grinning in the pattern on the wall
isn't a face –
'I'm not scared.'

That prickle on the back of my neck
is only the label on my pyjama jacket –
'I'm not scared.'
That moaning-moaning is nothing
but water in a pipe –
'I'm not scared.'

Everything's going to be just fine
as soon as I get into that bed of mine.
Such a terrible shame
it's always the same
it takes so long
it takes so long
it takes so long
to get there.

From the light switch
to my bed.
It's the Longest Journey in the World.

MICHAEL ROSEN
*Illustrated by* MICHAEL FOREMAN

# The Horrible Story

Outside it was quite dark, but inside the boys had a candle-lantern which cast a pale, flickering light on the tawny sides of the tent. You could not see much – only the long shapes of sleeping-bags and blankets, and the humpy shapes of heads and pillows.

The two longest shapes were Robert and Allan, who were by the door flap, which was fastened back tonight. They had told Christopher, Robert's little brother, that they wanted to look out into the garden and watch the stars, but really they had their own secret reasons for wanting to be together by the door, and for making him sleep on his own at the back of the tent. *His* bedtime shape was just blankets, for he had no sleeping-bag, and it was a shorter shape than Allan's or Robert's because he was only small – not quite seven – and they were ten.

Yesterday morning there had been no tent. A large parcel had arrived at lunch-time addressed to Mr Robert and Mr Christopher Johnson. Robert's eyes had shone with surprise and delight when it had been opened and its layers of paper and cardboard peeled back. It was a tent – not just a white tent such as you might see in any camp-ground either, but a tawny-brown tent that could belong to an Indian or an outlaw or some wild, fierce hero.

There had been the fun of fitting the poles together and

putting it up at the bottom of the garden, sheltered by the hedge, and the sudden excitement when they realized that they would be allowed to sleep out all night in it.

'Can Allan come too, Mum?' asked Robert, because Allan was his best friend, and they always shared adventures.

'Of course he may, if he is allowed,' Mother replied, smiling.

'Me too!' Christopher cried anxiously, for he knew that when Allan and Robert were together he was always just a little brother to be left behind or taken no notice of. 'It's *my* tent too, isn't it?'

Robert looked at him rather sourly. He said, 'You can come some other time. You've got lots of chances.'

His mother turned round sharply.

'Now, don't be difficult, Bob!' she said. 'Of course Christopher can camp out too. If there's no room for Christopher there's no room for Allan either.'

So here they were, the three of them, Allan and Robert, and Christopher on his own in the back of the tent, looking a bit lonely and small in the flickering shadows.

Secretly Allan nudged Robert as a sign that he was going to begin the Get-rid-of-Christopher plan . . . a plan they had made that afternoon riding their bicycles home from the river.

'Little kids get scared easy as easy in the dark,' Allan had said, his wet, red hair standing on end, his green eyes narrowed against the wind. He had glanced behind to see if Christopher was listening. The little boy had had his usual dreamy look and was practising his whistling. 'I bet when your little brother hears one of my famous horrible tales he'll run inside to Mummy and won't want to come into the tent ever again. Then we'll have a midnight feast, eh? I'll bring a tin of fruit salad, and a tin opener, and some luncheon sausage.'

'I'll buy a packet of biscuits,' Robert had replied. 'I've got ten pence.'

As he remembered this, he slid his hand under the pillow to feel the biscuits he'd hidden there. The paper crackled, and Christopher turned his head a little bit. Quickly Robert nudged Allan to show that he understood the plan was beginning. Allan blew out the candle in the lantern and for a moment everything went black as the night came, silent and sudden, into the tent.

'Hey,' said Allan, 'I know a story. It's pretty ghostly though . . .' He let his voice fade away uncertainly.

'Go on!' Robert said. 'Tell us! I'm not scared.'

'I'm not scared either,' said Christopher's piping voice from the back of the tent. He did not sound the least bit like a wild, fierce hero though.

'It's good you're not scared,' Allan declared, 'because it's a really horrible story, and it's about a boy called Christopher too. Now listen!

'This boy called Christopher lived in an old, dark house on the edge of a big forest. The forest was old too, and dark, like this tent, and full of creepy noises. Sometimes people went in, but no one ever came out again. Lots of rats lived in this forest, big as cats . . .' Allan paused, thinking out the next bit. In the little silence Robert was amazed to hear Christopher's small voice come in unexpectedly.

'When those rats ran around,' he said, 'their feet made a rustly sound, didn't they?' Outside, the hedge rustled in the wind, and Christopher added, '. . . a bit like that.'

'Huh!' said Allan crossly. 'And I suppose you think you
know what else lived in the forest?'

'Yes ... yes, I do, Allan.'

'Look, who's telling this story?' cried Allan indignantly.
Then he asked rather cautiously, 'Well, what else *did* live
there?'

'Spiders,' said Christopher. 'Big hairy spiders ... big as
footballs ... but hairy all over like dish mops, huge black
dish mops going scuttle, scuttle on lots of thin legs –'

Allan interrupted him fiercely, 'Hey shut *up*, will you!

This is my story, isn't it? Well then ... there weren't any spiders, but there was a dragon.'

Allan went on talking about the bigness and smokiness of the dragon, but Robert felt disappointed in it. Somehow it did not seem nearly as frightening as the scuttling, hairy spiders. On the other side of the tent something went *tap*, *tap*, *tap*! like quick little feet running over the canvas. Allan stopped and listened.

'It's just the wind,' Christopher said in a kind voice. 'It's just a scraping, twiggy piece from the hedge. Go on, Allan.'

Robert suddenly felt sorry for Christopher, lying there so trustingly staring into the dark with round black eyes like shoe buttons. Christopher was just not an adventurer. He was not the sort of boy who knew anything about the wild scaring life of the wide world. Christopher was the sort who would rather stay at home and read fairy stories than plan wars in the gorse or battles over the sand hills. Perhaps it was a bit mean to frighten him out of the tent, a tent which was really half his.

'Never mind!' thought Robert. 'He'll have lots of other chances.' Under his pillow the biscuit paper crackled faintly.

'And then, one night ...' Allan said mysteriously, 'the little boy was on his own in the old house when ... guess what happened?'

'Somebody knocked at the door,' said Christopher promptly. 'Three knocks, very slowly, KNOCK KNOCK KNOCK, like that.'

'Fair go!' replied Allan scornfully. 'Do you know who it was, Mr Smart?'

'Yes,' Christopher went on, 'the little boy opened the door and there was a man there all in black, at least it looked like a man, but you couldn't tell really, because he had a black thing over his face, a black silk scarf thing. And do you know what he said? He said, "Little boy, the time has come for you to follow *me*."' Christopher stopped, and the tent was quiet except for the sad-sea sound of the wind.

'Did the boy go?' asked Robert. He did not want to ask, but suddenly he felt he had to know. Allan said nothing. Christopher's voice was almost dreamy, as he replied,

'Yes, he did. He just couldn't help it. And as he went out of the door, it shut itself behind him. The gate did too. Then they were in that forest. Everywhere was the rustling noise of rats and spiders.'

'Hey . . .' began Allan.

'What?' squeaked Christopher. Allan turned over restlessly in the dark.

'Nothing! Go on!' he said.

'And *things* followed them,' Christopher went on, making his voice deep and mysterious. 'The man went first, and the boy followed the man, and if he looked back he saw things with *eyes* coming after him, but he couldn't see what things they were.'

'What were they?' asked Robert in a small voice.

'Just things!' said Christopher solemnly. 'Spooky things . . . with little red eyes,' he added thoughtfully. 'Then they came to a clearing place – there was a fire burning – not a yellow fire though, a blue one. All the flames were blue. It looked *ghastly*!' cried Christopher, pleased with his grown-up word. 'There were three heads – just heads, no arms or legs or bodies or anything – sticking out of the ground round the fire.' He stopped again. Allan and Robert could hear their own breathing. They did not ask any questions and Christopher went on with his story again. 'They were ugly, UGLY heads and they had these smiles on their faces' – Christopher was trying to think of words bad enough to describe the smiles – 'more horrible than anything you ever saw. They were yellow too, mind you, like cheese. One head looked at the man with cruel, mean eyes and said,

'"So you brought us some food."

'The man replied, "Yes, and it's very tender tonight."

'"Well, it's just as well," the head said, "or we'd have had to eat *you*."

'Then the second head said, "We'll have a good tuck-in tonight, eh, brothers? Bags I be the one to drink his blood." Then the third head opened its mouth, wide as wide, like a cat yawning, you know, and it had all these pointy teeth, like needles, some short and some long, and it didn't even say anything. It just began to scream, horrible, high-up screams . . .'

Christopher's voice got louder and higher with excitement, and at this very moment, almost it seemed at Robert's ear, a shrill furious howl arose from under the hedge. Allan scrambled to his feet with a cry of terror and went hopping madly out of the tent, too frightened to get out of his sleeping-bag first.

'The head!' yelled Robert and followed him, so frightened he felt sick and shaky in his stomach. Under the hedge were heads with teeth like needles waiting to bite him up as if he was an apple.

Christopher was alone in the tent. Quickly he hopped from under his blankets and stuck his head out through the tent flap. He saw Allan and Robert, still zipped in their sleeping-bags, hopping and stumbling up the lawn.

'It ends happily!' he shouted.

Then he thoughtfully put his hand under Allan's pillow and helped himself to the luncheon sausage hidden there.

Voices were talking on the veranda.

'It was only a cat fight!' Christopher's father was saying. 'Great Scott, if you're going to be scared by a cat fight, we'll never make campers of you.'

Christopher grinned to himself in the dark and quietly felt for the biscuits under Robert's pillow.

MARGARET MAHY
*Illustrated by* SHIRLEY HUGHES

# Night

The sun descending in the west,
    The evening star does shine;
The birds are silent in their nest,
    And I must seek for mine.
The moon, like a flower,
In heaven's high bower,
With silent delight
Sits and smiles on the night.

WILLIAM BLAKE

## The Adventures of Isabel

Isabel met an enormous bear,
Isabel, Isabel, didn't care;
The bear was hungry, the bear was ravenous,
The bear's big mouth was cruel and cavernous.
The bear said, Isabel, glad to meet you,
How do, Isabel, now I'll eat you!
Isabel, Isabel, didn't worry,
Isabel didn't scream or scurry,
She washed her hands and she straightened her hair up,
Then Isabel quietly ate the bear up.

Once in a night as black as pitch
Isabel met a wicked witch.
The witch's face was cross and wrinkled,
The witch's gums with teeth were sprinkled.
Ho ho, Isabel! the old witch crowed,
I'll turn you into an ugly toad!
Isabel, Isabel, didn't worry,
Isabel didn't scream or scurry,
She showed no rage, she showed no rancor,
But she turned the witch into milk and drank her.

Isabel once was asleep in bed
When a horrible dream crawled into her head.
It was worse than a dinosaur, worse than a shark,
Worse than an octopus oozing in the dark.
'Boo!' said the dream, with a dreadful grin,
'I'm going to scare you out of your skin!'
Isabel, Isabel, didn't worry,
Isabel didn't scream or scurry,
Isabel had a cleverer scheme;
She just woke up and fooled that dream.

OGDEN NASH
*Illustrated by* QUENTIN BLAKE

# 'Little Arabella Miller'

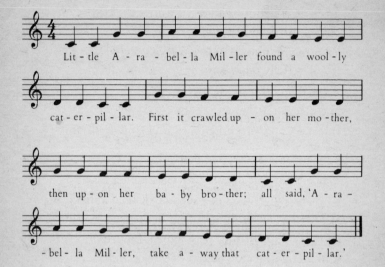

Little Arabella Miller
Found a woolly caterpillar.
First it crawled upon her mother,
Then upon her baby brother;
All said, 'Arabella Miller,
Take away that caterpillar.'

[*Pretend to pick up the caterpillar; walk fingers of right hand
up the left arm then vice versa; pretend to put the caterpillar down.*]

ANON.

# 'Jelly on a plate'

Jelly on a plate,
Jelly on a plate,
Wibble, wobble, wibble, wobble,
Jelly on a plate.

Sausages in the pan,
Sausages in the pan,
Turn them over, turn them over,
Sausages in the pan.

Ghostie in the house,
Ghostie in the house,
Turn him out, turn him out,
Ghostie in the house.

ANON.

# Where Arthur Sleeps

There was once a young man in west Wales who was the seventh son of a seventh son. All such, it is said, are born to great destinies, for with their forty-nine parts of man there is blended one part of Bendith y Mamau (Blessing of the Mothers, or fairies). It happened one day that he had a quarrel with his father and left home to seek his fortune in England. As he walked through Wales, he met a rich farmer who engaged him to take a herd of his cattle to London. 'For to my eyes,' said the farmer, 'you look a likely lad, and a lucky lad too. With a dog at your heels and a staff in your hand you would be a prince among drovers. Now here is a dog, but where in the world is a staff?'

'Leave that to me,' said our Welshman, and stepping aside to a rocky mound he cut himself the finest hazel stick he could find. It had to be fine, for as teeth to a dog so his staff to a drover. It was tall as his shoulder and mottled like a trout, and so hard of grain that when the sticks of his fellow-drovers were ragged as straws it showed neither split nor splinter.

He passed through England without losing a beast and disposed of his herd in London. A little later he was standing on London Bridge, wondering what to do next, when a stranger stopped alongside him and asked him from whence he came.

'From my own country,' he replied; for a Welshman does well to be cautious in England.

'And what is your name?' asked the stranger.

'The one my father gave me.'

'And where did you cut your stick, friend?'

'I cut it from a tree.'

'I approve your closeness,' said the stranger. 'Now what would you say if I told you that from that stick in your hand I can make you gold and silver?'

'I should say you are a wise man.'

'With Capital Letters at that,' said the stranger, and he went on to explain that his hazel stick had grown over a place where a vast treasure lay hidden. 'If only you can remember where you cut it, and lead me there, that treasure shall be yours.'

'I may well do that,' said the Welshman, 'for why am I here save to seek my fortune?'

Without more ado they set off together for Wales and at last reached Craig-y-Dinas (The Fortress Rock), where he showed the Wise Man (for such he was) the exact spot where he had cut his stick. It had sprung from the root of a large old hazel, and the knife-mark was still to be seen, as yellow as gold and broad as a broad-bean. With bill and mattock they dug this up and found underneath a big flat-stone; and when they lifted the stone they saw a passage and a gleam at the far end of it.

'You first,' said the Wise Man; for an Englishman does well to be cautious in Wales; and they crept carefully down the passage towards the gleam. Hanging from the passage roof was a bronze bell the size of a beehive, with a clanger as long as your arm, and the Wise Man begged the Welshman on no account to touch it, for if he did disaster would surely follow. Soon they reached the main cave, where they were amazed by the extent of it, and still more by what they saw there. For it was filled with armed warriors, all asleep on the floor. There was an outer ring of a thousand men, and an inner ring of a hundred, their heads to the wall and their feet to the centrè, each with sword, shield, battle-axe and spear; and outermost of all lay their horses, unbitted and unblinkered, with their trappings heaped before their noses. The reason why they could see this so clearly was because of the extreme brilliance of the weapons and the helmets glowing like suns and the hooves of the horses effulgent as autumn's moon. And in the middle of all lay a king and emperor at rest, as they knew by the glory of his array and the jewelled crown beneath his hand and the awe and majesty of his person.

Then the Welshman noticed that the cavern also contained two tall heaps of gold and silver. Gaping with greed he started towards them, but the Wise Man motioned to him to wait a moment first.

'Help yourself,' he warned him, 'from one heap or the other, but on no account from both.'

The Welshman now loaded himself with gold till he could not carry another coin. To his surprise the Wise Man took nothing.

'I have not grown wise,' he said, 'by coveting gold and silver.'

This sounded more wind than wisdom to the Welshman, but he said nothing as they started for the mouth of the cave. Again the Wise Man cautioned him about touching the bell. 'It might well prove fatal to us if one or more of the warriors should awake and lift his head and ask, "Is it day?" Should that happen there is only one thing to do. You must instantly answer, "No, sleep on!" and we must hope that he will lower his head again to rest, by which means we may escape.'

And so it happened. For the Welshman was now so bulging with gold that he could not squeeze past the bell without his elbow touching it. At once a sonorous sound of bronze bewrangled the passage, and a warrior lifted his head.

'Is it day?' he asked.

'No,' replied the Welshman, 'sleep on.'

At these prompt words the warrior lowered his head and slept, and not without many a backward glance the two companions reached the light of day and replaced the stone and the hazel tree. The Wise Man next took his leave of the Welshman, but gave him this counsel first. 'Use that wealth well,' he told him, 'and it will suffice you for the rest of your life. But if, as I suspect, you come to need more, you may return and help yourself from the silver heap. Try not to touch the bell, but if you do and a warrior awakes, he will ask, "Are the Cymry in danger?" You must then answer, "Not yet, sleep on!" But I should on no account advise you to return to the cave a third time.'

'Who are these warriors?' asked the Welshman. 'And who is their sleeping king?'

'The king is Arthur, and those that surround him are the men of the Island of the Mighty. They sleep with their steeds and their arms because a day will come when land and sky shall cower at the sound of a host, and the bell will tremble and ring, and then those warriors will ride out with Arthur at their head, and drive our foes headlong into the sea, and there shall be justice and peace among men for as long as the world endures.'

'That may be so, indeed,' said the Welshman, waving farewell. 'Meantime I have my gold.'

But the time soon came when his gold was all spent. A second time he entered the cave, and a second time took too great a load, only this time of silver. A second time his elbow touched the bell. Three warriors raised their heads. 'Are the Cymry in danger?' The voice of one was light as a bird's, the voice of another was dark as a bull's, and the voice of the third so menacing that he could hardly gasp out an answer.

'Not yet,' he said, 'sleep on!' Slowly, with sighs and mutterings, they lowered their heads, and their horses snorted and clashed their hooves before silence filled the cave once more.

For a long time after this escape he told himself that he would on no account return to the cave a third time. But in a year or two his silver went the way of his gold, and almost despite himself there he was, standing by the hazel with a mattock in his hand. A third time he entered the cave, and a third time his elbow touched the bell. As it boomed, all those warriors sprang to their feet, and the proud stallions with them, and what with the booming of the bell, the jangling of trappings, and the shrill neighing of the horses, never in the world's history was there more uproar in an enclosed place than that. Then Arthur's voice arose over the din, silencing them, and Cei and the one-handed Bedwyr, Owein, Trystan and Gwalchmei moved through the host and brought the horses to a stand.

'The time is not yet,' said Arthur. He pointed to the

Welshman, trembling with his gold and silver in the passage. 'Would you march out for him?'

At these words, Cei caught the intruder up by the feet and would have lashed him against the wall, but Arthur forbade it and said to put him outside, and so Cei did, flinging him like a wet rabbit-skin from the passage and closing the stone behind him. So there he was, without a penny to scratch with, blue as a plum with fright and bruises, flat on his back in the eye of the sun.

It was a long time before he could be brought to tell his story, and still longer before he grew well. One day, however, he returned, and some friends with him, to Craig-y-Dinas.

'Where is the hazel tree?' they asked, for it was not to be seen. 'And where is the stone?' they asked, for they could not find it. When he persisted in his story they jeered at him, and because he might not be silenced they beat him, and so it came about that for shame and wrath he left the countryside for ever. And from that day to this no one, though he were seven times over the seventh son of a seventh son, has beheld Arthur sleeping with his host, nor till the day of Britain's greatest danger shall any so behold him. So with the hope that that day is a long way off, we reach the end of our story.

GWYN JONES

# Granny

Through every nook and every cranny
The wind blew in on poor old Granny;
Around her knees, into each ear
(And up her nose as well, I fear).

All through the night the wind grew worse,
It nearly made the vicar curse.
The top had fallen off the steeple
*Just* missing him (and other people).

It blew on man; it blew on beast.
It blew on nun; it blew on priest.
It blew the wig off Auntie Fanny –
But most of all, it blew on Granny!!

SPIKE MILLIGAN

# 'Old Mother Twitchett'

Old Mother Twitchett has but one eye,
And a long tail which she can let fly,
And every time she goes over a gap,
She leaves a bit of her tail in a trap.

ANON.

*Illustrated by* RAYMOND BRIGGS

# 'Two legs sat upon three legs'

Two legs sat upon three legs
With one leg in his lap;
In comes four legs
And runs away with one leg;
Up jumps two legs,
Catches up three legs,
Throws it after four legs,
And makes him bring back one leg.

ANON.

*Illustrated by* RAYMOND BRIGGS

# 'Four stiff-standers'

Four stiff-standers,
Four dilly-danders,
Two lookers,
Two crookers,
And a wig-wag.

ANON.
*Illustrated by* RAYMOND BRIGGS

# I Saw a Jolly Hunter

I saw a jolly hunter
  With a jolly gun
Walking in the country
  In the jolly sun.

In the jolly meadow
  Sat a jolly hare,
Saw the jolly hunter
  Took jolly care.

Hunter jolly eager –
  Sight of jolly prey.
Forgot gun pointing
  Wrong jolly way.

Jolly hunter jolly head
  Over heels gone.
Jolly old safety-catch
  Not jolly on.

Bang went the jolly gun.
  Hunter jolly dead.
Jolly hare got clean away.
  Jolly good, I said.

CHARLES CAUSLEY

# Row, Row, Row Your Boat

## (ROUND FOR FOUR VOICES)

Row, row, row your boat
Gently down the stream.
Merrily, merrily, merrily, merrily
Life is but a dream.

ANON.

# Boredom

Oh dear! what shall I do?
Nothing lasts more than a minute or two,
Everything's silly, and nothing is fun,
And there doesn't seem anything left to be done.

Oh dear! what shall I do?
I've read all my fairy-tales seven times through,
I'm tired of my bricks and I'm sick of my train,
And my paint-box was left out all night in the rain.

Oh dear! what shall I do?
I don't *want* to go in the garden with you,
I don't *want* to sit down and play a nice game,
I want to do something that isn't the same.

Everything, everything *is* such a bore!
I don't enjoy being alive any more.
Why can't there sometimes be something that's new?
Oh dear! *what shall* I D O?

ELEANOR FARJEON

# Uninvited Ghosts

When the Browns moved to their new house, they left the old one empty. The rooms were swept and bare. The windows had no curtains. The walls had pale squares where the pictures had been.

The new house was like that, too. It seemed quite empty. The Browns spent a dreadful day moving in. It was all fuss and bustle. Mrs Brown broke her best teapot. Mr Brown fell off the ladder. Simon (who was eight) put his foot through the bathroom floor. Marian (who was nine) lost her pencil set. The cat took one look and ran away.

A chest of drawers and two removal men got stuck on the stairs for half an hour.

At last it was all done, and everybody was in a bad temper with everybody else. There was nothing but bread and margarine for supper. The cat came back and was sick on the kitchen floor. The television wouldn't work and the children were sent to bed.

It was then that they found the house was not empty.

First, Marian put her jersey in a drawer. She banged the drawer shut and a voice said 'Ouch!'

Marian said to Simon, 'I never touched you, stupid.'

Simon said, 'Stupid yourself!'

They were just about to get down to a proper battle, since both of them were tired and cross, when something else happened. The drawer slid slowly open, and out came a pale grey shape, about three feet high, smelling of wood-smoke. It sat down on a chair and began to hum to itself. It looked like a bundle of bedclothes, except that it was not solid. You could see, quite clearly, the cushion on the chair underneath it.

Marian took one huge jump into bed and shrieked, 'That's a ghost!'

The ghost said, 'It's not nice to call people names. Be quiet and go to sleep.'

It climbed on to the end of Simon's bed, took out a ball of wool and some needles and began to knit.

Have you ever tried telling your mother that you can't get to sleep because there is a ghost sitting on the end of your bed, clacking its knitting needles? I shouldn't. She would probably say the sort of things that Mrs Brown said to Simon.

The trouble was, the ghost only appeared to Simon and Marian. 'I like children,' it said cosily, 'always have. Eat up your dinner, there's a good boy.' At this point it was sitting on the kitchen table, breathing down Simon's neck.

They couldn't get away from it. When they were watching television, it sat itself down between them and talked loudly through all the best bits. When they wouldn't answer, it poked them in the ribs. That was like being nudged by a damp, cold cloud. It trailed round the garden after them when they were playing. It made remarks when they were trying to do their homework. 'Now then,' it would say sternly, 'no looking out of the window. No chewing the end of your pencil. When *I* was your age . . .'

'Go *away*, can't you!' yelled Simon. 'This is our house now.'

'No, it isn't,' said the ghost smugly. 'Always been here, I have. A hundred years or more. Seen plenty of families come and go, I have.'

At the end of the first week the children woke up to find the ghost on the wardrobe reading a newspaper. The newspaper had the date 1871 on it. The ghost was smoking a long, white clay pipe. Beside it there was a second, grey, cloudy shape.

'Morning,' said the ghost. 'Say how do you do to my Auntie Edna.'

'She can't come here,' roared the children.

'Oh, yes, she can,' said the ghost. 'She always comes here in August. Likes a bit of a change, does Auntie.'

Auntie Edna was even worse, if possible. She sucked peppermint drops which smelled so strong that Mrs Brown kept asking the children what they were eating. She sang hymns in a high, squeaky voice. She followed the children all over the house. She said she loved kiddies. It was nice to be where there were two such nice kiddies.

Two days later the children came up to bed to find a third ghost in their room. 'Meet Uncle Charlie,' said the first ghost. The children groaned. 'And Jip,' said the ghost. 'Here, Jip, good dog, say hello, then.'

A large grey dog that you could see straight through came out from under the bed, wagging its tail. The cat gave a howl and ran away again. The children howled, too, with rage, and got under the bedclothes. The ghosts chatted to each other all night and told long boring stories.

The children decided that something had to be done. They couldn't go on like this. 'We must get them to go and live somewhere else,' said Marian. The problem was where. And how.

That Sunday they were going to see their uncle, who lived by himself in a big house. Plenty of room for ghosts. The children were very cunning. They asked the ghosts if they would like a drive in the country. The ghosts said it might make a bit of a change.

On the way, the three ghosts and their dog sat on the back shelf of the car. Mr and Mrs Brown kept asking why there was such a strong smell of peppermint drops. They asked why the children were so restless, too. The fact was the ghosts kept shoving them.

The ghosts liked it at Uncle Dick's. They liked his colour television and they liked his fitted carpets. Nice and comfy, they said. 'Why not settle down here?' said Simon, in an offhand sort of way.

'Couldn't do that,' said the ghosts. 'No children. Dull. We like a place with a bit of life to it.'

All the way home in the car they ate toast. There were real toastcrumbs on the car floor and the children got the blame. Then the children had a brilliant idea. At the end of their road there lived a Mr and Mrs Clark, who had a baby. No other children. Just one baby. And all day long the baby was bored. It sat in its pram in the garden and threw its toys out and cried.

'I wonder . . .' said Simon and Marian to each other.

They made friends with Mrs Clark. They did her shopping for her and took the baby for walks and washed her car. Mrs Clark invited them to tea. They said to the ghosts, 'Would you like to go visiting again?' The ghosts said they wouldn't mind.

Mrs Clark gave the children ham sandwiches and choco-late cake. The ghosts watched the colour television. They said it was a nice big one, and they liked the big squashy sofa too. They went all round the house and said it wasn't at all a bad little place. Nice and warm, they said. Homely.

They *loved* the baby. 'Ah!' said Auntie Edna. 'There now

... bless its little heart. Give us a smile, then, darling.' They all sat round it and chattered at it and sang to it and told it stories.

And the baby loved the ghosts. It cooed and chuckled and smiled and it never cried all afternoon. Mrs Clark said she couldn't think what had come over it.

Well, I expect you can guess what happened. The ghosts moved down the road. Mrs Clark has the happiest baby in the world, Simon and Marian no longer have to share their bedroom with three other people, and the cat has come back.

PENELOPE LIVELY

# A Teeny-weeny Tale

Once upon a time there was a teeny-weeny woman who lived all by herself in a teeny-weeny house.

One day she went for a teeny-weeny walk. She had not gone far when she came to a teeny-weeny gate, so she opened the teeny-weeny gate and went into a teeny-weeny wood, and what should she find but a teeny-weeny bone under a teeny-weeny tree.

'I'll make a teeny-weeny pot of soup from this teeny-weeny bone,' said the teeny-weeny woman to her teeny-weeny self. So she put the teeny-weeny bone into her teeny-weeny pocket, and went out of the teeny-weeny wood to her teeny-weeny house. She put the teeny-weeny bone in her teeny-weeny cupboard, and then she went to her teeny-weeny bed.

But she had not been long in her teeny-weeny bed when

she heard a teeny-weeny voice come from the teeny-weeny cupboard, and the teeny-weeny voice said:

'Give me back my bone!'

When she heard this, the teeny-weeny woman was a teeny-weeny bit frightened. She hid under her teeny-weeny bedclothes, and went to sleep. Suddenly, the teeny-weeny woman woke to hear a teeny-weeny voice coming from the teeny-weeny cupboard again, and it said a teeny-weeny bit louder:

'Give me back my bone!'

This made the teeny-weeny woman more frightened than ever, and she hid her teeny-weeny self a teeny-weeny bit further under the teeny-weeny bedclothes. But she could not go to sleep, and after a teeny-weeny while she heard that teeny-weeny voice come from the teeny-weeny cupboard, but this time the teeny-weeny voice was a teeny-weeny bit louder, and it said:

'GIVE ME BACK MY BONE!'

This made the teeny-weeny woman nearly jump out of her teeny-weeny skin, but she poked her teeny-weeny head out of the teeny-weeny bedclothes and said in her loudest voice:

'TAKE IT!'

NORAH MONTGOMERIE

162

# The Dark House

In a dark, dark wood, there was a dark, dark house,
And in that dark, dark house, there was a dark, dark room,
And in that dark, dark room, there was a dark, dark
cupboard,
And in that dark, dark cupboard, there was a dark, dark
shelf,
And in that dark, dark shelf, there was a dark, dark box,
And in that dark, dark box, there was a GHOST!

ANON.

# Blind Alley

There's a turning I must pass
Often four times in a day,
Narrow, rather dark, with grass
Growing, a neglected way;

Two long walls, a tumbled shed,
Bushes shadowing each wall –
When I've wondered where it led
People say, Nowhere at all.

But if that is true, oh why
Should this turning be at all?
Some time, in the daylight, I
*Will* creep up along the wall;

For it somehow makes you think,
It has such a secret air,
It might lead you to the brink
Of – oh well, of anywhere!

Some time I will go. And see,
Here's the turning just in sight,
Full of shadows beckoning me!
Some time, yes. But not tonight.

ELEANOR FARJEON

# The Coronation Mob

'They've climbed Everest,' said my mother at breakfast on Coronation morning.

'Who's Everest?' said my brother. He was three. He didn't know about mountains.

'Who's climbed it?' said my father.

'Hillary and Tensing. It's in the paper, look.' She showed us the headline about Mount Everest and the photographs of the men who had climbed it.

'Is that actually them, actually on top of Mount Everest?' I said.

'I doubt it,' said my father. 'They'd be wearing special clothes and oxygen masks, I should think. The air's very thin, so high up.'

'I expect they'd have a flag to plant on top,' said my mother.

My brother drew a picture in the stop-press. He drew a circle with a wavy line coming out of it.

'What a lovely balloon,' said my mother.

'It's the Queen,' said my brother. He coloured the circle with marmalade.

'I thought that wavy line was a bit of string.'

'It's her leg.'

'Don't play with your food,' said my father. 'I think you'll find she has two legs.'

'No she hasn't. She goes hop, hop, hop,' said my brother.

He didn't know much about the Queen, either, because he had never seen her, even on television. There was only one television set on our side of the street. It belonged to the Savilles, three doors down, and everyone in our row was going to watch the Coronation on it; everyone, that is, except my father. He said he had some urgent work to do, but really it was because of Mrs Saville.

'I know you don't like Mrs S,' said my mother, 'but surely you could go down there just this once. It would be worth it, to see the Coronation.'

'No, it wouldn't,' said my father. 'I wouldn't watch the Last Judgement if it meant seeing it on Mrs Saville's T V.'

At ten o'clock my mother and brother and I went along to the Savilles'. There were chairs lined up in their living-room, but children were allowed to sit on the floor at the front; as a treat. It wasn't exactly a treat. The television set looked like a coffin stood on end, and the picture was right at the top.

Horses began to move across the screen, struggling through a blizzard of fizzing white spots. It was raining hard outside and I assumed it must be snowing in London, but Mr Saville said the picture was faulty.

'Gremlins, ha-ha-ha,' said Mr Saville. He took the tele-vision set by the shoulders and shook it. The blizzard got worse and the horses disappeared. It was like watching a funeral with a sock over your head.

I wondered how to get out. The room was dark, except for a sort of blue sheet-lightning from the television, and I thought I might crawl away unnoticed, but I was fenced in by a stockade of shins.

Next to me was my friend Barbara, who lived in the end house. Sometimes she was my friend, but not at the moment. I began to squeeze bits of Barbara between my new white sandals and the floor. Barbara squeaked. After a few minutes enough people noticed for my mother to get embarrassed and send me outside. I burrowed between the shins and stamped out of the room, looking cross. It was a terrible disgrace. I was spoiling the Coronation.

In the street the rain had stopped. My white sandals already had shiny grey patches on the toes, so I hopscotched from puddle to puddle, down the road towards the recreation ground, where rows of flags were snapping in the wind like wet washing. The pub on the corner was called the Star Inn, and its sign was a beautiful golden star that hung from a curly iron bracket. Now the bracket was golden and the star was red, white and blue.

The house next to the pub belonged to the dentist. His brass plate was still brass but he had red, white and blue flowers in his window-box this summer, instead of dead wallflowers; and a loyal bush in a tub at the top of the steps that ran up to the front door.

There was a tunnel under these steps and someone was sitting in it. It was my friend, Billy Chapman, wearing the black school cap with an orange peak that made him look like a penguin. He wasn't at the Savilles' house because his mother thought that television was common.

I didn't ask him what he was doing in the tunnel, because I knew it was his gateway to stirring adventures. He would go in one end, plain Billy Chapman, and stagger out at the other, riddled with bullets.

'Just been climbing Everest,' said Billy, casually.

'Why aren't you on top, then?' I asked. I thought he ought to be up on the summit, in the porch.

Billy beckoned me into the tunnel.

'Keep your head down,' he said. There wasn't really room to do anything else. I edged in beside him. 'I was on top,' he went on. 'Then I saw the Swaffers coming, so I had to lie low.'

'Where are they?' I said. I noticed that Billy had his shoes on the wrong feet again. His mother was trying to cure his pigeon toes.

'They're lying in wait round the corner of the pub,' said Billy.

'Why don't you run away, then?' I asked, because I knew he would have to in the end and it seemed only sensible to do it now.

'Trust a girl to say that,' said Billy. 'I've got to see this thing through.'

I didn't argue. I knew that he was quoting from one of the manly books that his mother got him from the library, in which the hero always emerged from terrible fights without a scratch on him. None of the heroes in Billy's books was nine years old with pigeon toes, but Billy hadn't noticed that.

A bug-eyed face squinted round the corner and was quickly withdrawn.

'There's Gordon,' said Billy.

'How do you know?'

'It's Gordon's turn for the gas-mask. Norman had it last week.'

Norman and Gordon Swaffer lived in Pudds Cottages, down an alley at the end of our street. Norman was the elder, but Gordon was the brains of the outfit. When he went into battle he used Norman as a gun-limber, a sandbag or a tank-trap; any piece of military hardware that happened to be needed. Their uncle Tom had been a Desert Rat, among other things, and the Swaffers went about dressed in army cast-offs; leather jerkins, khaki gaiters, tin hats, and the gas-mask which they had to share between them. My father said that Montgomery only won at El Alamein because he sent Tom Swaffer on ahead, to frighten the enemy.

I could see the snout of Gordon's gas-mask sticking out beyond the brickwork. A little higher up was another head, in goggles and a leather helmet. Norman. Evidently Gordon had disguised him as a human being today.

The gas-mask lunged forward and the Swaffers charged round the corner. Uncle Tom hadn't been able to swipe them a machine-gun, so Gordon had to make his own weapons. They were carrying spears; gardening canes, tipped with gramophone needles. Gordon had a box of matches as well, his flame-thrower. Striking them in quick succession, he threw them into the tunnel.

'They're going to smoke us out,' gasped Billy, between gritted teeth. Already he felt the choking vapour invade his lungs, although the wind extinguished the matches almost before they left Gordon's hand.

'Save yourself,' cried Billy, nobly. Norman was blocking his end of the tunnel and he couldn't get out at the other until I did. I stood up and Gordon waved his gramophone needle at me.

'Thass'our tunnel,' he said, removing the gas-mask.

'No it's not,' said Billy. 'It belongs to the dentist. It's his steps.'

Norman said a rude word. 'Spawn,' he said. I don't know why he thought it was rude, but I could tell he did from the way he said it. Also he wrote it on walls: SPORN. Perhaps it just looked rude.

'It's wrong to swear at girls,' said Billy, crawling out of the tunnel.

'Ha, you should know. You're a girl,' said Gordon.

Billy began his manly act, dancing about on his toes, a warrior penguin.

'Geh'ahvit,' said Norman, levelling his spear, and Billy did get out of it, not from fear of Norman, of course, but because he was not allowed to speak to the Swaffers, and going home full of holes would be an admission of guilt.

None of us was allowed to speak to the Swaffers. Our mothers were afraid that we would learn rude words.

Billy knew that a man should defend his honour, but he also knew when to be diplomatic.

'Are you coming to the Coronation party?' he asked.

'Coming to it? Ho, not half we aren't,' said Gordon. 'We're the Coronation Mob. When there's a Coronation we smash it up.'

'You can't be very busy,' I said.

'The Coronation's in London,' said Billy.

'I mean this here Coronation, after dinner,' said Gordon.

There was to be a party that afternoon in the recreation ground, for everyone in our street, but before we could get on with it we had to see Jane Hodgkiss crowned Queen of Sussex Street. All the girls had put their names in a hat to see who would be Queen, and Jane had won. No one had invited Norman and Gordon to draw for the honour of being the Duke of Edinburgh. The mothers said that Pudds Cottages were really part of Essex Avenue, not Sussex

Street, and we all knew what a lie that was, because in Essex Avenue the houses weren't even joined together. Our road was terraced, but the houses were not much like Pudds Cottages. Everyone would have been shocked at the idea of the Swaffers being left out, but they weren't let in, either.

'We'll wop it all up,' said Gordon. 'And the fancy dress, and the tea-party.'

'How?' said Billy. 'There's only two of you and there's hundreds of us.' He meant seventy-three including the scout master, who was going to be Archbishop of Canterbury and crown Queen Jane. 'Our fathers won't let you. They'll call the police.'

Billy's remedy for everything was calling the police, which was odd in someone who won the war single-handed every day before lunch.

'We got a gang,' said Gordon. He hadn't.

'I say,' said Billy. 'Surely you don't want to spoil things for everyone else?'

'Yus,' said Norman. Billy decided to try some more diplomacy.

'Are you jealous?' he asked, tactfully. 'Do you want to be in the Coronation? I'd let you be Duke of Edinburgh instead of me. Only I'm not Duke of Edinburgh,' he added.

'No, you're Winston Churchill,' said Gordon.

'I know,' said Billy. 'I'll fight you for it. Fair fight, mind. No kicking. If I win, you must swear not to smash up the Coronation.'

Gordon lay down on the pavement and pretended to die laughing. If I had been Billy I'd have taken this opportunity to jump on Gordon, but Billy was put out by this unsporting reply to his challenge.

'I'll kill y' by meself,' Norman had offered helpfully.

'I'll pull y'apart.'

At that moment, Mrs Chapman appeared in her front garden. Television wasn't the only thing that she considered common, but when she was angry, she stood at the gate with her hands on her hips, like anyone else's mother.

'Oh heck,' murmured Billy. This was the worst word he knew, in spite of talking to the Swaffers. He stepped over the dying Gordon and started for home. I walked with him to provide moral support.

'This is serious,' said Billy. He meant the Coronation Mob, not his mother, though I didn't agree with him there. 'We've got to save the Coronation,' he said, thumping palm with fist. 'We must warn everyone, so they'll be ready.'

'Does your mother know where you've been?' demanded Mrs Chapman, as she hauled Billy indoors. That was all she ever said to me. That and, 'Don't pick our privet,' when I was only looking for caterpillars.

All through our Coronation a wet wind scoured the awning above the throne, but when the crown was on, a ray of sunlight shone down just where Queen Jane was standing. That bit got into the *Kentish Express:* SUN SHINES ON SUSSEX STREET QUEEN.

Billy and I stood at the back of the crowd, keeping an eye open for a sight of the gas-mask among the horseradish leaves that bordered the recreation ground.

'They're getting ready to do a mad rush, later on,' said Billy. 'When they think no one's expecting it.'

We were all lined up for the fancy-dress parade. Billy was Lord Nelson with a patch over one eye, which impaired his efficiency as a look-out, although he had a telescope. My brother was done up as a frog, in long underwear dyed green, with a buckram mask from Woolworths. We couldn't get a frog mask so my mother bought a monkey mask, steamed it over the kettle and pinched it into frog shape. I was the Spirit of England, in bits of butter-muslin dyed red, white and blue.

'She looks like the Spirit of Being Hard Up,' said my father. He was going up and down the lines of children, finding out what everyone was supposed to be. This was just as well since it was rather hard to guess, in some cases. Several people pointed out my brother as that dear little dragon.

'Tell them you're a frog,' my mother kept hissing, so he did, but inside the frog skin he was probably being a train.

We all had to walk past the judges' table, little ones first. My brother went by, legs going up and down like pistons. I was right; he was being a train. Then Christopher Saville, with his head in a box.

'A television set,' my father called out, for the judges' benefit. 'A shepherdess, the Queen of Hearts, a hot – no, surely not – yes, a hot-water bottle.' It was my turn. 'The Spirit of England.'

As I passed the table I saw the gas-mask peering through the horseradish leaves. I left the line and ran over to my father.

'The Coronation Mob's here,' I said. Billy had told him all about it beforehand. I looked round for Billy and by good luck he was busy walking the quarter-deck.

'Lord Nelson,' shouted my father. 'Hang on a moment.' He walked over to the horseradish and addressed the gas-mask.

'What a way to come to a party.'

'Spawn,' said Norman, behind another leaf. Billy came cantering up, waving his telescope.

'Sir, Sir!' My father didn't like being called 'Sir' away from school, but Billy wouldn't learn. 'Sir, they're going to smash us up.'

'Go away,' said my father. He dragged the Coronation Mob out of the horseradish. They were in full battledress: gas-mask, goggles, gaiters, helmet, boots and jerkins, spears at the trail. They reminded me of something, but I couldn't think what. My father could. He yanked a Union Jack off the back of the throne and hung it on Gordon's gramophone needle. Then he took the Mob, one in each hand, and

tacked them on to the end of the fancy-dress parade. As they went past the judges he called out, 'Hillary and Tensing on top of Mount Everest.' There was a tremendous cheer and Norman and Gordon won first prize for the most original costume.

Norman's prize was a moneybox shaped like a crown and Gordon got an autograph book with the Queen on the cover.

'Though what you'll do with it I don't know,' said my father. 'I imagine most of your heroes are in the Chamber of Horrors.'

The Coronation Mob wouldn't stay for tea, and left as soon as they could.

'They're not a bit grateful,' complained Billy, watching them go. Gordon was already converting Norman's money-box into an offensive weapon.

'Of course they aren't,' said my father. 'They came to smash us up and then I went and made them win first prize.'

'You should have smashed them up, Sir,' said Billy, regret-fully.

'Why?' said my father. 'They're not exactly a threat to civilization as we know it. What did you want, a massacre?' Billy gave him a headache. I think he preferred the Corona-tion Mob, even if they did come from Pudds Cottages.

As it happened, the Mob left off being a mob soon after-wards. That autumn Gordon started at the Grammar School, and after that we didn't get the chance not to speak to him.

He wouldn't speak to us.

JAN MARK
*Illustrated by* DAVID PARKINS

# A Fishy Tale,
## or How I Joined the Mixed
## Maggots and Bottom Feeders,
## Told to Gene Kemp
## by John Sweet

My Dad says the best thing to do is to forget all about it. Especially as I lost my wellingtons. I suppose he's right, really, but since you asked about it, here goes, Mzz Kemp.

I was getting tired, I reckon, and my concentration slipped and so did I, into the canal, at the edge where all the tall plants and reeds line the bank, deep and green and mysterious, full of insects and weird crawlies. And there in the middle of the canal is the deep channel where all the fish swim along. Yes, I love fishing. I like going fishing with my Dad better than anything else. Better even than football, I think ... All them fish, browny red dace, roach with orange fins, spotted perch, all spiky, you need a rag to protect your hands when you get him off the hook, and down at the bottom of the centre channel there's the spotted brown gudgeon, a bottom feeder, and the stone loach with stick-out lips, like this, whuwh, see? Of course, you do get the nobs putting in a grand appearance some-times, the salmon and the silver brown trout, but not for me with my licence at £1.50. If you do nabble one, you put it back quick.

Oh, it's a fantastic sport.

And the sport isn't just to catch the fish, but to land it, easy, easy. If you wind in too quickly the line will break, because of the friction, so you must do it slowly to let it move around in angles which tires the fish, and it's easier to pull out smoothly. Don't let the line go loose or the fish jumps, the hook slides and the fish escapes.

You need the feel, like.

This Sunday I'm telling you about, my Dad took me out about four. It was a smashing day, hot for October, with brown and yellow leaves lying in heaps to shuffle your feet through, scrunch, scrunch. I was glad to go, not only because, as I've told you, I like going fishing with my Dad better than anything, but because it had been that sort of a Sunday. My elder brother was out of the house some-where, but the rest were hanging about all over the place, shouting and bossing me about, that's the worst of having four sisters, and you know what our Sandra is like, Mzz Kemp. Our house isn't very big neither, and my Mum made me do jobs, but it didn't really matter, not inside, because I knew I was going fishing with my Dad.

We set off, and it was still warm and sunny, though the mist was beginning to stir in little smoky spirals as we walked down the long hill that goes to the river and beyond to the canal. It's called Fore Street, and our teacher, you, Mzz Kemp, told us the Romans marched down there, long ago, and people before that, and it's a pretty steep hill, though that didn't bother me, *then*.

At last we reached the canal, and there's a road on one side for cars, and a path on the other for people and dogs, but half-way to Double Locks is a bridge, a really narrow bridge, and there the road crosses over, becoming a path, and the path becomes the road on the other side, bit daft really, not that it bothered me and Dad, because we were walking anyway, but it is tricky to drive across. Two posts stop cars trying to drive on to the path. Just beyond the bridge, where it's fine for fishing with the banks all green and quiet and beautiful, I sat down with my tackle and Dad wandered on a bit. I put down my bag for the fish and my rag to handle them with, then I made sure the eyes were level, pulled the lines up through them, fixed the little round band, the float and the hook, judged the weights, put them on, stood up straight and cast without maggots. Then I got the maggots on to the hook, pushing them with my thumb, and cast. My landing net was ready and the float was okay. The red bit goes under when you've got a bite.

Only I hadn't. And I didn't. I waited and I waited and I waited.

The sun painted the sky, pink and purple and orange and red, while I sat there on my little folding stool, waiting. No bite at all. Not a sausage. Not a dicky bird. Not a dicky bird of a sausage. Not a nibble.

I could feel a nibble inside, though.

I was hungry. I was very hungry. I was starving.

Roast pork with apple sauce and crackling when we got home, Mum had said. I thought about roast pork and apple sauce and crackling. I pictured it on my plate. I pictured me eating it. I felt even hungrier.

The sun pushed off to the other side of the world or wherever it goes, taking all the colour with it. Grey mist trailed everywhere. My fingers grew cold and stiff. Dad came along and asked how I was doing, no good I said, him neither, we'd pack it in soon and go home.

'Another minute, Dad,' I asked, as he turned away. I

didn't want to return with no catch and Sandra laughing
like a drain, and I don't know why, but at the very thought
of Sandra, my chair slipped, so did I, and there I was, slip,
sliding away on my back into the reeds, and down, down,
down into the water, coming up over my wellies, colder
than cold, shock, horror. Somehow I turned, grabbed a
rough and unkind sort of plant and yelled for Dad, who
had gone some way away.

And a car came over the bridge, a man's head stuck out
of the window, yelling, 'Look at that little kid. He's gonna
drown! Stop!'

It didn't stop. It came roaring on. Towards me. My cold
hands were slipping. Any minute now, I'd be among the
fish I'd been after, earlier, and I didn't fancy the idea much.
I didn't want to meet the bottom feeders on their own
level. I didn't think we'd have much to say to each other
down there amongst all that cold mud. 'Dad!' I yelled even
louder. I couldn't see him, and I was slipping further all
the time.

But if I couldn't see Dad, I could see the car. It was heading straight towards me and it didn't look as if it knew how to stop. It seemed as if I had a choice. Either be run over or drowned. I thought fast, very fast. And there was only one way to go so I went. Backwards into the canal. Right up to my neck in cold slimy canal right down into what seemed enough mud to submerge a submarine. I thought I could hear the fishes laughing all the way to Double Locks.

The car swerved, hitting the posts, one went into the water, just missing me, the other stayed put and the car rose up on it. The back door flew open and out jumped a man.

'Don't worry, son. I'm here.'

He certainly was. Water splashed everywhere, as if some huge whale was spouting off. He grabbed me by the neck and headed for the bank.

'I'm all right. I can swim,' I shouted, but he wasn't listening. Holding me like he was a dog with his favourite bone, he stumbled on, then fell forward, me with him.

'I can't swim,' he shouted, dropping me, and waving his arms about.

'I'm coming,' shouted another man, leaping towards us. I managed to move just in time. This splash was more like a freak tidal wave. Nowhere was left untouched. But I'd seen Dad on the bank and I was getting to him fast.

'It's all right,' shouted my Dad. 'Don't all go in!'

Too late. Another flying body hit the water, now full of bodies and one post. The canal was having a busy evening. Together we arrived at the bank where Dad pulled us out one by one. A lot of panting and spitting and coughing went on. That canal water doesn't taste nice at all.

'We saved your boy,' said one.

'Yeah,' said my Dad.

'Aren't you gonna thank us?'

'Well, thank you, yes, and I hope you enjoyed your bit of fun in there, but I feel I must say that first of all, he's the school swimming champion, and next, you couldn't drown a rabbit in there, let alone three big blokes like you. John, where's your wellingtons?'

'In the mud, Dad. They came off.'

'Well, we'd better get walking then, before you catch cold. It's a fair step.'

The driver had righted the car by now. The others climbed in dripping wet.

'We can't offer you a lift,' one said.

'Funny you not being able to swim, Reg. I never knew that,' I heard one of them say. Reg made a sort of angry roaring noise as the car drove off.

It was a long way home. Especially in wet-socked feet. And I thought I'd got a fish down my back, but it turned out to be a slimy weed. I kept thinking of them Roman soldiers as we walked back up that hill, Mzz Kemp, and how they had to keep going when they didn't feel like it. Once a dog came out and barked at us, but he soon stopped when my Dad said a few words to him. But it was a long way home.

Roast pork and apple sauce and crackling's scrumptious when you eat it in front of a hot fire after a bath. Even Sandra was nice to me. She didn't laugh. Much.

Guess what I'm doing next Sunday?

Going fishing, of course.

GENE KEMP

# The Silver Fish

While fishing in the blue lagoon,
I caught a lovely silver fish,
And he spoke to me, 'My boy,' quoth he,
'Please set me free and I'll grant your wish;
A kingdom of wisdom? A palace of gold?
Or all the fancies your mind can hold?'
And I said, 'O.K.,' and I set him free,
But he laughed at me as he swam away,
And left me whispering my wish
Into a silent sea.

Today I caught that fish again
(That lovely silver prince of fishes),
And once again he offered me,
If I would only set him free,
Any one of a number of wishes
If I would throw him back to the fishes.

He was delicious.

SHEL SILVERSTEIN

# Daddy Fell into the Pond

Everyone grumbled. The sky was grey.
We had nothing to do and nothing to say.
We were nearing the end of a dismal day,
And there seemed to be nothing beyond,
        THEN
   *Daddy fell into the pond!*

And everyone's face grew merry and bright,
And Timothy danced for sheer delight.
'Give me the camera, quick, oh quick!
He's crawling out of the duckweed.' *Click*!

Then the gardener suddenly slapped his knee,
And he doubled up, shaking quietly,
And the ducks all quacked as if they were daft
And it sounded as if the old drake laughed.

O, there wasn't a thing that didn't respond
                    WHEN
            Daddy fell into the pond!

                            ALFRED NOYES
                    *Illustrated by* VICTOR AMBRUS

## Well Bread

If you cast your bread on the waters,
It returns a thousandfold,
So it says in the Bible,
That's what I've been told.

(So) I cast my bread on the waters,
It was spotted by a froggy,
And the bits of bread *he* didn't eat
Just floated back all soggy.

                    SPIKE MILLIGAN

# The Fool of the World and the Flying Ship

There were, once upon a time, an old peasant and his wife, and they had three sons. Two of them were clever young men who could borrow money without being cheated, but the third was the Fool of the World. He was as simple as a child, simpler than some children, and he never did anyone a harm in his life.

Well, it always happens like that. The father and mother thought a lot of the two smart young men; but the Fool of the World was lucky if he got enough to eat, because they always forgot him unless they happened to be looking at him, and sometimes even then.

But, however it was with his father and mother, this is a story that shows that God loves simple folk, and turns things to their advantage in the end.

For it happened that the Tsar of that country sent out messengers along the highroads and the rivers, even to huts in the forest like ours, to say that he would give his daughter, the Princess, in marriage to anyone who could bring him a flying ship – ay, a ship with wings, that should sail this way and that through the pale blue sky, like a ship sailing the sea.

'This is a chance for us,' said the two clever brothers; and that same day they set off together, to see if one of them could not build the flying ship and marry the Tsar's daughter, and so be a great man indeed.

And their father blessed them, and gave them finer clothes than ever he wore himself. And their mother made them up hampers of food for the road, soft white rolls, and several kinds of cooked meats, and bottles of corn brandy. She went with them as far as the highroad, and waved her hand to them till they were out of sight. And so the two clever brothers set merrily off on their adventure, to see what could be done with their cleverness. And what happened to them I do not know, for they were never heard of again.

The Fool of the World saw them set off, with their fine parcels of food, and their fine clothes, and their bottles of corn brandy.

'I'd like to go too,' says he, 'and eat good meat, with soft white rolls, and drink corn brandy, and marry the Tsar's daughter.'

'Stupid fellow,' says his mother, 'what's the good of your going? Why, if you were to stir from the house you would walk into the arms of a bear; and if not that, then the wolves would eat you before you had finished staring at them.'

But the Fool of the World would not be held back by words.

'I am going,' says he. 'I am going. I am going. I am going.'

He went on saying this over and over again, till the old woman his mother saw there was nothing to be done, and was glad to get him out of the house so as to be quit of the sound of his voice. So she put some food in a bag for him to eat by the way. She put in the bag some crusts of dry black bread and a flask of water. She did not even bother to go as far as the footpath to see him on his way. She saw the last of him at the door of the hut, and he had not taken two steps before she had gone back into the hut to see to more important business.

No matter. The Fool of the World set off with his bag over his shoulder, singing as he went, for he was off to seek his fortune and marry the Tsar's daughter. He was sorry his mother had not given him any corn brandy; but he sang merrily for all that. He would have liked white rolls instead of the dry black crusts; but, after all, the main thing on a journey is to have something to eat. So he trudged merrily along the road, and sang because the trees were green and there was a blue sky overhead.

He had not gone very far when he met an ancient old man with a bent back, and a long beard, and eyes hidden under his bushy eyebrows.

'Good-day, young fellow,' says the ancient old man.

'Good-day, grandfather,' says the Fool of the World.

'And where are you off to?' says the ancient old man.

'What!' says the Fool; 'haven't you heard? The Tsar is going to give his daughter to anyone who can bring him a flying ship.'

'And you can really make a flying ship?' says the ancient old man.

'No, I do not know how.'

'Then what are you going to do?'

'God knows,' says the Fool of the World.

'Well,' says the ancient, 'if things are like that, sit you down here. We will rest together and have a bite of food. Bring out what you have in your bag.'

'I am ashamed to offer you what I have here. It is good enough for me, but it is not the sort of meal to which one can ask guests.'

'Never mind that. Out with it. Let us eat what God has given.'

The Fool of the World opened his bag, and could hardly believe his eyes. Instead of black crusts he saw fresh white rolls and cooked meats. He handed them out to the ancient, who said, 'You see how God loves simple folk. Although your own mother does not love you, you have not been done out of your share of the good things. Let's have a sip at the corn brandy . . .'

The Fool of the World opened his flask, and instead of water there came out corn brandy, and that of the best. So the Fool and the ancient made merry, eating and drinking; and when they had done, and sung a song or two together, the ancient says to the Fool,

'Listen to me. Off with you into the forest. Go up to the first big tree you see. Make the sacred sign of the cross three times before it. Strike it a blow with your little hatchet. Fall backwards on the ground, and lie there, full length on your back, until somebody wakes you up. Then you will find the ship made, all ready to fly. Sit you down in it, and fly off whither you want to go. But be sure on the way to give a lift to everyone you meet.'

The Fool of the World thanked the ancient old man, said goodbye to him, and went off to the forest. He walked up to a tree, the first big tree he saw, made the sign of the cross three times before it, swung his hatchet round his head, struck a mighty blow on the trunk of the tree, instantly fell backwards flat on the ground, closed his eyes, and went to sleep.

A little time went by, and it seemed to the Fool as he slept that somebody was jogging his elbow. He woke up and opened his eyes. His hatchet, worn out, lay beside him. The big tree was gone, and in its place there stood a little ship, ready and finished. The Fool did not stop to think. He jumped into the ship, seized the tiller and sat down. Instantly the ship leapt up into the air, and sailed away over the tops of the trees.

The little ship answered the tiller as readily as if she were sailing in water, and the Fool steered for the highroad, and sailed along above it, for he was afraid of losing his way if he tried to steer a course across the open country.

He flew on and on, and looked down, and saw a man lying in the road below him with his ear on the damp ground.

'Good-day to you, uncle,' cried the Fool.

'Good-day to you, Sky-fellow,' cried the man.

'What are you doing down there?' says the Fool.

'I am listening to all that is being done in the world.'

'Take your place in the ship with me.'

The man was willing enough, and sat down in the ship with the Fool, and they flew on together singing songs.

They flew on and on, and looked down, and there was a man on one leg, with the other tied up to his head.

'Good-day, uncle,' says the Fool, bringing the ship to the ground. 'Why are you hopping along on one foot?'

'If I were to untie the other, I should move too fast. I should be stepping across the world in a single stride.'

'Sit down with us,' says the Fool.

The man sat down with them in the ship, and they flew on together singing songs.

They flew on and on, and looked down, and there was a man with a gun, and he was taking aim, but what he was aiming at they could not see.

'Good health to you, uncle,' says the Fool. 'But what are you shooting at? There isn't a bird to be seen.'

'What!' says the man. 'If there were a bird that you could see, I should not shoot at it. A bird or a beast a thousand versts away, that's the sort of mark for me.'

'Take your seat with us,' says the Fool.

The man sat down with them in the ship, and they flew on together. Louder and louder rose their songs.

They flew on and on, and looked down, and there was a man carrying a sack full of bread on his back.

'Good health to you, uncle,' says the Fool, sailing down. 'And where are you off to?'

'I am going to get bread for my dinner.'

'But you've got a full sack on your back.'

'That — that little scrap! Why, that's not enough for a single mouthful.'

'Take your seat with us,' says the Fool.

The Eater sat down with them in the ship, and they flew on together, singing louder than ever.

They flew on and on, and looked down, and there was a man walking round and round a lake.

'Good health to you, uncle,' says the Fool 'What are you looking for?'

'I want a drink, and I can't find any water.'

'But there's a whole lake in front of your eyes. Why can't you take a drink from that?'

'That little drop!' says the man. 'Why, there's not enough water there to wet the back of my throat if I were to drink it at one gulp.'

'Take your seat with us,' says the Fool.

The Drinker sat down with them, and again they flew on, singing in chorus.

They flew on and on, and looked down, and there was a man walking towards the forest, with a faggot of wood on his shoulders.

'Good-day to you, uncle,' says the Fool. 'Why are you taking wood to the forest?'

'This isn't simple wood,' says the man.

'What is it, then?' says the Fool.

'If it is scattered about, a whole army of soldiers leaps up.'

'There's a place for you with us,' says the Fool.

The man sat down with them, and the ship rose up into the air, and flew on, carrying its singing crew.

They flew on and on, and looked down, and there was a man carrying a sack of straw.

'Good health to you, uncle,' says the Fool; 'and where are you taking your straw?'

'To the village.'

'Why, are they short of straw in your village?'

'No; but this is such straw that if you scatter it abroad in the very hottest of the summer, instantly the weather turns cold, and there is snow and frost.'

'There's a place here for you too,' says the Fool.

'Very kind of you,' says the man, and steps in and sits down, and away they all sail together, singing like to burst their lungs.

They did not meet anyone else, and presently came flying up to the palace of the Tsar. They flew down and cast anchor in the courtyard.

Just then the Tsar was eating his dinner. He heard their loud singing, and looked out of the window and saw the ship come sailing down into his courtyard. He sent his servant out to ask who was the great prince who had brought him the flying ship, and had come sailing down with such a merry noise of singing.

The servant came up to the ship, and saw the Fool of the World and his companions sitting there cracking jokes. He saw they were all moujiks, simple peasants, sitting in the ship; so he did not stop to ask questions, but came back quietly and told the Tsar that there were no gentlemen in the ship at all, but only a lot of dirty peasants.

Now the Tsar was not at all pleased with the idea of giving his only daughter in marriage to a simple peasant, and he began to think how he could get out of his bargain. Thinks he to himself, 'I'll set them such tasks that they will not be able to perform, and they'll be glad to get off with their lives, and I shall get the ship for nothing.'

So he told his servant to go to the Fool and tell him that before the Tsar had finished his dinner the Fool was to bring him some of the magical water of life.

Now, while the Tsar was giving this order to his servant, the Listener, the first of the Fool's companions, was listening, and heard the words of the Tsar and repeated them to the Fool.

'What am I to do now?' says the Fool, stopping short in his jokes. 'In a year, in a whole century, I never could find that water. And he wants it before he has finished his dinner.'

'Don't you worry about that,' says the Swift-goer, 'I'll deal with that for you.'

The servant came and announced the Tsar's command.

'Tell him he shall have it,' says the Fool.

His companion, the Swift-goer, untied his foot from beside his head, put it to the ground, wriggled it a little to get the stiffness out of it, ran off, and was out of sight almost before he had stepped from the ship. Quicker than I can tell it you in words he had come to the water of life, and put some of it in a bottle.

'I shall have plenty of time to get back,' thinks he, and down he sits under a windmill and goes off to sleep.

The royal dinner was coming to an end, and there wasn't a sign of him. There were no songs and no jokes in the flying ship. Everybody was watching for the Swift-goer, and thinking he would not be in time.

The Listener jumped out and laid his right ear to the damp ground, listened a moment, and said, 'What a fellow! He has gone to sleep under the windmill. I can hear him snoring. And there is a fly buzzing with its wings, perched on the windmill close above his head.'

'This is my affair,' says the Far-shooter, and he picked up his gun from between his knees, aimed at the fly on the windmill, and woke the Swift-goer with the thud of the bullet on the wood of the mill close by his head. The Swift-goer leapt up and ran, and in less than a second had brought the magic water of life and given it to the Fool. The Fool gave it to the servant, who took it to the Tsar.

The Tsar had not yet left the table, so his command had been fulfilled as exactly as ever could be.

'What fellows these peasants are,' thought the Tsar. 'There is nothing for it but to set them another task.' So the Tsar said to his servant, 'Go to the captain of the flying ship and give him this message: "If you are such a cunning fellow, you must have a good appetite. Let you and your companions eat at a single meal twelve oxen roasted whole, and as much bread as can be baked in forty ovens!"'

The Listener heard the message, and told the Fool what was coming. The Fool was terrified, and said, 'I can't get through even a single loaf at a sitting.'

'Don't worry about that,' said the Eater. 'It won't be more than a mouthful for me, and I shall be glad to have a little snack in place of my dinner.'

The servant came, and announced the Tsar's command.

'Good,' says the Fool. 'Send the food along, and we'll know what to do with it.'

So they brought twelve oxen roasted whole, and as much bread as could be baked in forty ovens, and the companions had scarcely sat down to eat before the Eater had finished the lot.

'Why,' said the Eater, 'what a little! They might have given us a decent meal while they were about it.'

The Tsar told his servant to tell the Fool that he and his companions were to drink forty barrels of wine, with forty bucketfuls in every barrel.

The Listener told the Fool what message was coming.

'Why,' says the Fool, 'I never in my life drank more than one bucket at a time.'

'Don't worry,' says the Drinker. 'You forget that I am thirsty. It'll be nothing of a drink for me.'

They brought the forty barrels of wine, and tapped them, and the Drinker tossed them down one after another, one gulp for each barrel. 'Little enough,' says he. 'Why, I am thirsty still.'

'Very good,' says the Tsar to his servant, when he heard that they had eaten all the food and drunk all the wine. 'Tell the fellow to get ready for the wedding, and let him go and bathe himself in the bath-house. But let the bath-house be made so hot that the man will stifle and frizzle as soon as he sets foot inside. It is an iron bath-house. Let it be made red hot.'

The Listener heard all this and told the Fool, who stopped with his mouth open in the middle of a joke.

'Don't you worry,' says the moujik with the straw.

Well, they made the bath-house red hot, and called the Fool, and the Fool went along to the bath-house to wash himself, and with him went the moujik with the straw.

They shut them both into the bath-house, and thought that that was the end of them. But the moujik scattered his straw before them as they went in, and it became so cold in there that the Fool of the World had scarcely time to wash himself before the water in the cauldrons froze to solid ice. They lay down on the very stove itself, and spent the night there, shivering.

In the morning the servants opened the bath-house, and there were the Fool of the World and the moujik, alive and well, lying on the stove and singing songs.

They told the Tsar, and the Tsar raged with anger. 'There is no getting rid of this fellow,' says he. 'But go and tell him that I send him this message: "If you are to marry my daughter, you must show that you are able to defend her. Let me see that you have at least a regiment of soldiers." ' Thinks he to himself, 'How can a simple peasant raise a troop? He will find it hard enough to raise a single soldier.'

The Listener told the Fool of the World, and the Fool began to lament. 'This time,' says he, 'I am done indeed. You, my brothers, have saved me from misfortune more than once, but this time, alas, there is nothing to be done.'

'Oh, what a fellow you are!' says the peasant with the faggot of wood. 'I suppose you've forgotten about me. Remember that I am the man for this little affair, and don't you worry about it at all.'

The Tsar's servant came along and gave his message.

'Very good,' says the Fool; 'but tell the Tsar that if after this he puts me off again, I'll make war on his country, and take the Princess by force.'

And then, as the servant went back with the message, the whole crew on the flying ship set to their singing again, and sang and laughed and made jokes as if they had not a care in the world.

During the night, while the others slept, the peasant with the faggot of wood went hither and thither, scattering his sticks. Instantly where they fell there appeared a gigantic army. Nobody could count the number of soldiers in it – cavalry, foot soldiers, yes, and guns, and all the guns new and bright, and the men in the finest uniforms that ever were seen.

In the morning, as the Tsar woke and looked from the windows of the Palace, he found himself surrounded by troops upon troops of soldiers, and generals in cocked hats bowing in the courtyard and taking orders from the Fool of the World, who sat there joking with his companions in the flying ship. Now it was the Tsar's turn to be afraid. As quickly as he could he sent his servants to the Fool with presents of rich jewels and fine clothes, invited him to come to the palace and begged him to marry the Princess.

The Fool of the World put on the fine clothes, and stood there as handsome a young man as a princess could wish for a husband. He presented himself before the Tsar, fell in love with the Princess and she with him, married her the same day, received with her a rich dowry and became so clever that all the court repeated everything he said. The Tsar and the Tsaritsa liked him very much, and as for the Princess, she loved him to distraction.

ARTHUR RANSOME

# Juba: A Chant

Juba this and juba that
Juba killed a yellow cat
Juba up and juba down
Juba running all around.

[*The leader recites the verse and the group repeats it several times.
The actions are added one at a time.*]

*First time:*  repeat verse slowly and very loudly in singsong
cadence

*Second:*  repeat verse a little faster and a little more softly,
and clap hands in rhythm.

*Third:*  repeat verse a little faster and even more softly.
Slap both hands on knees and then clap hands
together in rhythm.

*Fourth:*  repeat verse very fast and in a very soft voice.
At the same time, slap hands on knees, clap hands
together, clap hands to both cheeks, clap hands
together again, in rhythm.

ANON.

# First Day at School

A millionbillionwillion miles from home
Waiting for the bell to go. (To go where?)
Why are they all so big, other children?
So noisy? So much at home they
must have been born in uniform.
Lived all their lives in playgrounds.
Spent the years inventing games
that don't let me in. Games
that are rough, that swallow you up.

And the railings.
All around, the railings.
Are they to keep out wolves and monsters?
Things that carry off and eat children?
Things you don't take sweets from?
Perhaps they're to stop us getting out.
Running away from the lessins. Lessin.
What does a lessin look like?
Sounds small and slimy.
They keep them in glassrooms,
Whole rooms made out of glass. Imagine.

I wish I could remember my name.
Mummy said it would come in useful.
Like wellies. When there's puddles.
Lellowwellies. I wish she was here.
I think my name is sewn on somewhere.
Perhaps the teacher will read it for me.
Tea-cher. The one who makes the tea.

ROGER MCGOUGH

# Bad Report – Good Manners

My daddy said, 'My son, my son,
This school report is bad.'
I said, 'I did my best I did,
My dad my dad my dad.'

'Explain, my son, my son,' he said,
'Why *bottom* of the class?'
'I stood aside, my dad my dad,
To let the others pass.'

SPIKE MILLIGAN

# Send Three and Fourpence
# We are Going to a Dance

Mike and Ruth Dixon got on well enough, but not so well that they wanted to walk home from school together. Ruth would not have minded, but Mike, who was two classes up, preferred to amble along with his friends so that he usually arrived a long while after Ruth did.

Ruth was leaning out of the kitchen window when he came in through the side gate, kicking a brick.

'I've got a message for you,' said Mike. 'From school. Miss Middleton wants you to go and see her tomorrow before assembly, and take a dead frog.'

'What's she want *me* to take a dead frog for?' said Ruth. 'She's not my teacher. I haven't got a dead frog.'

'How should I know?' Mike let himself in. 'Where's Mum?'

'Round Mrs Todd's. Did she really say a dead frog? I mean, really say it?'

'Derek told me to tell you. It's nothing to do with me.'

Ruth cried easily. She cried now. 'I bet she never. You're pulling my leg.'

'I'm not, and you'd better do it. She said it was important – Derek said – and you know what a rotten old temper she's got,' said Mike, feelingly.

'But why me? It's not fair.' Ruth leaned her head on the window-sill and wept in earnest. 'Where'm I going to find a dead frog?'

'Well, you can peel them off the road sometimes when they've been run over. They go all dry and flat, like pressed flowers,' said Mike. He did think it a trifle unreasonable to demand dead frogs from little girls, but Miss Middleton *was* unreasonable. Everyone knew that. 'You could start a pressed frog collection,' he said.

Ruth sniffed fruitily. 'What do you think Miss'll do if I don't get one?'

'She'll go barmy, that's what,' said Mike. 'She's barmy anyway,' he said. 'Nah, don't start howling again. Look, I'll go down the ponds after tea. I know there's frogs there because I saw the spawn, back at Easter.'

'But those frogs are alive. She wants a dead one.'

'I dunno. Perhaps we could get it put to sleep or something, like Mrs Todd's Tibby was. And don't tell Mum. She doesn't like me down the ponds and she won't let us have frogs indoors. Get an old box with a lid and leave it on the rockery, and I'll put old Froggo in it when I come home. *And stop crying!*'

After Mike had gone out Ruth found the box that her summer sandals had come in. She poked air holes in the top and furnished it with damp grass and a tin lid full of water. Then she left it on the rockery with a length of darning wool so that Froggo could be fastened down safely until morning. It was only possible to imagine Froggo alive; all tender and green and saying croak-croak. She could not think of him dead and flat and handed over to Miss Middleton, who definitely must have gone barmy. Perhaps Mike or Derek had been wrong about the dead part. She hoped they had.

She was in the bathroom, getting ready for bed, when Mike came home. He looked round the door and stuck up his thumbs.

'Operation Frog successful. Over and out.'

'Wait. Is he . . . alive?'

'Shhh. Mum's in the hall. Yes.'

'What's he like?'

'Sort of frog-shaped. Look, I've got him; O.K.? I'm going down now.'

'Is he green?'

'No. More like that pork pie that went mouldy on top. Good night!'

Mike had hidden Froggo's dungeon under the front hedge, so all Ruth had to do next morning was scoop it up as she went out of the gate. Mike had left earlier with his friends, so she paused for a moment to introduce herself. She tapped quietly on the lid. 'Hullo?'

There was no answering cry of croak-croak. Perhaps he *was* dead. Ruth felt a tear coming and raised the lid a fraction at one end. There was a scrabbling noise and at the other end of the box she saw something small and alive, crouching in the grass.

'Poor Froggo,' she whispered through the air holes. 'I

won't let her kill you, I promise,' and she continued on her way to school feeling brave and desperate, and ready to protect Froggo's life at the cost of her own.

The school hall was in the middle of the building and classrooms opened off it. Miss Middleton had Class 3 this year, next to the cloakroom. Ruth hung up her blazer, untied the wool from Froggo's box, and went to meet her doom. Miss Middleton was arranging little stones in an aquarium on top of the bookcase, and jerked her head when Ruth knocked, to show that she should come in.

'I got him, Miss,' said Ruth, holding out the shoe box in trembling hands.

'What, dear?' said Miss Middleton, up to her wrists in water-weed.

'Only he's not dead and I won't let you kill him!' Ruth cried, and swept off the lid with a dramatic flourish. Froggo, who must have been waiting for this, sprung out, towards Miss Middleton, landed with a clammy sound on that vulnerable place between the collar bones, and slithered down inside Miss Middleton's blouse.

Miss Middleton taught Nature Study. She was not afraid of little damp creatures, but she was not expecting Froggo. She gave a squawk of alarm and jumped backwards. The aquarium skidded in the opposite direction; took off; shattered against a desk. The contents broke over Ruth's new sandals in a tidal wave, and Lily the goldfish thrashed about in a shallow puddle on the floor. People came running with mops and dustpans. Lily Fish was taken out by the tail to recover in the cloakroom sink. Froggo was arrested while trying to leave Miss Middleton's blouse through the gap between two buttons, and put back in his box with a weight on top in case he made another dash for freedom.

Ruth, crying harder than she had ever done in her life, was sent to stand outside the Headmaster's room, accused of playing stupid practical jokes; and cruelty to frogs.

Sir looked rather as if he had been laughing, but it seemed unlikely, under the circumstances, and Ruth's eyes were so swollen and tear-filled that she couldn't see clearly. He gave her a few minutes to dry out and then said,

'This isn't like you, Ruth. Whatever possessed you to go throwing frogs at poor Miss Middleton? And poor frog, come to that.'

'She told me to bring her a frog,' said Ruth, stanching another tear at the injustice of it all. 'Only she wanted a dead one, and I couldn't find a dead one, and I couldn't kill Froggo. I won't kill him,' she said, remembering her vow on the way to school.

'Miss Middleton says she did not ask you to bring her a frog, or kill her a frog. She thinks you've been very foolish and unkind,' said Sir, 'and I think you are not telling the truth. Now . . .'

'Mike told me to,' said Ruth.

'Your brother? Oh, come now.'

'He did. He said Miss Middleton wanted me to go to her before assembly with a dead frog and I did, only it wasn't dead and I won't!'

'Ruth! Don't grizzle. No one is going to murder your frog, but we must get this nonsense sorted out.' Sir opened his door and called to a passer-by, 'Tell Michael Dixon that I want to see him at once, in my office.'

Mike arrived, looking wary. He had heard the crash and

kept out of the way, but a summons from Sir was not to be ignored.

'Come in, Michael,' said Sir. 'Now, why did you tell your sister that Miss Middleton wanted her to bring a dead frog to school?'

'It wasn't me,' said Mike. 'It was a message from Miss Middleton.'

'Miss Middleton told you?'

'Nō, Derek Bingham told me. She told him to tell me – I suppose,' said Mike, sulkily. He scowled at Ruth. All her fault.

'Then you'd better fetch Derek Bingham here right away. We're going to get to the bottom of this.'

Derek arrived. He too had heard the crash.

'Come in, Derek,' said Sir. 'I understand that you told Michael here some tarradiddle about his sister. You let him think it was a message from Miss Middleton, didn't you?'

'Yes, well ...' Derek shuffled. 'Miss Middleton didn't tell *me*. She told, er, someone, and they told me.'

'Who was this someone?'

Derek turned all noble and stood up straight and pale. 'I can't remember, Sir.'

'Don't let's have any heroics about sneaking, Derek, or I shall get very *cross*.'

Derek's nobility ebbed rapidly. 'It was Tim Hancock, Sir. He said Miss Middleton wanted Ruth Dixon to bring her a dead dog before assembly.'

'A dead *dog*?'

'Yes, Sir.'

'Didn't you think it a bit strange that Miss Middleton should ask Ruth for a dead dog, Derek?'

'I thought she must have one, Sir.'

'But why should Miss Middleton want it?'

'Well, she does do Nature Study,' said Derek.

'Go and fetch Tim,' said Sir.

Tim had been playing football on the field when the aquarium went down. He came in with an innocent smile which wilted when he saw what was waiting for him.

'Sir?'

'Would you mind repeating the message that you gave Derek yesterday afternoon?'

'I told him Miss Middleton wanted Sue Nixon to bring her a red sock before assembly,' said Tim. 'It was important.'

'Red sock? Sue Nixon?' said Sir. He was beginning to look slightly wild-eyed. 'Who's Sue Nixon? There's no one in this school called Sue Nixon.'

'I don't know any of the girls, Sir,' said Tim.

'Didn't you think a red sock was an odd thing to ask for?'

'I thought she was bats, Sir.'

'Sue Nixon?'

'No, Sir. Miss Middleton, Sir,' said truthful Tim.

Sir raised his eyebrows. 'But why did you tell Derek?'

'I couldn't find anyone else, Sir. It was late.'

'But why Derek?'

'I had to tell someone or I'd have got into trouble,' said Tim, virtuously.

'You are in trouble,' said Sir. 'Michael, ask Miss Middleton to step in here for a moment, please.'

Miss Middleton, frog-ridden, looked round the door.

'I'm sorry to bother you again,' said Sir, 'but it seems that Tim thinks you told him that one Sue Nixon was to bring you a red sock before assembly.'

'Tim!' said Miss Middleton, very shocked. 'That's a naughty fib. I never told you any such thing.'

'Oh Sir,' said Tim. 'Miss didn't tell me. It was Pauline Bates done that.'

'*Did* that. I think I see Pauline out in the hall,' said Sir. 'In the P.T. class. Yes? Let's have her in.'

Pauline was very small, and very frightened. Sir sat her on his knee and told her not to worry. 'All we want to know,' he said, 'is what you said to Tim yesterday. About Sue Nixon and the dead dog.'

'Red sock, Sir,' said Tim.

'Sorry. Red sock. Well, Pauline?'

Pauline looked as if she might join Ruth in tears. Ruth had just realized that she was no longer involved, and was crying with relief.

'You said Miss Middleton gave you a message for Sue Nixon. What was it?'

'It wasn't Sue Nixon,' said Pauline, damply. 'It was June Nichols. It wasn't Miss Middleton, it was Miss Wimbledon.'

'There *is* no Miss Wimbledon,' said Sir. 'June Nichols, yes. I know June, but Miss Wimbledon ...?'

'She means Miss Wimpole, Sir,' said Tim. 'The big girls call her Wimbledon 'cause she plays tennis, Sir, in a little skirt.'

'I thought you didn't know any girls,' said Sir. 'What did Miss Wimpole say to you, Pauline?'

'She didn't,' said Pauline. 'It was Moira Thatcher. She said to tell June Nichols to come and see Miss Whatsit before assembly and bring her bed socks.'

'Then why tell Tim?'

'I couldn't find June. June's in his class.'

'I begin to see daylight,' said Sir. 'Not much, but it's there. All right, Pauline. Go and get Moira, please.'

Moira had recently had a new brace fitted across her front teeth. It caught the light when she opened her mouth.

'Yeth, Thir?'

'Moira, take it slowly, and tell us what the message was about June Nichols.'

Moira took a deep breath and polished the brace with her tongue.

'Well, Thir, Mith Wimpole thaid to thell June to thee her before athembly with her wed fw – thw – thth –'

'Frock?' said Sir. Moira nodded gratefully. 'So why tell Pauline?'

'Pauline liveth up her thtweet, Thir.'

'No I don't,' said Pauline. 'They moved. They got a council house, up the Ridgeway.'

'All right, Moira,' said Sir. 'Just ask Miss Wimpole if she could thp – spare me a minute of her time, please?'

If Miss Wimpole was surprised to find eight people in Sir's office, she didn't show it. As there was no longer room to get inside, she stood at the doorway and waved. Sir waved back. Mike instantly decided that Sir fancied Miss Wimpole.

'Miss Wimpole, I believe you must be the last link in the chain. Am I right in thinking that you wanted June Nichols to see you before assembly, with her red frock?'

'Why, yes,' said Miss Wimpole. 'She's dancing a solo at the end-of-term concert. I wanted her to practise, but she didn't turn up.'

'Thank you,' said Sir. 'One day, when we both have a spare hour or two, I'll tell you why she didn't turn up.

As for you lot,' he said, turning to the mob round his desk, 'you seem to have been playing Chinese Whispers without knowing it. You also seem to think that the entire staff is off its head. You may be right. I don't know. Red socks, dead dogs, live frogs – we'll put your friend in the school pond, Ruth. Fetch him at break. And now, someone had better find June Nichols and deliver Miss Wimpole's message.'

'Oh, there's no point, Sir. She couldn't have come anyway,' said Ruth. 'She's got chicken-pox. She hasn't been at school for ages.'

JAN MARK
*Illustrated by* DAVID PARKINS

## *'If you don't put your shoes on . . .'*

If you don't put your shoes on before I count fifteen
then we won't go to the woods to climb the chestnut tree.
One.
    But I can't find them.
Two.
    I can't.
They're under the sofa. Three.
    No ... O yes.
Four Five Six.

Stop – they've got knots they've got knots.
You should untie the laces when you take your shoes off.
Seven.

Will you do one shoe while I do the other then?
Eight. But that would be cheating ...

Please.
All right.

It always ...
Nine.

It always sticks – I'll use my teeth.
Ten.

It won't it won't ... It has – look.
Eleven.

I'm not wearing any socks.
Twelve.

Stop counting stop counting. (Mum where are my socks
mum?)
THEY'RE IN YOUR SHOES. WHERE YOU
LEFT THEM.

I didn't.
Thirteen.

O they're inside out and upside down and bundled up.
Fourteen.

Have you done the knot on the shoe you were ...
Yes. Put it on the right foot.

But socks don't have right and wrong foot.
The shoes, silly ... Fourteen and a half.

I am I am. Wait.

Don't go to the woods without me.

Look that's one shoe already.
Fourteen and three quarters.

There!
You haven't tied the bows yet.
    We could do them on the way there?
No we won't. Fourteen and seven eighths.
    Help me then –
    You know I'm not fast at bows.
Fourteen and fifteen sixteenths.
    A single bow is all right, isn't it?
Fifteen. We're off.
See I did it.

Didn't I?

                                    MICHAEL ROSEN

# What Did You Put in Your Pocket?

What did you put in your pocket
What did you put in your pocket
    in your pockety pockety pocket
Early Monday morning?

I put in some chocolate pudding
I put in some chocolate pudding
    slushy glushy pudding
Early Monday morning.

*Refrain*: SLUSHY GLUSHY PUDDING!

What did you put in your pocket
What did you put in your pocket
   in your pockety pockety pocket
Early Tuesday morning?

I put in some ice-cold water
I put in some ice-cold water
   nicy icy water
Early Tuesday morning.

   *Refrain*: SLUSHY GLUSHY PUDDING!
         NICY ICY WATER!

What did you put in your pocket
What did you put in your pocket
   in your pockety pockety pocket
Early Wednesday morning?

I put in a scoop of ice cream
I put in a scoop of ice cream
   slurpy glurpy ice cream
Early Wednesday morning.

   *Refrain*: SLUSHY GLUSHY PUDDING!
         NICY ICY WATER!
         SLURPY GLURPY ICE CREAM!

What did you put in your pocket
What did you put in your pocket
   in your pockety pockety pocket
Early Thursday morning?

I put in some mashed potatoes
I put in some mashed potatoes
    fluppy gluppy potatoes
Early Thursday morning.

    *Refrain*: SLUSHY GLUSHY PUDDING!
            NICY ICY WATER!
            SLURPY GLURPY ICE CREAM!
            FLUPPY GLUPPY POTATOES!

What did you put in your pocket
What did you put in your pocket
  in your pockety pockety pocket
Early Friday morning?

I put in some sticky treacle
I put in some sticky treacle
  sticky icky treacle
Early Friday morning.

> *Refrain*: SLUSHY GLUSHY PUDDING!
>              NICY ICY WATER!
>              SLURPY GLURPY ICE CREAM!
>              FLUPPY GLUPPY POTATOES!
>              STICKY ICKY TREACLE!

What did you put in your pocket
What did you put in your pocket
  in your pockety pockety pocket
Early Saturday morning?

I put in my five fingers
I put in my five fingers
  funny finny fingers
Early Saturday morning.

> *Refrain*: SLUSHY GLUSHY PUDDING!
>              NICY ICY WATER!
>              SLURPY GLURPY ICE CREAM!
>              FLUPPY GLUPPY POTATOES!
>              STICKY ICKY TREACLE!
>              FUNNY FINNY FINGERS!

What did you put in your pocket
What did you put in your pocket
   in your pockety pockety pocket
Early Sunday morning?

I put in a clean white handkerchief
I put in a clean white handkerchief
   a spinky spanky handkerchief
Early Sunday morning.

> *Refrain*: SLUSHY GLUSHY PUDDING!
>             NICY ICY WATER!
>             SLURPY GLURPY ICE CREAM!
>             FLUPPY GLUPPY POTATOES!
>             STICKY ICKY TREACLE!
>             FUNNY FINNY FINGERS!
>             SPINKY SPANKY
>                HANDKERCHIEF!

BEATRICE SCHENK DE REGNIERS
*Illustrated by* DAVID MCKEE

# The Dinner Lady
# Who Made Magic

Frogover Road Primary School is housed in an old and ugly building. It has windows that are too high to look out of, a yard like iron that you daren't fall down on, bogs that always need plumbing, and more wild kids than good books. There is so much noise coming in from outside, where there is a busy road one way and a railway line the other, that it is murder when the windows have to be wedged open in summer. In winter, when the windows are shut tight, it is like hell, getting hotter and hotter all the time. There was a time when the boilers that clattered and bumbled from below sounded as if they were just going to blow up. That was the time when the school was a pretty dreadful place to be in.

In those days, the Frogover Road kids were a really nasty lot. They pinched one another's dinner money to buy stink bombs to drop at Assembly, they wrote rude things about the teachers in school chalk on the outside walls and blamed other people when they were caught, and they told lies and used swear words and few of them ever spoke below a shout.

The tough kids were always making new gangs and busting up the old ones and, when that happened, there'd be blacks and whites and Asians and Chinese and Cypriots and Arabs all mixed up, bashing each other up and down the playground and over the classrooms; boys and girls punching and clawing, teachers yelling and screaming at them to stop, and the little tiddlers in the Reception class crying and wanting to go home. As for the kids who weren't tough – they'd just keep out of everyone's way as much as possible, and pretend to read books with their fingers in their ears. The only thing no one ever did at that school was learn anything.

At dinner-time, the dinner ladies were as cross as two sticks: they dunked out the potatoes and sloshed the stew and pushed out the plates of prunes and custard without looking anyone in the face, and, as soon as another job came their way, they gave in their notices at once. And the children were so horrible and the teachers so bad-tempered that no one even noticed when they went.

And it might have gone on like that: on and on for ever and ever, getting worse and worse, if it hadn't been for a bit of magic.

Now, you'd never have believed that any kind of magic would have been likely to find its way into that part of London. All those miserable, treacherous pavements with the cracks and dips in them, and the houses with several families jammed together under one roof, and the shops with windows full of ugly posters, and the old men who spat at the street corners. 'Magic?' you'd have said. 'Why, even the colour tellies in the hire-shop windows aren't magic any more – everyone has them now.'

But there *was* a bit of magic all right. It came over from the West Indies with a boy called Gerry's grandmam. This boy called Gerry's grandmam flew over for a visit one summer and man, was *she* something special? She was a real witch. Nothing creepy or turning you into something horrible if you upset her or anything – just an old black lady who was good at spells. She knew about things: what spices to mix together, the right knots to tie in pig's chitterlings, how many black chicken's feathers to burn at one go, and why you couldn't brew spells over a gas-ring – things like that. Mild stuff for making the odd friendly spell.

Gerry's grandmam was so black that she shone, and so fat that she walked with a bounce like an air-balloon, and so kind that the meanest, crossest check-out girl in the dingiest supermarket had to smile with her. And when she laughed, which she often did, her chuckles gurgled and bubbled like a Lakeland beck and everyone around laughed to hear her.

Now, around the time Gerry's grandmam was over, there was a crisis at Frogover Road, a *serious* crisis – a walk-out. There had been trouble in the dinner-hour, real trouble. It had started when a girl called Lucy Wilkins, who had yellow hair with green slides in it, had pushed in front of a girl called Carmen Melinski and tried to take her place in the dinner queue.

Lucy was a big 'I'm-the-boss-lady-around-here' sort of girl, with a strong gang behind her, who liked and expected to be treated as Queen of the School. Carmen was a new girl, little and quiet, with black hair and deep blue eyes and very red lips, who looked like she couldn't blow fluff off a milkshake. No one had expected Carmen to be anything but meek, but instead, quick as a flash, Carmen's olive fingers dug themselves into Lucy's gold mop, the green slides skittered to the floor, Lucy fell hard against Horace Loss, a pale-brown West Indian with long eyelashes and a quick temper, and before you could say 'battle' they were all at it. Mashed potato flew across the hall, creamed carrots slithered beneath the struggling bodies, and custard dripped from the table-tops. And then five terrified little first-years, running for refuge among the alarmed dinner ladies, upset the fish fingers on to the stove and set them alight!

If the school secretary hadn't phoned at once for the police and the fire brigade, someone might have been killed. The hot, food-plastered children stood in disgraced rows while first the police sergeant, then the fire chief and then the Head-mistress gave them good tellings-off. By rights they should have been sent home in disgrace but, as most of their mothers were working, they'd have had nowhere to go and might have got into more trouble. So there they had to stay, dinner-bedecked and depressed, until it was time for school to finish for the day. The only ones who went home, at once and for ever, were the angry dinner ladies, who resigned in a bunch.

'And now what shall we do?' the school secretary asked the Headmistress.

The Headmistress rang the Chief Education Officer. 'What *shall* we do about dinners in future for Frogover Primary? We can manage with one lady short if we have to, but not the lot. Oh, my!'

But all the Chief Education Officer could say was, 'Ad-vertise, advertise!'

So, whether they liked it or not, the best that could be done for Frogover Road's midday meal was bread and cheese and apples, which made the kids mutinous and their parents ask what they were supposed to be paying for. But what else could be done? Dinner ladies don't grow on trees! The word had gone round and so, in spite of the advertisements that the Headmistress put in the local paper, and the ones that the school secretary placed on the paper-shop boards, and in spite of the phone calls to the Job Centre, no one wanted to work in a school with a reputation as bad as Frogover Road's.

So it went on being bread and cheese cut into lumps by the overworked secretary, and specky apples from the market, and no one daring to grumble aloud because they knew they'd gone too far. What with that Carmen Melinski behaving like a smug mouse, and a thankful gang of previously persecuted nonentities going home in a posse, and Lucy Wilkins with sticking plaster down the side of her face where she had been scratched smouldering in the middle of her lot, and Horace Loss and his mates sulking all playtime down by the dustbins, and Achmed, Shemsha and Mouki and their crowd going off into corners and whispering, it's a wonder that the secretary didn't walk out too.

But she was a nice lady – worried, but nice. The kids quite liked her. One or two of the better-natured ones even felt sorry for her, sorry enough to help with the cheese-cutting. But of course it couldn't go on. The situation was explosive.

The third morning after the walk-out of the dinner ladies, while she was waiting at Tesco's check-out with a trolley full of cut loaves and cheese, the harassed school secretary looked across at the queue opposite and saw a face. If the sun had been black, that was how it would have beamed! Springy grey curls under a hat like a crown of coloured veils bobbed and nodded above a broad and all-encompassing smile.

'Don' look so down, secretary Miss,' said Gerry's grand-mam, who knew the secretary by sight, for wasn't her

grandson a second-year Frogover Roader? 'Seems to me
now those children have been punished enough. Too much
misery can lead to real bad doings. It's time something nice
happened in that miserable old school for a change.'

They met as soon as they had passed through the check-
outs, and the school secretary told Gerry's grandmam what
was in her heart: all about how old the school was and how
crowded and noisy, how the teachers were edgy and how
there wasn't even a proper dining-room, only the assembly
hall with temporary tables down the middle. 'It's not the
children, really,' she said. 'It's Things. But you can't blame
the dinner ladies either,' she went on. 'Those children were
very, very naughty. Do you know, the caretaker says that

little bits of dried potato are still dropping off the light bulbs?'

Gerry's grandmam listened, and then she laughed, so that the secretary laughed too, and so did the other shoppers, and even the passers-by in the High Street who couldn't hear through the glass found themselves smiling as they hurried by.

'I'm having a fine holiday in this old U.K.,' the witch-grandmam said. 'I've been to Brighton, and Buckingham Palace, the Commonwealth Institute and the Oval and to visit my sister and her family in Birmingham. But I ain't never been in a school. So, I'll tell you what, I'll come and help with those dinners for a week or two before I fly home again. That *will* be something to talk about when I get back! And I'll look around and find a couple or so other folk to help me.'

And that's what happened. That evening Gerry's grandmam went down to the fried chicken take-away and talked to a couple of rather posh little old white sister-ladies who were waiting for potato fritters, and somehow these old ladies found themselves offering to help out as dinner ladies.

'It's an emergency – like in the war-time,' said one. 'I remember making cocoa for the air raid wardens.'

'We must do our bit for the children,' said the other, and they giggled with pleasure.

Gerry's grandmam knew a girl called Winnie Wong, who sat about all day painting her nails, so she called and asked her if she'd like to help in the school kitchen as a change from nail-painting and idling. And, although she'd never meant to, somehow Winnie Wong found herself saying, 'Yes, all right.'

'Three good helpers will be enough, I guess,' that old witch-grandmam said.

That night Gerry's grandmam got busy in the small trodden yard behind the house where Gerry's family lived. On a black skillet over a fire of wood-chips she frizzled feathers and burned spices and whispered spells as old as Africa. With a long iron spoon she stirred and mashed the growing magic, turning it over and over to ensure that every bit received its appropriate incantation, until the fire died and fell away to white ash, and the skillet cooled and all that remained was a bare spoonful of glittery powder.

Next morning at nine o'clock the new dinner helpers arrived: Gerry's grandmam in her magnificent hat and a flowing overall patterned with birds of paradise, the pale old sisters in frilly pink aprons with streamers that had once been worn by a long-ago parlourmaid, and Winnie Wong in the dark blue trousers and tunic of a Chinese worker, with a red carnation tucked behind her ear for luck. There they were, all ready to heat and dish up the school dinners.

For the first time for days a good warm smell rose up from the kitchen and penetrated the classrooms. That day the Central Kitchen had delivered stew, which now bubbled over the gas-rings.

'Hi-yee-ah,' said Gerry's grandmam as she raised the heavy lids and looked down upon the mutton and vegetables. 'Hi-yee-ah,' she said again, and a pinch of something small and glittery and magic slipped from the end of her wooden spoon and was lost to sight as she stirred the pot.

In the meantime, one of the posh old ladies and Winnie Wong put up the tables and arranged the chairs, while the other sister popped out to the market and came back with a couple of bunches of pink daisies, which she divided out into empty milk bottles and put on each table. 'There!' she said. 'The children will like those!'

The Frogover kids came eagerly to dinner, their noses twitching. For them, they were fairly quiet. There was a hushed feeling in the air and, as they fell into line, they spoke in whispers.

Gerry's grandmam in her rainbow hat served up the mouth-watering stew and beamed as each child carried its plate to where Miss Wong waited, her beautiful fluttering pale hands with their painted nails poised to spoon out the mash and lay it delicately and deliciously beside the meat and veg.

The little old ladies, twittering and tottering, wandered round with fresh jugs of water and helped the little ones to

cut their meat and offered cubes of bread like dear old-fashioned grannies, speaking so politely in their posh soft voices that the startled children spoke softly if not poshly back.

And, as they ate, the magic worked; it sank into angry stomachs and soothed and petted them into kindness. Querulous teachers suddenly hushed and smiled at each other. Lucy Wilkins peeled off the sticking plaster which she'd only been wearing for effect – for the marks of Carmen's nails had healed days before – and, rolling it neatly, dropped it in her pocket. Horace Loss and his mates, who had recently formed themselves into the Horseshoe Gang, rose as one boy and, without being asked, collected the empty plates of the Reception class and fetched the helpings of jam roll to save the little things from having to queue. And the Asian children, who were mostly vegetarians, smiled at everyone for, although they had not tasted the stew themselves, the magic working away inside everyone else had created a friendliness they were only too pleased to share.

After dinner, Gerry's grandmam and her helpers washed up and stacked away the dishes, singing happily together. The blended voices of the witch-grandmam, the posh old ladies and the lovely Winnie Wong filled the school as pleasantly as the scent of the midday stew, and the kids and the teachers smiled as they listened, and then went on with the lessons in the smoothest way imaginable.

So, day after day, until it was time for her to fly home, Gerry's grandmam and her helpers served the school dinners, dispensing magic until the miserable old building became bright and colourful, the outside noises sounded as pleasant as early-morning bird songs, and the rumbles of the downstairs boiler seemed like the drowsy chuckles of a slumbering giant. Now the school was talked about as a place in a million. Somewhere where it was good to be. Somewhere where the kids liked learning and the teachers liked teaching.

News of its transformation spread through the neighbour-hood. In a body, just as they had walked out, the dinner ladies returned to plead for their old jobs back. By now the magic had truly worked. It had penetrated every crack and cranny of the old school building and soaked into the hearts of all who entered it. The Headmistress knew that it would soon be time for Gerry's grandmam to go back home, and that the posh old sisters would be leaving to join the W.V.S., and that Winnie Wong was soon to marry Mr Ah Foo from the Chinese diner, and so she graciously wel-comed the dinner ladies back. And now, so good were the children and so pleasant the teachers, that the dinner ladies found themselves beaming as they dished out the dinners.

Before she left, Gerry's grandmam gave the chief dinner lady a small tinful of magic. 'Just drop a bit in now and again,' she said. 'You may as well use it up.'

But the chief dinner lady didn't believe in spells and she threw the tin away next day. It didn't really matter, though, for the magic had done its work and goes on making things better and better. When the time comes for those kids to grow up and make their own lives among those old streets and houses, they'll have so much magic in them that they'll make the place a paradise!

DOROTHY EDWARDS
*Illustrated by* JILL BENNETT

# Turtle Soup

Beautiful soup, so rich and green,
Waiting in a hot tureen!
Who for such dainties would not stoop?
Soup of the evening, beautiful soup!
Soup of the evening, beautiful soup!
 Beau—ootiful soo—oop!
 Beau—ootiful soo—oop!
Soo—oop of the e—e—evening,
 Beautiful, beautiful soup!

Beautiful soup! Who cares for fish,
Game, or any other dish?
Who would not give all else for two
Pennyworth only of beautiful soup?
Pennyworth only of beautiful soup?
 Beau—ootiful soo—oop!
 Beau—ootiful soo—oop!
Soo—oop of the e—e—evening,
 Beautiful, beauti—FUL SOUP!

LEWIS CARROLL

# Dear Bren

*Dear Bren,*

*Don't drop dead because I'm writing to you. In Quiet Time we've got to write our letters to our mums and dads. It's boring — worse than being at Gran's when she's having her sleep — so at the same time as writing to them I'm writing a secret letter to you.*

Sunday, 25th May

Dear Mum and Dad,

I arrived safely on School Journey. I'm glad I came. The beds are hard and the food's horrible. I'm having a great time.

In this letter I'll tell you some of the things we've been doing.

The other envelope is for Brenda. It's private!

*What you said about this place was right. It's a good laugh. I only cried one night, but I had a headache. The worst one for crying is Lorraine Cooper's brother, Marvin. He keeps crying all the time. It gets on your nerves. He says his dog's ill, but Sandra Brown says he hasn't even got one.*

We went to the zoo on Monday. It's not all that big. They've only got one lion. Mr Cox had a load of work cards, and my group had to do all about giraffes. It was all right, except the giraffe didn't want to come out of his shed.

*Dragging round and round the zoo really makes your feet ache. Like you said, this one's dead crummy, and we all got fed up. Then Jason Ring told us to go and see what the monkeys were doing. It was great, watching them – till Miss Blake found us. She made our group go back to the giraffe. How boring!*
*But we kept on laughing about the monkeys . . .*

In the dinner-hall we get all the meal on one tray, like in those prison films. You'll be pleased to know I'm eating all my food up. We get cooked breakfasts and the dinners here are just like at school – except there the mash is lumpy and the custard's runny, and down here they go in for lumpy custard and runny mash.

*Don't you get starving down here, Bren? They don't give you half enough. Still, in Free Time, if you squeeze through the hedge at the back of the playing-field, you can run down the village shop for crisps. Did you used to do that? Half the camp's in there some nights. One of the kids said there's only one reason why we don't get caught. The teachers are all down the pub buying pies!*

On Tuesday we went to look at a big white horse drawn

on a hill. You can see it for miles. From the coach it looked like a big painting, but up close it's the chalk, still showing through after hundreds of years. It's really something, I reckon, lasting all that time.

*You're supposed to keep off of that big white horse. There's notices there. But Tony Smith went on it and dug up a bit of chalk with his heel. He wanted it to take home for his mum, but he got scared and dropped it out the coach window. It went under this lorry's wheel and got squashed to nothing on the road.*

There's eight girls in our dormitory. We get points for keeping it tidy. You get three for making your bed properly, and one for leaving the sink clean. But you lose points if you leave sweet-papers and clothes on the floor. Up to today I'm number five.

*We're not all that bothered about Miss Blake's points. Stella Camp worked out our own system. You get one point for going out on the landing in your nightie, two for knocking on the boys' door and running away, and five for going down the stairs or doing something else daring. Stella's winning, but I'm second — and I've got a couple of good ideas for next week.*

On Wednesday we went horse riding. We had to wear the proper hats. I went round the field twice on mine, and he galloped quite fast. The lady said I was very good.

If we cleared our shed out, we'd have room for a little pony, wouldn't we? I could go out every day and collect grass off the verge for him to eat, and wouldn't I save a lot on bus fares?

*Sandra Brown said she knew all about horse riding. She reckons she goes every week. She really fancies herself, and she sat on*

*her horse like those girls do in the pony books, with a face like
some statue. But then her horse wouldn't go! He kept eating the
grass, and she had to pretend she was letting him.*

Our school played some games against one of the other
schools on Thursday. The boys played football and the girls
played netball. I was in the netball team. We won 14–6,
but the boys lost 10–0. If the teachers still want to, our
school's going to play them at rounders next week.

*In the football game this other school kept calling our boys a
load of rubbish. And when Prakash Patel got the ball they made
jungle noises. Even the teachers had a row about it. The other
school won the match, but we won the fights after the teachers
went in.*

On Friday we saw loads of animals at the market. Mr
Cox said he thought he'd bought a cow when he blew his
nose in the Auction Ring. We saw all the sheep up close,
and a pig as big as our bath. But I felt really sad, seeing
all the animals going off to be killed.

*At the market one man was really cruel to this calf. He kept
prodding it hard with a sharp stick, and when he pushed it in
the back of a van he made it knock its head. Anyway, when the
man was having a drink, Raymond Smith gave him a sandwich.
It was one the cows had licked. And the man ate it up! We felt
better then. But I'm definitely going to be a vegetarian when I'm
not so hungry.*

Do you remember that film, *Valley of Time*? Well, we
had it down here on Friday night, in the dinner-hall. It would
have been good, but there were some little kids here from
one of the other schools, and the teacher put his hand over

the picture every time the prehistoric monster came on. We said it wasn't fair. If they weren't old enough to watch it, they should have been in bed.

*In films these little cissy kids stopped us seeing the monsters. So after lights-out Tommy Dove and Raymond Smith got dressed up in sheets and crawled into their bedroom – just to make up for what they missed!*

*I've never heard screaming like it – anyhow, not since that spider walked across your pillow.*

Yesterday we went to the seaside. We did a project on the harbour. We had to draw the fishermen's sheds. We saw one of the boats come in and unload the catch. We made a list of all the different things they caught. Then we had fish and chips in a café. At the end, we had an hour of Free Time while we waited for the coach.

*The harbour's good, isn't it, Bren? Especially the Amusements over the road. Stella and I were sick on the coach back and Miss Blake blamed the fish supper. But we'd had six goes on the Octopus. We found out if you scream a lot they let you stay on for nothing!*

Well, that's nearly all I've got time for. Miss Blake says I've got to keep up the same behaviour next week.

Oh! She's just coming round to check our spellings and handwriting, and collect up all the spare bits of paper.

Sorry about screwing this page up. I made a mistake, thought it was some other bit of paper. Tell Bren I'm sorry there isn't a letter for her after all. But say it's been great on School Journey. I've really learned a lot down here.
See you on Saturday.

Your loving daughter, Lyn

BERNARD ASHLEY

# Snake in the Grass

Robin could tell, right from the beginning, that he was going to enjoy the picnic. To begin with, Uncle Joe and Auntie Joy had brought him a present, a bugle.

He took a long, testing blow. The note went on and on and on – and on. He saw Auntie Joy shudder and his cousin Nigel put his hands to his ears. Nigel was twelve, and Robin hardly even came up to his shoulder.

'We'll be off now,' Uncle Joe said, climbing into his car. 'See you there.'

Robin got into the back seat of his father's car.

'It's lovely at Miller's Beck,' his mother said. 'You'll love it, Robin.'

Robin did not reply. The picnic hamper was on the back seat, too, and he was trying to squint between the wicker-work to see what was in there. In the end he gave up squinting, and sniffed. Ham, was it? Tomatoes? Oranges, definitely, and was it – could it be – strawberries?

He sat back and began to practise the bugle. He kept play-ing the same three notes over and over again, and watched the back of his father's neck turning a dark red.

'D'ye *have* to play that thing now?' he growled at last. 'We shall all end up in a ditch!'

'I'm only trying to learn it, Dad,' said Robin. 'I've always wanted a bugle.'

An hour later, when they reached Miller's Beck, he had invented a tune that he really liked and had already played it about a hundred times. It was a kind of cross between 'Onward Christian Soldiers' and 'My Old Man's a Dustman'.

The minute the car stopped, Robin got out and ran down to the stream. He pulled off his shoes and socks and paddled in. The water was icy cold and clear as tap water, running over stones and gravel and small boulders.

Robin began to paddle downstream after a piece of floating bark he wanted for a boat, when:

'Ooooooooch!' he yelled. 'Owwwwch!'

A sharp pain ran through his foot. He balanced on one leg and lifted the hurt foot out of the water. He could see blood dripping from it.

'Ooooowh!' he yelled again. 'Help!'

He began to sway round and round on his good leg, like a spinning-top winding down. He threw out his arms, yelled again and was down, flat on his bottom in the icy beck.

'Robin,' he heard his father scream. 'Robin.'

He sat where he was with the water above his waist and the hurt foot lifted above the water, still dripping blood. He couldn't even feel the foot any more. He just sat and stared at it as if it belonged to somebody else.

His father was pulling off his shoes and socks and next minute was splashing in beside him and had lifted him clean up out of the water. Robin clutched him hard and water squelched between them. Robin's elbow moved sharply and he heard his father's yell.

'Hey, my glasses.'

Robin twisted his head and saw first that he was dripping

blood all over his father's trousers, second that the bottoms of his father's trousers were in the water because he hadn't had time to roll them up, and third that lying at the bottom of the beck were his father's spectacles. Robin could see at a glance that they were broken – at least, one of the lenses was.

His father staggered blindly out of the water, smack into Uncle Joe who was hopping on the bank.

'Here! Take him!' he gasped.

Then Robin was in Uncle Joe's arms, dripping blood and water all over *him*, and was carried back up the slope with his mother and Auntie Joy dancing and exclaiming around them.

It was half an hour before the picnic could really begin. By then, Robin was sitting on one of the folding chairs with his foot resting on a cushion on the other chair. This meant that both his parents were sitting on the grass. Robin's foot was bandaged with his father's handkerchief and the blood had soaked right through it and had made a great stain on the yellow cushion. Robin's shorts were hanging over the car bumper, where they were dripping on to Nigel's comic; Robin was wearing his swimming trunks and had his mother's new pink cardigan draped round his shoulders. There was blood on that, too.

'*Everyone's* got a bit of blood,' he noted with satisfaction.

Admittedly, his father and Uncle Joe had come off worst. His father sat half on the rug and half off with his trousers dripping. He had to keep squinting about him and twisting his head round to see through the one remaining lens of his glasses. Robin kept staring at him, thinking how queer he looked with one small squinting eye and one familiar

large one behind the thick pebble lens. It made him look
a different person – more a creature than a person, really,
like something come up from under the sea.

'Are you comfy, dear?' asked his mother.

Robin nodded.

'Are you hungry?'

Robin nodded.

'Ravenous.'

'Pass Robin a sandwich, Nigel!' said Auntie Joy sharply.
'Sitting there stuffing yourself! And you'd better not have
any more till we see how many Robin wants. Bless his heart!
Does he look pale to you, Myra?'

The picnic got better and better every minute. Robin had
at least three times his share of strawberries, and Auntie Joy
made Nigel give Robin his bag of crisps because she caught

him sticking out his tongue at Robin. Nigel went off in a huff and found blood all over his comic and the minute he tried to turn the first page, it tore right across.

'That hanky's nearly soaked,' Robin said, watching Auntie Joy helping herself to the last of the strawberries. 'I've never seen so much blood. You should have seen it dripping into the water. It turned the whole stream a sort of horrible streaky red.'

Auntie Joy carried on spooning.

'If I'd been in the sea, I expect it'd have turned the whole *sea* red,' Robin went on. 'It was the thickest blood I ever saw. Sticky, thicky red blood – streams of it. Gallons. I bet it's killed all the fishes.'

Auntie Joy gulped and bravely spooned out the remaining juice.

'I won't bleed to death, will I?' he went on. 'Bleed and bleed and bleed till there isn't another drop of blood left in my whole body, and I'm dead. Just like an empty bag, I'd be.'

Auntie Joy turned pale and put down her spoon.

'Just an empty bag of skin,' repeated Robin thoughtfully. 'That's what I'll be.'

'Of course you won't, darling!' cried his mother.

'Well, this handkerchief certainly is bloody,' said Robin. 'There must've been a bucket of blood. A *bowlful* anyway!'

Auntie Joy pushed away her bowl of strawberries.

'I wonder what it could've been?' went on Robin. 'That cut me, I mean.'

'Glass!' his mother said. 'It must have been. It's disgraceful, leaving broken glass lying about like that. Someone might have been crippled for life.'

'Dad,' said Robin, after a pause. At first his father did

not hear. He had stretched out at full length and was peering closely at his newspaper with his one pebble eye.

'Dad!' His father looked up. 'Dad, hadn't you better go and pick *your* glass up? From your specs, I mean? Somebody else might go and cut themselves.'

'The child's right!' his mother cried. 'Fancy the angel thinking of that! Off you go, George, and pick it up, straight away!'

Robin's father got up slowly. His trousers flapped wetly about his legs and his bloodstained shirt clung to him.

'And mind you pick up every little bit!' she called after him. 'Don't you want those strawberries, Joy?'

She shook her head.

'Could you manage them, Robin?'

Robin could. He did. When he had finished, he licked the bowl.

Once the tea things were cleared away, everyone settled down. Auntie Joy was knitting a complicated lacy jacket that meant she had to keep counting under her breath. His mother read, Uncle Joe decided to wash his car, and his father was searching for the sports pages of his newspaper that had blown away while he was down at the beck picking up his broken spectacles. Nigel had a new model yacht and took it down to the stream. Robin watched him go. All *he* had was a sodden comic and the bugle.

He played the bugle until the back of his father's neck was crimson again and Auntie Joy had twice lost count of her stitches and had to go right back to the beginning of the row again. For a change, he tried letting her get half-way across a row and then, without warning, gave a deafening blast. She jumped, the needles jerked, and half the stitches came off.

After the third time, even that didn't seem funny any more. Robin swung his legs down and tested the bad foot. Surprisingly, it hardly hurt at all. He stood right up and took a few steps. His mother looked up.

'Robin!' she squealed. 'Darling! What are you doing?'

'It's all right, Mum,' he said. 'It doesn't hurt. It's stopped bleeding now. It looks worse than it is, the handkerchief being all bloody.'

'I really think you should sit still,' she said.

Robin took no notice and went limping down to the beck. Nigel was in mid-stream, turning his yacht. It was a beauty.

'Swap you it for my bugle,' he said, after a time.

'What?' Nigel turned to face him. 'You're crazy. Crazy little kid!'

'I'll swap,' repeated Robin.

'Well, I *won't*.' Nigel turned his back again.

Robin stayed where he was. Lying by his feet were Nigel's shoes, with the socks stuffed inside them. Gently, using the big toe of his bandaged foot, he edged them off the bank and into the water. They lay there, the shoes filled and the socks began to balloon and sway. Fascinated, Robin watched. At last the socks, with a final graceful swirl, drifted free of the shoes and began to float downstream.

Robin watched them out of sight. After that, there seemed nothing he could do. What *could* you do, with your foot all bandaged up? The picnic was going all to pieces.

He felt a little sting on his good leg and looked down in time to see a gnat making off. He swatted hard at it, and with a sudden inspiration clapped a hand to his leg, fell to his knees and let out a blood-curdling howl.

'Robin!' He heard his mother scream. 'Robin!'

They were thundering down the slope towards him now, all of them, even Uncle Joe, wash-leather in hand.

'Darling! what is it?'

'Snake!' gasped Robin, squeezing his leg tight with his fingers.

'Where?' cried Auntie Joy. He pointed upstream, towards the long grass. He noticed that her wool was wound round her waist and her knitting trailing behind her, both needles missing.

'Where did it *bite* you?' she cried.

Robin took his hands away from the leg. Where they had clutched it, the skin was red and in the middle of the crimson patch was the tiny prick made by the gnat.

'Oooooh!' He heard his mother give an odd, sighing moan and looked up in time to see that she was falling. His father leapt forward and caught her just in time and they both fell to the ground together.

'Biting the dust,' thought Robin, watching them.

'Here!' cried Auntie Joy. 'We'll have to suck the poison out!'

She dropped to her knees beside him, her hair awry and face flushed. Next minute she had her mouth to Robin's leg and was sucking it, with fierce, noisy sucks. He tried to jerk his leg away but she had it in an iron grip. At last she stopped sucking and turning her head aside spat fiercely right into the stream. It was almost worth having her suck, to see her spit.

'Carry him up to the car!' she gasped, scrambling up. 'I must see to Myra!'

Uncle Joe picked him up for the second time that day and carried him away. Over his shoulder Robin could see the others bending over his mother, trying to lift her. Best of all, he could see Nigel beating round in the long grass with a stick while his boat, forgotten, sailed slowly off downstream.

'Gone,' Robin thought. 'Gone for ever.'

Uncle Joe put him down in the driving seat of his own car.

'Be all right for a minute, old chap?' he asked.

Robin nodded.

'Have a mint.' He fished one from his pocket. 'Back in a minute. Better go and see if I can find that brute of a snake. Don't want Nigel bitten.'

Then he was gone. Robin stared through the windscreen towards the excited huddle by the bank. It seemed to him that everyone was having a good time except himself. There he sat, quite alone, scratching absently at the gnat bite.

Idly he looked about the inside of the car. Usually he wasn't allowed in. It was Uncle Joe's pride and joy. The dashboard glittered with knobs and dials. He twiddled one or two of them, and got the radio working, then a green light on, then a red, then the windscreen wipers working. He pushed the gearstick and it slotted smoothly into place. To his left, between the bucket seats, was the handbrake. He knew how to release it – his father had shown him.

The brake was tightly on, and it was a struggle. He was red in the face and panting by the time he sat upright again. The car was rolling forward, very gently, down the grassy slope, then gathering speed as it approached the beck.

By the time they saw him it was too late. The car lurched, then bounced off the bank and into the water. It stopped, right in mid-stream.

Robin looked out and saw himself surrounded by water.

'The captain goes down with his ship!' he thought.

He saw his mother sit up, stare, then fall straight back again. He saw the others, wet, bloodstained and horror-struck, advancing towards him.

With a sigh he let his hands fall from the wheel. It was the end of the picnic, he could see that. He wound down the window and put out a hand to wave. Instead, it met glass and warm flesh. He heard a splash and a tinkle. Level with the window, he saw his father's face. Now *both* his eyes were small and squinting. Small, squinting and murderous.

The picnic was definitely over.

HELEN CRESSWELL
*Illustrated by* JAN ORMEROD

## You Tell Me

Here are the football results:
League Division Fun
Manchester United won, Manchester City lost.
Crystal Palace 2, Buckingham Palace 1
Millwall Leeds nowhere
Wolves 8 A cheese roll and had a cup of tea 2
Aldershot 3 Buffalo Bill shot 2
Evertonill, Liverpool's not very well either
Newcastle's Heaven Sunderland's a very nice place 2
Ipswhich one? You tell me.

MICHAEL ROSEN

# *Freddie, the Toothbrush Cheat*

Freddie sat at the kitchen table collecting crumbs and arranging them in a circle around the rim of his plate. His mother was at the sink, elbow-deep in foam washing the dishes after supper, and Freddie looked up at her feeling warm and full and sleepy. It would soon be bedtime; Freddie didn't mind going to bed too much in the winter when it was dark and cold outside and he could wriggle down in the bed like a snake with his comics and have a little read and a laugh before the light went out. But then his heart sank; he would have to have a bath and clean his teeth. Ugh.

Now Freddie was a friendly boy, very pleasant company and fun to be with, but he hated soap and water with all his heart and, even more, hated cleaning his teeth. The whole business bored and annoyed him so much that the thought of it made him want to hide from his mother, or even run away rather than have to go through with it again. He felt depressed and stuck his thumb in his mouth and gave it a good suck, at the same time twirling a strand or two of hair with his other hand. His mother had just finished putting away the last knife and fork in the drawer when she saw him from the corner of her eye.

'Come on, Freddie, you look tired, darling. It's half past eight, I'll just go and run your bath.' And she went upstairs.

Freddie let out a groan and felt himself sag. 'Here we

go again,' he thought. 'All that palaver. Soap in my eyes, up my nose, in my mouth, and that awful, boring toothbrush.' He could bear it no longer and furtively climbed into the kitchen waste-bin and pulled the lid over himself. It was a bit smelly in there. There'd been kippers for tea and the bones crunched under his shoes, but it was preferable he thought to the smell of rose-pink soap. He heard his mother re-enter the kitchen. She called him, then sighed when he didn't answer. Lifting the flap of the waste-bin an inch or two, he found himself gazing at her flowery apron and he quickly shut it again, but she heard the thud and pulled him out without ceremony and chased him up the stairs whacking his bottom with a loofah.

Freddie was in a frightful rage by now; he shouted and wailed, whilst his mother soaped and scrubbed him. The flannel got in his mouth, and his ears filled with bubbles, hot angry tears dripped into the lather as he slipped and slithered in an attempt to escape his mother's grasp, but she held him firmly and didn't let him escape until he was rosy and clean, and wrapped in a warm white towel.

'Oh, Freddie,' sighed his mother, rubbing his hair dry, 'I'm sick of you being so naughty at bath-time; it really wears me out. You can clean your own teeth, I'm going downstairs to see if Daddy's in yet.'

Freddie sat on the bathroom floor sucking his thumb. He was surrounded by little pools of water and patches of foam, the result of his battle. He hadn't won round one, but he was determined to win round two. He picked up his toothbrush, ran it under the tap, took the top off the tube, spread it here and there as if he'd spat it out in the bottom of the basin, and then got into bed feeling rather pleased with himself. He didn't know why, but he didn't enjoy his comic that night; he couldn't smile once, not even at Korky the Cat, who was usually his favourite.

The next morning, after breakfast, his mother said, 'Go and clean your teeth, Freddie. I don't want to have to start the day with a quarrel, so you can do them by yourself.'

Freddie climbed the stairs with a sly grin. He put his tooth-brush under the tap, made a few splashing and spitting noises, spread a bit of toothpaste around the bottom of the basin and gazed triumphantly at himself in the mirror. He smiled gleefully, but quickly closed his mouth when he noticed that his teeth were pale yellow.

For pudding that day, Mother had made blackberry pie

and for supper they finished with chocolate mousse. Freddie was quite good in the bath that night and said he would clean his own teeth. After splashing the toothbrush around for a while he grinned in the mirror and was surprised to see his teeth were brownish-grey with blackberry seeds stuck between the spaces. He didn't sleep well at all.

The next morning after the same performance had gone on, Freddie bared his teeth in the mirror and found to his dismay that his teeth were pale green, and dotted with blackberry seeds. Still, it was better than the boring business of teeth-cleaning, and he was careful not to smile at anyone that day and only spoke with his hand over his mouth, much to everyone's amazement.

That night he spent ages making teeth-cleaning noises, spitting and sploshing about. He was afraid to look at his teeth, which was hardly surprising for they were now quite black and tasted foul – and little did he know, but the blackberry seeds had started to take root.

The next few days were misery; little shoots began to grow around his gums, and tendrils with small green leaves kept popping out of his mouth. He had to keep pushing them back in again in case anyone noticed. He was afraid to speak, of course, and just answered his parents with a 'Mmmmm' or a nod. His mother didn't mention his teeth, but he couldn't help feeling he wished she would.

After four weeks of not cleaning his teeth, Freddie was a dreadful sight. His mouth was a tangle of weeds and he was so thin through not eating, and so lonely through not speaking, that his heart was breaking.

His mother, greatly distressed, called the doctor.

His examination was brief. 'This child has not been

cleaning his teeth!' he said, shaking his thermometer gravely and trying to part the branches to insert it in to his mouth. 'There's nothing I can do for him I'm afraid. He'll have to go to the dentist!'

Freddie's mother was horrified. 'Why, Freddie,' she exclaimed, 'you are a silly boy. You think you've been cheating me but really you've been cheating yourself, and look what it's led to. I've never seen such a ghastly sight in my life. Put on your coat. We're off to the dentist at once.'

The dentist was a jolly chap. 'This is the worst case of non-teeth-cleaning I've ever come up against, my boy,' he said, and set to work with his probes and files and tweezers, disentangling the jungle in Freddie's mouth.

Freddie was half an hour in the dentist's chair and his teeth were given a final polish with a tickly brush whizzing round on the end of the drill. Then the dentist handed him a mirror and said, 'Now smile, Freddie – that's how your teeth should look.'

They were rows of gleaming white pearls set in firm pink gums – a lovely sight. Nobody ever had to tell Freddie to clean his teeth again!

WENDY CRAIG

# The Owl and the Pussy-Cat

The Owl and the Pussy-Cat went to sea
In a beautiful pea-green boat;
They took some honey, and plenty of money,
Wrapped up in a five-pound note.
The Owl looked up to the stars above,
And sang to a small guitar,
'O lovely Pussy! O Pussy, my love,
What a beautiful Pussy you are,
                    You are,
                    You are!
What a beautiful Pussy you are!'

Pussy said to the Owl, 'You elegant fowl!
How charmingly sweet you sing!
O let us be married! too long we have tarried:
But what shall we do for a ring?'

They sailed away for a year and a day,
To the land where the Bong-tree grows,
And there in a wood a Piggy-wig stood,
With a ring at the end of his nose.
                    His nose
                    His nose,
With a ring at the end of his nose.

'Dear Pig, are you willing to sell for one shilling
Your ring?' Said the Piggy, 'I will.'
So they took it away, and were married next day
By the Turkey who lives on the hill.
They dined on mince, and slices of quince,
Which they ate with a runcible spoon;
And hand in hand, on the edge of the sand,
They danced by the light of the moon,
                    The moon
                    The moon,
They danced by the light of the moon.

*Written and illustrated by* EDWARD LEAR

# The Dutch Cheese

Once – once upon a time there lived, with his sister Griselda, in a little cottage near the Great Forest, a young farmer whose name was John. Brother and sister, they lived alone except for their sheepdog, Sly, their flock of sheep, the numberless birds of the forest, and the 'fairies'. John loved his sister beyond telling; he loved Sly; and he delighted to listen to the birds singing at twilight round the darkening margin of the forest. But he feared and hated the fairies. And, having a very stubborn heart, the more he feared, the more he hated them; and the more he hated them, the more they pestered him.

Now these were a tribe of fairies, sly, small, gay-hearted and mischievous, and not of the race of fairies noble, silent, beautiful and remote from man. They were a sort of gipsy-fairies, very nimble and of aery and prankish company, and partly for mischief and partly for love of her they were always trying to charm John's dear sister Griselda away, with their music and fruits and trickery. He more than half believed it was they who years ago had decoyed into the forest not only his poor father, who had gone out faggot-cutting in his sheepskin hat with his ass; but his mother too, who soon after had gone out to look for him.

But fairies, even of this small tribe, hate no man. They mocked him and mischiefed him; they spilt his milk, rode astraddle on his rams, garlanded his old ewes with sow-thistle and briony, sprinkled water on his kindling wood, loosed his bucket in the well, and hid his great leather shoes. But all this they did, not for hate – for they came and went like evening moths about Griselda – but because in his fear and fury he shut up his sister from them, and because he was sullen and stupid. Yet he did nothing but fret himself. He set traps for them, and caught starlings; he fired his blunderbuss at them under the moon, and scared his sheep; he set dishes of sour milk in their way, and sticky leaves and brambles where their rings were green in the meadows; but all to no purpose. When at dusk, too, he heard their faint, elfin music, he would sit in the door blowing into his father's great bassoon till the black forest re-echoed with its sad, solemn, wooden voice. But that was of no help either. At last he grew so surly that he made Griselda utterly miserable. Her cheeks lost their scarlet and her eyes their sparkling. Then the fairies began to plague John in earnest – lest their lovely, loved child of man, Griselda, should die.

Now one summer's evening – and most nights are cold in the Great Forest – John, having put away his mournful bassoon and bolted the door, was squatting, moody and gloomy, with Griselda, on his hearth beside the fire. And he leaned back his great hairy head and stared straight up the chimney to where high in the heavens glittered a host of stars. And suddenly, while he lolled there on his stool moodily watching them, there appeared against the dark sky a mischievous elvish head secretly peeping down at him; and busy fingers began sprinkling dew on his wide upturned face. He heard the laughter too of the fairies miching and gambolling on his thatch, and in his rage he started up, seized

a round Dutch cheese that lay on a platter, and with all his force threw it clean and straight up the sooty chimney at the faces of mockery clustered above. And after that, though Griselda sighed at her spinning wheel, he heard no more. Even the cricket that had been whistling all through the evening fell silent, and John supped on his black bread and onions alone.

Next day Griselda woke at dawn and put her head out of the little window beneath the thatch, and the day was white with mist.

''Twill be another hot day,' she said to herself, combing her beautiful hair.

But when John went down, so white and dense with mist were the fields, that even the green borders of the forest were invisible, and the whiteness went to the sky. Swathing and wreathing itself, opal and white as milk, all the morning the mist grew thicker and thicker about the little house. When John went out about nine o'clock to peer about him, nothing was to be seen at all. He could hear his sheep bleating, the kettle singing, Griselda sweeping, but straight up above him hung only, like a small round fruit, a little cheese-red beamless sun — straight up above him, though the hands of the clock were not yet come to ten. He clenched his fists and stamped in sheer rage. But no one answered him, no voice mocked him but his own. For when these idle, mischievous fairies have played a trick on an enemy they soon weary of it.

All day long that little sullen lantern burned above the mist, sometimes red, so that the white mist was dyed to amber, and sometimes milky pale. The trees dripped water from every leaf. Every flower asleep in the garden was neckleted with beads; and nothing but a drenched old forest crow visited the lonely cottage that afternoon to cry: 'Kah, Kah, Kah!' and fly away.

But Griselda knew her brother's mood too well to speak of it, or to complain. And she sang on gaily in the house, though she was more sorrowful than ever.

Next day John went out to tend his flocks. And wherever he went the red sun seemed to follow. When at last he found his sheep they were drenched with the clinging mist and were huddled together in dismay. And when they saw him it seemed that they cried out with one unanimous bleating voice:

'O ma-a-a-ster!'

And he stood counting them. And a little apart from the rest stood his old ram Soll, with a face as black as soot; and there, perched on his back, impish and sharp and scarlet, rode and tossed and sang just such another fairy as had mocked John from the chimney-top. A fire seemed to break out in his body, and, picking up a handful of stones, he rushed at Soll through the flock. They scattered, bleating, out into the mist. And the fairy, all-acockahoop on the old ram's back, took its small ears between finger and thumb, and as fast as John ran, so fast jogged Soll, till all the young farmer's stones were thrown, and he found himself alone in a quagmire so sticky and befogged that it took him till afternoon to grope his way out. And only Griselda's singing over her broth-pot guided him at last home.

Next day he sought his sheep far and wide, but not one could he find. To and fro he wandered, shouting and calling and whistling to Sly till, heartsick and thirsty, they were both wearied out. Yet bleatings seemed to fill the air, and a faint beautiful bell tolled on out of the mist; and John knew the fairies had hidden his sheep, and he hated them more than ever.

After that he went no more into the fields, brightly green beneath the enchanted mist. He sat and sulked, staring out of the door at the dim forests far away, glimmering faintly red beneath the small red sun. Griselda could not sing any more, she was too tired and hungry. And just before twilight she went out and gathered the last few pods of peas from the garden for their supper.

And while she was shelling them, John, within doors in the cottage, heard again the tiny timbrels and the distant horns, and the odd, clear, grasshopper voices calling and calling her, and he knew in his heart that, unless he relented and made friends with the fairies, Griselda would surely one day run away to them and leave him forlorn. He scratched his great head, and gnawed his broad thumb. They had taken his father, they had taken his mother, they might take his sister – but he *wouldn't* give in.

So he shouted, and Griselda in fear and trembling came in out of the garden with her basket and basin and sat down in the gloaming to finish shelling her peas.

And as the shadows thickened and the stars began to shine, the malevolent singing came nearer, and presently there was a groping and stirring in the thatch, a tapping at the window, and John knew the fairies had come – not alone, not one or two or three, but in their company and bands – to plague him, and to entice away Griselda. He shut his mouth and stopped up his ears with his fingers, but when, with great staring eyes, he saw them capering like bubbles in a glass, like flames along straw, on his very doorstep, he could contain himself no longer. He caught up Griselda's bowl and flung it – peas, water and all – full in the snickering faces of the Little Folk! There came a shrill, faint twitter of laughter, a scampering of feet, and then all again was utterly still.

Griselda tried in vain to keep back her tears. She put her arms round John's neck and hid her face in his sleeve.

'Let me go!' she said, 'let me go, John, just a day and a night, and I'll come back to you. They are angry with us. But they love me; and if I sit on the hillside under the boughs of the trees beside the pool and listen to their music just a little while, they will make the sun shine again and drive back the flocks, and we shall be as happy as ever. Look at poor Sly, John dear, he is hungrier even than I am.' John heard only the mocking laughter and the tap-tapping and the rustling and crying of the fairies, and he wouldn't let his sister go.

And it began to be marvellously dark and still in the cottage. No stars moved across the casement, no waterdrops glittered in the candleshine. John could hear only one low, faint, unceasing stir and rustling all round him. So utterly dark and still it was that even Sly woke from his hungry dreams and gazed up into his mistress's face and whined.

They went to bed; but still, all night long, while John lay tossing on his mattress, the rustling never ceased. The old kitchen clock ticked on and on, but there came no hint of dawn. All was pitch-black and now all was utterly silent. There wasn't a whisper, not a creak, not a sigh of air, not a footfall of a mouse, not a flutter of moth, not a settling of dust to be heard at all. Only desolate silence. And John at last could endure his fears and suspicions no longer. He got out of bed and stared from his square casement. He could see nothing. He tried to thrust it open; it would not move. He went downstairs and unbarred the door and looked out. He saw, as it were, a deep, clear, green shade, from behind which the songs of the birds rose faint as in a dream.

And then he sighed like a grampus and sat down, and knew that the fairies had beaten him. Like Jack's beanstalk, in one night had grown up a dense wall of peas. He pushed and pulled and hacked with his axe, and kicked with his shoes, and buffeted with his blunderbuss. But it was all in vain. He sat down once more in his chair beside the hearth and covered his face with his hands. And at last Griselda, too, awoke, and came down with her candle. And she comforted her brother, and told him if he would do what she bade she would soon make all right again. And he promised her.

So with a scarf she bound tight his hands behind him; and with a rope she bound his feet together, so that he could neither run nor throw stones, peas or cheeses. She bound his eyes and ears and mouth with a napkin, so that he could neither see, hear, smell, nor cry out. And, that done, she pushed and pulled him like a great bundle, and at last rolled him out of sight into the chimney-corner against the wall. Then she took a small sharp pair of needlework scissors that her godmother had given her, and snipped and snipped, till at last there came a little hole in the thick green hedge of peas. And putting her mouth there she called softly through the little hole. And the fairies drew near the doorstep and nodded and nodded and listened.

And then and there Griselda made a bargain with them for the forgiveness of John — a lock of her golden hair;

seven dishes of ewes' milk; three and thirty bunches of currants, red, white and black; a bag of thistledown; three handkerchiefs full of lambs' wool; nine jars of honey; a peppercorn of spice. All these (except the hair) John was to bring himself to their secret places as soon as he was able. Above all, the bargain between them was that Griselda would sit one full hour each evening of summer on the hillside in the shadow and greenness that slope down from the great forest towards the valley, where the fairies' mounds are, and where their tiny brindled cattle graze.

Her brother lay blind and deaf and dumb as a log of wood. She promised everything.

And then, instead of a rustling and a creeping, there came a rending and a crashing. Instead of green shade, light of amber; then white. And as the thick hedge withered and shrank, and the merry and furious dancing sun scorched and scorched and scorched, there came, above the singing of the birds, the bleatings of sheep – and behold sooty Soll and hungry Sly met square upon the doorstep; and all John's sheep shone white as hoar-frost on his pastures; and every lamb was garlanded with pimpernel and eyebright; and the old fat ewes stood still, with saddles of moss; and their laughing riders sat and saw Griselda standing in the doorway in her beautiful yellow hair.

As for John, tied up like a sack in the chimney-corner, down came his cheese again crash upon his head, and, not being able to say anything, he said nothing.

WALTER DE LA MARE

## The Fairies

Up the airy mountain,
   Down the rushy glen,
We daren't go a-hunting
   For fear of little men;
Wee folk, good folk,
   Trooping all together;
Green jacket, red cap,
   And white owl's feather!

Down along the rocky shore
   Some make their home,
They live on crispy pancakes
   Of yellow-tide foam;
Some in the reeds
   Of the black mountain lake,
With frogs for their watch-dogs
   All night awake.

## THE FAIRIES

High on the hill-top
　　The old King sits;
He is now so old and grey
　　He's nigh lost his wits.
With a bridge of white mist
　　Columbkill he crosses,
On his stately journeys
　　From Slieveleague to Rosses;
Or going up with music
　　On cold starry nights,
To sup with the Queen
　　Of the gay Northern Lights.

They stole little Bridget
　　For seven years long;
When she came down again
　　Her friends were all gone.
They took her lightly back,
　　Between the night and morrow,
They thought that she was fast asleep,
　　But she was dead with sorrow.
They have kept her ever since
　　Deep within the lakes,
On a bed of flag-leaves,
　　Watching till she wakes.

By the craggy hill-side,
  Through the mosses bare,
They have planted thorn-trees
  For pleasure here and there.
Is any man so daring
  As dig them up in spite,
He shall find their sharpest thorns
  In his bed at night.

Up the airy mountain,
  Down the rushy glen,
We daren't go a-hunting
  For fear of little men;
Wee folk, good folk,
  Trooping all together;
Green jacket, red cap,
  And white owl's feather!

WILLIAM ALLINGHAM

## Calico Pie

Calico Pie,
   The little Birds fly
Down to the calico tree.
   Their wings were blue
   And they sang 'Tilly-loo' –
   Till away they all flew,
And they never came back to me!
   They never came back!
   They never came back!
They never came back to me!

Calico Jam,
The little Fish swam
Over the syllabub sea,
He took off his hat,
To the Sole and the Sprat,
And the Willeby-wat, –
But he never came back to me!
He never came back!
He never came back!
He never came back to me!

Calico Ban
The little Mice ran,
To be ready in time for tea,
Flippity Flup,
They drank it all up,
And danced in the cup, –

But they never came back to me!
    They never came back!
    They never came back!
But they never came back to me!

    Calico Drum,
    The Grasshoppers come,
The Butterfly, Beetle, and Bee,
    Over the ground,
    Around and round,
    With a hop and a bound,
But they never came back!
    They never came back!
    They never came back!
They never came back to me!

*Written and illustrated by* EDWARD LEAR

# The Well of the World's End

Once upon a time, and a very long time ago it was, there was a girl called Rosemary. She was a good girl but not very clever, and a merry girl but not too pretty; and all would have been well with her but that she had a cruel stepmother. So instead of having pretty dresses to wear and sweet cakes to eat and idle friends to play with, as all girls should, she was made to do the housework: to go down on her knees and scrub the stone floors, and roll up her sleeves to the elbows and do the washing. And the better she did the work, the worse her stepmother hated her. If she got up early in the morning, it was not early enough; if she cooked the dinner, it was not cooked right. Poor Rosemary! She worked all the day, yet everything she did was wrong.

Well, one day her stepmother decided to be rid of her.

'Child,' said she, 'take this sieve and go to the Well of the World's End; and when you have found it, fill the sieve with water and bring it back to me. Mind now, and see that you don't spill a drop. Be off with you!'

So Rosemary, who never dared answer her stepmother back, nor even ask her a question hardly, took the sieve and went out to look for the Well of the World's End.

Presently she met a carter, who had stopped to tighten his horse's reins.

'Where are you off to?' asked he. 'And what have you got in your hand?'

'I am trying to find the Well of the World's End,' she answered, 'and this is a sieve that I must fill with water.'

The carter laughed heartily and said she was a foolish girl and that he had no idea where the well was. So saying, he jumped back upon his cart, whipped up the horse and left poor Rosemary standing in the road.

She walked on a while, and soon she saw three little boys bowling their hoops in the yard before an inn.

'Where are you off to?' one of them shouted. 'And what have you got in your hand?'

'I am trying to find the Well of the World's End,' she answered, 'and this is a sieve that I have to fill with water.'

All the three boys laughed aloud at this and told her she was stupid and that there was no such well in the world.

So Rosemary trudged on, asking everybody she met if they could tell her where the well was; but no one knew. Some were rude, some laughed at her and others said they would have helped her if they could, but they knew not how.

At last she spied an old ragged woman, bent nearly double, looking for something in a cart-rut. She had a torn bonnet, very nearly no teeth at all, and a crooked stick. With this she was poking about in the mud.

'What are you looking for?' asked Rosemary.

'I had two groats that I was going to buy bread with, and if I don't find them I shall have nothing to eat tonight.'

So Rosemary helped her look for the two groats, and presently her sharp eyes caught sight of them.

'Thank you,' said the old woman in her creaky voice. 'I should never have found them by myself, I do declare. Now tell me where you are going and what you are doing with that sieve.'

'I am going to the Well of the World's End,' said Rosemary, 'but I am afraid there is no such place in the world. When I get there, I must fill the sieve with water and take it home to my stepmother.'

'Why, indeed,' said the old woman, 'there is a Well of the World's End, and I will tell you how to find it. As for what you are going to do when you get there, that is another matter.'

So, pointing with her stick, she showed Rosemary the way.

'Through the gap in that hedge,' she said, 'over the far hill, up the stony path along the hazel wood, and along the valley – that will take you there. God speed you, and may the way seem short.'

Rosemary thanked her, and the old woman hobbled off, clutching her stick in one bony hand and her two groats in the other.

Through the gap in the hedge went Rosemary with her sieve, up the hill, along the stony path by the hazel wood, until she came to a deep valley, all wet underfoot, and very green and lonesome. And at the very end of the valley was a well. It was so overgrown with ivy and moss that she nearly missed it. But there it was, sure enough: and this was the Well of the World's End.

Rosemary knelt down on the bank beside the well, and dipped her sieve into the water. Many times she dipped it, but each time the water ran out through the holes in the sieve, so that not a drop was left to take home to her stepmother. She sat down and cried.

'I shall never do it,' she sobbed. 'I shall never have a sieveful of water to take home.'

Just as she was beginning to think that her misery would never end, something croaked, and a fat green frog hopped out from under a fern leaf.

'What's the matter?' asked the frog.

Rosemary told him.

'If you promise,' said the frog, 'to do everything I ask for a whole night, I can help you.'

'Yes, of course I will,' said Rosemary eagerly. 'I'll promise whatever you like – only *do* help me, *please*.'

The frog considered for a moment or two, gulped once or twice, and spoke:

> 'Stop it with moss, and daub it with clay,
> And then it will carry the water away.'

Quickly Rosemary gathered soft, green moss from the mouth of the well and covered the bottom of the sieve with

it. Then she scooped up some damp clay from the bank and spread it on top of the moss, pressing it down until all the holes in the sieve were filled. Next, she dipped the sieve into the water, and this time not a drop ran out.

'I must get home as quickly as I can,' she said, turning to go. 'Thank you, thank you, dear frog, for helping me. I should never have thought of that for myself.'

'No, I don't suppose you would,' croaked the frog. 'Carry the water carefully – and don't forget your promise.'

Rosemary remembered that she had promised the frog to do anything he wanted for a whole night. She didn't suppose that any harm would come of a promise made to a frog, so she told him she would not forget, and went gratefully on her way.

You can imagine how surprised her stepmother was to see her when she got home. She had hoped to get rid of the girl for good and all. But here she was, none the worse for her journey, carrying a sieve full of water, just as she had been told. The stepmother didn't say much, because she was too angry. Instead, she made her get the supper for them both and wash the dishes afterwards, just as if nothing had happened.

As night was falling, they were surprised to hear the sound of knocking at the door.

'Who can it be?' asked the stepmother.

Rosemary went to the door and called out:

'Who's there, and what do you want at this time of day?'

There was a little croaking noise, and a voice said:

'Open the door and let me in,
Let me in, my heart of gold;

Remember the words we spoke so true
Down by the water green and cold.'

It was the frog. Rosemary had almost forgotten him. Her stepmother asked her who it was at the door, and Rosemary told her all about the frog and the promise she had made him.

'Well, let him in,' said the stepmother, 'and do as he tells you. Girls must keep their promises.'

She rather liked the idea of her stepdaughter having to obey the commands of a frog. So Rosemary opened the door, and the frog hopped in. He looked at her, and then he spoke again. This is what he said:

'Lift me, lift me up to your knee,
Up to your knee, my heart of gold;
Remember the words we spoke so true
Down by the water green and cold.'

Rosemary did not much like the idea of having a damp frog sitting on her knee, but her stepmother said:

'Do as he tells you. Girls must keep their promises.'

So the girl lifted the frog up, and he sat perched on her knee. Then once more he spoke to her:

'Give me, O give me meat and drink,
Meat and drink, my heart of gold;
Remember the words we spoke so true
Down by the water green and cold.'

'Do as he tells you,' ordered the stepmother. 'Girls must keep their promises.'

Rosemary fetched from the larder the food that had been

left from supper and put it on a plate in front of the frog, and he bent his head down and ate every scrap of it. Then once more he spoke:

> 'Take me, take me into your bed,
> Into your bed, my heart of gold;
> Remember the words we spoke so true
> Down by the water green and cold.'

'No,' said Rosemary, 'I will never have such a cold, clammy creature in bed with me. Get away, you nasty animal!'

At this the stepmother almost screamed with laughter.

'Go on!' she cried. 'Do as the frog bids. Remember your promise. Young girls must keep their promises.'

With that she went off to her room, and Rosemary was left with the frog. Well, she got into bed, took the frog in beside her, but kept him as far away as she could. After a while she slept soundly.

In the morning, before the break of day, she was awakened by a croaking sound close to her ear.

'Everything I have asked, you have done,' said the frog. 'One more thing I ask, then you will have kept your promise. Take an axe and chop off my head!'

Rosemary looked at the frog, and her heart went cold.

'Dear frog,' she said, 'don't ask me to do that. You have been so kind to me. Don't ask me to kill you.'

'Do as I ask,' said the frog. 'Remember your promise. The night is not yet over. Fetch an axe, and cut off my head.'

So very sadly Rosemary went into the kitchen and fetched the chopper that was used to cut up logs for the fire. She could scarcely bear to look at the poor frog, but somehow she managed to raise the chopper and cut off his head.

Then she had the greatest surprise of her life. For the frog was no more: in his place stood a young and handsome man. She stepped back in amazement, dropping the chopper to the floor. The young man was smiling at her.

'Don't be afraid,' he said in a soft and musical voice. 'I am not here to hurt or alarm you. Once I was a prince, but a foul enchantress turned me into a frog; and her wicked spell could not be unspelled until a young girl should do my bidding for a whole night.'

At these words the stepmother, who had been woken up by the sound of voices, came into the room. Great was her astonishment to see the young Prince there instead of the slimy frog.

'Madam,' said the Prince, 'your daughter has had the kindness to unspell the spell that made me a frog; for that I am going to marry her. I am a powerful prince, and you shall not deny me. You wanted to get rid of your step-daughter. Well, you have done so, for now I am going to take her away to be my wife.'

For once the stepmother had nothing to say. She looked at the Prince and opened her mouth, but no words came; then she looked at Rosemary and opened her mouth, but still no words came. So she turned away and began to get some breakfast for them all. It was the only thing she could do.

Not long afterwards the Prince and Rosemary were married, and very happy they were. As for the stepmother, she had tried to get rid of her daughter, so that she had the pleasure of knowing that by this means she had caused her to rescue the Prince from enchantment and find herself a kind and loving husband.

JAMES REEVES

## The Witches' Call

Come, witches, come, on your hithering brooms!
The moorland is dark and still
Over the church and the churchyard tombs
To the oakwood under the hill.

Come through the mist and the wandering cloud,
Fly with the crescent moon;
Come where the witches and warlocks crowd,
Come soon . . . soon!

Leave your room with its shadowy cat,
Your cauldron over the hearth;
Seize your cloak and pointed hat,
Come by the witches' path.
Float from the earth like a rising bird,
Stream through the darkening air,
Come at the sound of our secret word,
Come to the witches' lair!

CLIVE SANSOM

# If All the Seas

If all the seas were one sea,
What a great sea that would be!
If all the trees were one tree,
What a great tree that would be!
And if all the axes were one axe,
What a great axe that would be!
And if all the men were one man,
What a great man that would be!
And if the great man took the great axe
And cut down the great tree,
And let it fall into the great sea,
What a splish–splash that would be!

ANON.

# The Parrot Pirate Princess

The King and Queen were quarrelling fiercely over what the baby Princess was to be called when the fairy Grisel dropped in. Grisel, that is to say, did not drop in – to be more accurate, she popped out of one of the vases on the mantelpiece, looked round, saw the baby and said:

'What's this?'

'Oh, good afternoon,' said the King uncomfortably.

'We were just putting you on the list of people to be invited to the christening,' said the Queen, hastily doing so. She had presence of mind.

'Mmmmm,' said Grisel. 'Is it a boy or a girl?'

'It's a girl, and the sweetest little –'

'*I'm* the best judge of that,' interrupted the fairy, and she hooked the baby out of its satin cradle. 'Well, let's have a look at you.'

The baby was a calm creature, and did not, as the Queen had dreaded, burst into loud shrieks at the sight of Grisel's wizened old face. She merely cooed.

'Well, you can't say she's very handsome, can you? Takes too much after both of you,' Grisel said cheerfully. The baby laughed. 'What are you going to call her?'

'We were just wondering when you came in,' the Queen said despairingly. She knew that Grisel had a fondness for suggesting impossible names, and then being extremely angry if the suggestions were not taken. Worse – she might want the baby called after herself.

'Then I'll tell you what,' said Grisel, eagerly leaning forward. 'Call it –'

But here she was interrupted, for the baby, which she still held, hit her a fearful whack on the front teeth with its heavy silver rattle.

There was a terrible scene. The King and Queen were far too well-bred to laugh, but they looked as if they would

have liked to. The Queen snatched the baby from Grisel, who was stamping up and down the room, pale with rage, and using the most unladylike language.

'That's right – laugh when I've had the best part of my teeth knocked down my throat,' she snarled. 'And as for you you –' She turned to the baby, who was chuckling in the Queen's arms.

'Goo goo,' the baby replied affably.

'Goo goo, indeed. I'll teach you to repeat what I say,' the fairy said furiously. And before the horrified Queen could make a move, the baby had turned into a large grey parrot and flown out of the window.

Grisel smiled maliciously round the room and said: 'You can take me off the christening list now.'

She went, leaving the King and Queen silent.

The parrot turned naturally to the south, hunting for an island with palm trees, or at least a couple of coconuts to eat. After some time she came to the sea. She was disconcerted. She did not feel that she could face flying all the way over that cold grey-looking water to find an island that would suit her. So she sat down on the edge to think. The edge where she sat happened to be a quay, and presently a sailor came along, said 'Hullo, a parrot', and picked her up.

She did not struggle. She looked up at him and said in a hoarse, rasping voice: 'Hullo, a parrot.'

The sailor was delighted. He took her on board his ship, which sailed that evening for the South Seas.

This was no ordinary ship. It was owned by the most terrible pirate then in business, who frightened all the ships off the seas. And so fairly soon the parrot saw some surprising things.

The pirates were quite kind to her. They called her Jake, and took a lot of interest in her education. She was a quick learner, and before the end of the voyage she knew the most shocking collection of swear words and nautical phrases that ever parrot spoke. She also knew all about walking the plank and the effects of rum. When the pirates had captured a particularly fine ship, they would all drink gallons of rum and make her drink it too, whereupon the undignified old fowl would lurch about all over the deck and in the rigging, singing '*Fifteen men on a dead man's chest, Yo, ho, ho and a bottle of rum,*' and the pirates would shout with laughter.

One day they arrived at the island where they kept their treasure, and it was all unloaded and rowed ashore. It took them two days to bury it, and the parrot sat by, thinking: 'Shiver my timbers, but I'd like to get away and live on this island!' But she could not, for one of the pirates had thoughtfully tied her by the ankle to a tree. She sat swearing under her breath and trying to gnaw through the rope, but it was too thick.

Luck, however, was with her. The second day after they had left the island, a great storm sprang up, and the pirates' ship was wrecked.

'Brimstone and botheration and mercy me!' chorused the pirates, clinging frantically to the rigging. They had little time for more, because with a frightful roar the ship went to the bottom, leaving Jake bobbing about on the waves like a cork.

'Swelp me,' she remarked, rose up and flew with the wind, which took her straight back to the island.

'Well, blow me down,' she said when she got there. 'This

is a bit better than living on biscuit among all those unrefined characters. Bananas and mangoes, bless my old soul! This is the life for me.'

She lived on the island for some time, and became very friendly with a handsome grey gentleman parrot already there, called Bill. Bill seemed to know as much about pirates as she did, but he was always rather silent about his past life, so she gathered that he did not want it mentioned. They got on extremely well, however, and lived on the island for about twenty years, which did not change them in the least, as parrots are notoriously long-lived.

Then one day, as they were sharing a bunch of bananas, a frightful hurricane suddenly arose, and blew them, still clutching the bananas, out to sea.

'Hold on tight!' shrieked Bill in her ear.

'I am holding on,' she squawked back. 'Lumme, Bill, you do look a sight. Just like a pin-cushion!'

The wretched Bill was being fluffed out by the wind until his tail-feathers stood straight up. 'Well, you're not so pretty yourself,' he said indignantly, screwing his head round to look at her. 'Don't half look silly, going along backwards like that.'

'Can't you see, you perishing son of a sea-cook,' squawked Jake, 'it stops the wind blowing your feathers out – have a try.'

'It makes me feel funny,' complained Bill, and he went back to his former position, still keeping a tight hold on the bananas.

'Mountains ahead – look out!' he howled, a moment or two later. They were being swept down at a terrific speed towards a range of hills.

'Is it the mainland?' asked Jake, swivelling round to get a glimpse. 'Doesn't the wind make you giddy?'

'Yes. It's the mainland, I reckon,' said Bill. 'There's houses down there. Oh, splice my mainbrace, we're going to crash into them. Keep behind the bananas.' Using the great bunch as a screen, they hurtled downwards.

'Mind last week's washing,' screamed Jake, as they went through a low belt of grey cloud. 'I never in all my life saw anything to beat this. Talk about seeing the world.' They were only twenty feet above ground now, still skimming along, getting lower all the time.

'Strikes me we'd better *sit* on the bananas if we don't want our tail feathers rubbed off,' said Jake. 'Oh my, look where we're going.'

Before Bill had time to answer, they went smack through an immense glass window, shot across a room, breaking three vases on the way, and came to rest on a mantelpiece, still mixed up with the bananas, which were rather squashed and full of broken glass.

'Journey's end,' said Jake. 'How are you, Bill?'

'Not so bad,' said Bill, wriggling free of the bananas and beginning to put his feathers to rights.

Then they were both suddenly aware of the fairy Grisel, sitting in one corner of the room, where she had been knocked by a vase, and glaring at them. She picked herself up and came and looked at them closely.

'It's you again is it,' she said. 'I might have known it.'

'Pleased to meet you,' said Jake, who had no recollection of her. 'I'm Jake, and this is my husband Bill.'

'I know you, don't you worry,' said Grisel. Then Jake suddenly remembered where she had seen Grisel before.

'Oh lor – don't you go changing me into a princess

again,' she cried in alarm, but hardly were the words out of her beak when, bang, she was back in her father's palace, in the throne-room. She looked down at herself, and saw that she was human once more.

'Well! Here's a rum go,' she said aloud. 'Who'd have thought it?' She glanced round the room and saw, through a french window, the King and Queen, a good deal older, having tea on the terrace. There was also a girl, not unlike herself. She went forward to them with a very nautical gait, and hitching up her trousers – only it was a long and flowing cloth-of-gold skirt.

'Hello, Pa! Pleased to meet you!' she cried, slapping the King on the back. 'Shiver my timbers, Ma, it's a long time since we met. Not since I was no longer than a marline spike. Who's this?'

They were all too dumbfounded to speak. 'Hasn't anyone got a tongue in their head?' she asked. 'Here comes the prodigal daughter, and all they can do is sit and gawp!'

'Are you – are you that baby?' the Queen asked faintly. 'The one that got taken away?'

'That's me!' Jake told her cheerfully. 'Twenty years a parrot, and just when I'm beginning to enjoy life, back I comes to the bosom of my family. Shunt my backstay, it's a funny life.'

She sighed.

The King and Queen looked at one another in growing horror.

'And this'll be my little sissy, if I'm not mistaken,' said Jake meditatively. 'Quite a big girl, aren't you, ducks? If you'll excuse me, folks, I'm a bit thirsty. Haven't had a drink for forty-eight hours.'

She rolled indoors again.

'Well, I suppose it might be worse,' said the Queen doubtfully, in the horrified silence. 'We can *train* her, can't we? I suppose she'll have to be the heir?'

'I'm afraid so,' said the King. 'I hope she'll take her position seriously.'

'And what happens to *me*?' demanded the younger sister shrilly.

The King sighed.

During the next two months the royal family had an uncomfortable time. Jake obviously meant well, and was kindly disposed to everyone, but she did make a bad Crown Princess. Her language was dreadful, and she never seemed to remember not to say 'Stap my vitals' or something equally unsuitable, when she trod on her skirt. She said that trains were a nuisance.

'You don't want to traipse round with the drawing-room curtains *and* the dining-room tablecloth pinned to your tail. I'm used to flying. Splice my mainbrace!' she would cry.

She rushed about and was apt to clap important court officials and ambassadors on the back and cry, 'Hallo! How's the missus, you old son of a gun?' Or if they annoyed her, she loosed such a flood of epithets on them ('You lily-livered, cross-eyed, flop-eared son of a sea-cook') that the whole Court fled in horror, stopping their ears. She distressed the King and Queen by climbing trees, or sitting rocking backwards and forwards for hours at a time, murmuring, 'Pretty Poll. Pretty Jake. Pieces of eight, pieces of eight, pieces of eight.'

'Will she *ever* turn into a presentable Queen?' said the King despairingly, and the Queen stared hopelessly out of the window.

'Perhaps she'll marry and settle down,' she suggested, and so they advertised for princes in the *Monarchy's Marriage Mart*, a very respectable paper.

'We'll have to think of Miranda too,' the King said. 'After all, she was brought up to expect to be Queen. It's only fair that she should marry some eligible young prince and come into a kingdom that way. She's a good girl.'

Eventually a Prince arrived. He came quite quietly, riding on a fiery black horse, and stayed at an inn near the palace. He sent the King a note, saying that he would be only too grateful for a sight of the Princess, whenever it was convenient.

'Now, we must really try and make her behave presentably for once,' said the Queen, but there was not much hope in her voice.

A grand ball was arranged, and the court dressmakers spent an entire week fitting Jake to a white satin dress, and Miranda obligingly spent a whole evening picking roses in the garden to put in Jake's suspiciously scarlet hair.

Finally the evening came. The throne-room was a blaze of candlelight. The King and Queen sat on the two thrones, and below them on the steps, uncomfortably but gracefully posed, were the two princesses. A trumpet blew, and the Prince entered. The crowd stood back, and he walked forward and bowed very low before the thrones. Then he kissed Miranda's hand and said:

'Will you dance with me, Princess?'

'Hey, young man,' interrupted the King, 'you've made a mistake. It's the other one who's the Crown Princess.'

Jake roared with laughter, but the Prince had gone very pale, and Miranda was scarlet.

'I didn't know *you* were the Prince of Sitania,' she said.

'*Aren't* you the Princess, then?' he said.

'Have you two met before?' the King demanded.

'Last night in the Palace gardens,' said Miranda. 'The Prince promised he'd dance the first dance with me. But I didn't know, truly I didn't, that he was *that* Prince.'

'And I thought you were the Crown Princess,' he said.

There was an uncomfortable silence. Jake turned away and began humming *'Yo ho ho and a bottle of rum'*.

'Your Majesty, I am sorry to be so inconvenient,' said the Prince desperately, 'but may I marry *this* princess?'

'How large is your kingdom?' asked the King sharply.

'Well, er, actually I am the youngest of five sons, so I have no kingdom,' the Prince told him, 'but my income is pretty large.'

The King shook his head. 'Won't do, Miranda must have a kingdom. I'm afraid, young man, that it's impossible. If you wanted to marry the other princess and help reign over this kingdom, that would be different.'

The Prince hung his head, and Miranda bit her lip. Jake tried to put her hands in her white satin pockets, and whistled. The crowd began to shuffle, and to quiet them the Royal Band struck up. And then Jake gave a shriek of delight, and fairly skated across the marble floor.

'*Bill*, my old hero! I'd know you anywhere!' A burly pirate with a hooked nose and scarlet hair was standing in the doorway.

'Well, well, well!' he roared. 'Looks like I've bumped into a party. You and I, ducks, will show them how the hornpipe ought to be danced.' And solemnly before the frozen Court they broke into a hornpipe, slow at first, and then faster and faster. Finally they stopped, panting.

'I'm all of a lather. Haven't got a wipe, have you, Jake?' Bill asked.

'Here, have half the tablecloth.' She tore a generous half from her twelve-foot train and gave it to him. They both mopped their brows vigorously. Then Jake took Bill across to where the King and Queen were standing with horror-struck faces.

'Here's my husband,' said Jake. The Court turned as one man and fled, leaving the vast room empty but for the King and Queen, Jake and Bill, and Miranda and the Prince.

'Your husband? But you never said anything about him. And here we were, searching for Princes,' the Queen began.

'I don't think you ever asked me for *my* news,' said Jake. 'And now, if you'll excuse us, we'll be going. I've waited these two months for Bill, and a dratted long time he took to get here. Told him my address when we were parrots together, before all this happened, and a nasty time I've had, wondering if he'd forgotten it. But I needn't have worried. Slow but sure is old Bill,' she patted his shoulder, 'aren't you, ducks?'

'But –' said the Queen.

'Think I really stayed here all this time learning how to be a lady?' Jake said contemptuously. 'I was waiting for Bill. Now we'll be off.'

'But –' began the King.

'Don't be crazy,' said Jake irritably. 'You don't think I could stop and be queen *now* – when all the Court have seen me and Bill dancing like a couple of young grass-hoppers? You can have those brats –' she nodded towards Miranda and the Prince, who were suddenly looking hope-ful. 'Well, so long, folks.' She took Bill's hand and they went out.

And now, if you want to know where they are, all you have to do is go to the island where they lived before, and directly over the spot where the treasure was hidden, you will see a neat little pub with a large signboard: 'The Pirate's Rest', and underneath: *'By Appointment to Their Majesties'*.

JOAN AIKEN
*Illustrated by* SUSAN HUNTER

# The Cow

The cow is of the bovine ilk;
One end is moo, the other, milk.

OGDEN NASH

*Illustrated by* QUENTIN BLAKE

## The Camel

The camel has a single hump;
The dromedary, two;
Or else the other way around.
I'm never sure. Are you?

OGDEN NASH
*Illustrated by* QUENTIN BLAKE

# Hare and Tortoise

When Tortoise was very little, his mother said to him, 'You will never be able to go very fast. We Tortoises are a slow-moving family, but we get there in the end. Don't try to run. Remember, "steady and slow" does it.' Tortoise remembered these words.

One day when he was grown-up, he was walking quietly round in a field minding his own business; and Hare thought he would have some fun, so he ran round Tortoise in quick circles, just to annoy him. Hare was proud of himself because everyone knew he was one of the swiftest of animals. But Tortoise took no notice, so Hare stopped in front of him and laughed.

'Can't you move faster than *that*?' said Hare. 'You'll *never* get anywhere at that rate! You should take a few lessons from *me*.'

Tortoise lifted his head slowly and said:

'I don't want to get anywhere, thank you. I've no need to go dashing about all over the place. You see, my thick shell protects me from my enemies.'

'But how *dull* life must be for you,' Hare went on. 'Why, it takes you half an hour to cross one field, while I can be away out of sight in half a minute. Besides, you really do look silly, you know! You ought to be ashamed of yourself.'

Well, at this Tortoise was rather annoyed. Hare was really very provoking.

'Look here,' said Tortoise, 'if you want a race I'll give you one; and I don't need any start either.'

Hare laughed till the tears ran down his furry face, and his sides shook so much that he rolled over backwards. Tortoise just waited till Hare had finished, then he said:

'Well, what about it? I'm not joking.'

Several other animals had gathered round, and they all said: 'Go on Hare. It's a challenge. You'll have to race him.'

'Certainly,' said Hare, 'if you want to make a fool of yourself. Where shall we race to?'

Tortoise shaded his eyes with one foot and said:

'See that old windmill on the top of the hill yonder? We'll race to that. We can start from this tree-stump here. Come on, and may the best animal win!'

So as soon as they were both standing beside the tree-stump, Chanticleer the Cock shouted 'Ready – steady – go!' and Tortoise began to crawl towards the far-off windmill. The other animals had hurried on ahead so as to see the finish.

Hare stood beside the tree-stump watching Tortoise waddle away across the field. The day was hot, and just beside the tree-stump was a pleasant, shady place, so he sat down and waited. He guessed it would take him about two and a half minutes to reach the windmill, even without trying very hard, so there was no hurry – no hurry at all. Presently he began to drop off to sleep. Two or three minutes passed, and Hare opened one eye lazily. Tortoise had scarcely crossed the first field. 'Steady and slow,' he said to himself under his breath. 'Steady and slow. That's what mother said.' And he kept on towards the far-off windmill.

'At that rate,' said Hare to himself sleepily, 'it'll take him just about two hours to get there – if he doesn't drop dead on the way.'

He closed his eye again and fell into a deep sleep.

After a while Tortoise had crossed the first field and was making his way slowly over the second.

'Steady and slow does it,' he muttered to himself.

The sun began to go down, and at last Hare woke up, feeling chilly.

'Where am I?' he thought. 'What's happened? Oh yes, I remember.'

He got to his feet and looked towards the windmill. But where was Tortoise? He was nowhere to be seen. Hare jumped on to the tree-stump and strained his eyes to gaze into the distance. There, half-way across the very last field before the windmill, was a tiny black dot. Tortoise!

'This won't do,' said Hare. 'I must have overslept. I'd better be moving.'

So he sprang from the stump and darted across the first field, then the second, then the third. It was really much farther than he had thought.

At the windmill the other animals were waiting to see the finish. At last Tortoise arrived, rather out of breath and wobbling a little on his legs.

'Come on, Tortoise!' they shouted.

Then Hare appeared at the far side of the last field, streaking along like the wind. How he ran! Not even Stag, when he was being hunted, could go faster. Even Swallow could scarcely fly faster through the blue sky.

'Steady and slow,' said Tortoise to himself, but no one could hear him, for he had very, very little breath left to walk with.

'Come on, Tortoise!' cried some animals, and a few cried, 'Come on, Hare! He's beating you!'

Hare put on extra speed and ran faster than he had ever run before. But it was no good. He had given Tortoise too much start, and he was still twenty yards behind when Tortoise crawled over the last foot of ground and tumbled up against the windmill. He had won the race!

All the animals cheered, and after that Hare never laughed at Tortoise again.

AESOP, *adapted by* JAMES REEVES

# The Monkey and the Crocodile

Beside a river in the jungle stood a tall mango tree. In the tree lived many monkeys. They swung from branch to branch, eating fruit and chattering to each other. Hungry crocodiles swam in the river and sunned themselves on the banks.

One young crocodile was hungrier than all the rest. He could never get enough to eat. The young crocodile watched the monkeys for a long time. Then one day he said to a wise old crocodile: 'I'd like to catch a monkey and eat him!'

'How would you ever catch a monkey?' asked the old crocodile. 'You do not travel on land and monkeys do not go into the water. Besides, they are quicker than you are.'

'They may be quicker,' said the young crocodile, 'but I am more cunning. You will see!'

For days the crocodile swam back and forth, studying the monkeys all the while. Then he noticed one young monkey who was quicker than all the others. This monkey loved to jump to the highest branches of the tree and pick the ripe mangoes at the very top. 'He's the one I want,' the crocodile said to himself. 'But how am I going to catch him?'

The crocodile thought and thought, and at last he had an idea. 'Monkey,' he called, 'wouldn't you like to come with me over to the island, where the fruit is so ripe?'

'Oh, yes,' said the monkey. 'But how can I go with you? I do not swim.'

'I will take you on my back,' said the crocodile, with a toothy smile.

The monkey was eager to get to the fruit, so he jumped down on the crocodile's back. 'Off we go!' said the crocodile, gliding through the water.

'This is a fine ride you are giving me,' said the monkey.

'Do you think so? Well, how do you like this?' asked the crocodile. And suddenly he dived into the water.

'Oh, please don't!' said the monkey as he went under. He was afraid to let go and he did not know what to do. When the crocodile came up, the monkey sputtered and choked. 'Why did you take me under the water, Crocodile?' he asked. 'You know I can't swim!'

'Because I am going to drown you,' replied the crocodile. 'And then I am going to eat you.'

The monkey shivered in fear. But he thought quickly, and before the crocodile dived again he said: 'I wish you had told me you wanted to eat me. If I had known that, I would have brought my heart.'

'Your heart?' asked the crocodile.

'Yes, it is the tastiest part of me. But I left it behind in the tree.'

'Then we must go back and get it,' said the crocodile, turning round.

'But we are so near the island,' said the monkey. 'Please take me there first.'

'No,' said the crocodile. 'First I am taking you straight to your tree. You will get your heart and bring it to me at once. Then we will see about going to the island.'

'Very well,' said the monkey. And the crocodile headed back to the river bank.

No sooner did the monkey jump on to the bank than

up he swung into the tree. From the highest branch he called
down to the crocodile: 'My heart is way up here. If you
want it, come for it! Come for it!' And he laughed and
laughed while the crocodile thrashed his tail in anger. That
night the monkey moved far down the river from the mango
tree. He wanted to get away from the crocodile so he could
live in peace.

But the crocodile was still determined to catch him. He
searched and searched and finally he found the monkey, living in another tree. Here a large rock rose out of the water,
half-way between the monkey's new home and the island.
The crocodile watched the monkey jumping from the river
bank to the rock, and then to the island where the fruit
trees were. 'Monkey will stay on the island all day,' the
crocodile thought to himself. 'And I'll catch him on his way
home tonight.'

The monkey had a fine feast, while the crocodile swam
about watching him all day. Towards night, the crocodile
crawled out of the water and lay on the rock, perfectly still.
When it grew dark among the trees, the monkey started
for home. He ran down to the river bank, and there he
stopped. 'What is the matter with the rock?' the monkey

wondered. 'I never saw it so high before. Something must be lying on it.'

The monkey went to the water's edge and called: 'Hello, Rock!' No answer. He called again: 'Hello, Rock!' Still no answer. Three times the monkey called, and then he said: 'Why is it, friend Rock, that you do not answer me tonight?'

'Oh,' said the crocodile to himself, 'the rock must talk to the monkey at night. I'll have to answer for the rock this time.'

So he answered: 'Yes, Monkey! What is it?'

The monkey laughed and said: 'Oh, it's you, Crocodile, is it?'

'Yes,' said the crocodile, 'I am waiting here for you. And I am going to eat you up!'

'You have certainly caught me this time,' said the monkey, sounding afraid. 'There is no other way for me to go home. Open your mouth wide so I can jump right into it.'

Now the monkey knew very well that when crocodiles open their mouths wide, they shut their eyes. So while the crocodile lay on the rock with his mouth open and his eyes shut, the monkey jumped. But NOT into his mouth! He landed on top of the crocodile's head, and then sprang quickly to the river bank. Up he ran into his tree.

When the crocodile saw the trick the monkey had played on him, he said: 'Monkey, I thought I was cunning, but you are much more cunning than I. And you know no fear. I will leave you alone after this.'

'Thank you, Crocodile,' said the monkey. 'But I shall be on the watch for you just the same.'

. . . And so he was, and the crocodile never, never caught him.

PAUL GALDONE

## The Crocodile

How doth the little crocodile
Improve his shining tail,
And pour the waters of the Nile
On every golden scale!

How cheerfully he seems to grin,
How neatly spreads his claws,
And welcomes little fishes in,
With gently smiling jaws!

**LEWIS CARROLL**

# If You Should Meet a Crocodile

If you should meet a crocodile,
Don't take a stick and poke him;
Ignore the welcome in his smile,
Be careful not to stroke him.

For as he sleeps upon the Nile,
He thinner gets and thinner;
And whene'er you meet a crocodile
He's ready for his dinner.

ANON.

# Two Octopuses

Two octopuses got married and walked down the aisle
arm in arm in arm in arm in arm in arm in arm in arm
in arm in arm in arm in arm in arm in arm in arm in arm.

**REMY CHARLIP**

## 'One finger, one thumb, keep moving'

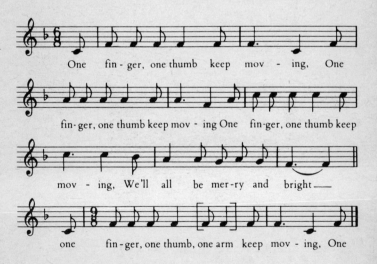

One finger, one thumb, keep moving,
One finger, one thumb, keep moving,
One finger, one thumb, keep moving,
We'll all be merry and bright.

One finger, one thumb, one arm, keep moving,
One finger, one thumb, one arm, keep moving,
One finger, one thumb, one arm, keep moving,
We'll all be merry and bright.

One finger, one thumb, one arm, one leg, keep moving, etc.

One finger, one thumb, one arm, one leg, one nod of the head, keep moving, etc.

ANON.

## 'Peter hammers with one hammer'

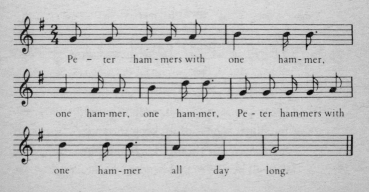

Pe - ter ham - mers with one ham - mer,
one ham - mer, one ham - mer, Pe - ter ham-mers with
one ham - mer all day long.

Peter hammers with one hammer,
  [*Bang on the floor with one foot*]
One hammer, one hammer,
Peter hammers with one hammer,
All day long.

Peter hammers with two hammers
  [*two fists*]
Two hammers, two hammers,
Peter hammers with two hammers,
All day long.

Peter hammers with three hammers, etc.
  [*fists and one foot*]

Peter hammers with four hammers, etc.
  [*fists and both feet*]

Peter hammers with five hammers, etc.
  [*fists, feet and nodding head*]

ANON.

# I Had a Hippopotamus

I had a hippopotamus; I kept him in a shed
And fed him upon vitamins and vegetable bread;
I made him my companion on many cheery walks,
And had his portrait done by a celebrity in chalks.

His charming eccentricities were known on every side,
The creature's popularity was wonderfully wide;
He frolicked with the Rector in a dozen friendly tussles,
Who could not but remark upon his hippopotamuscles.

If he should be afflicted by depression or the dumps,
By hippopotameasles or hippopotamumps,
I never knew a particle of peace till it was plain
He was hippopotamasticating properly again.

# I HAD A HIPPOPOTAMUS

I had a hippopotamus; I loved him as a friend;
But beautiful relationships are bound to have an end;
Time takes, alas! our joys from us and robs us of our blisses;
My hippopotamus turned out a hippopotamissis.

My housekeeper regarded him with jaundice in her eye;
She did not want a colony of hippopotami;
She borrowed a machine-gun from her soldier-nephew
  Percy,
And showed my hippopotamus no hippopotamercy.

My house now lacks the glamour that the charming
  creature gave,
The garage where I kept him is as silent as the grave;
No longer he displays among the motor-tyres and spanners
His hippopotamastery of hippopotamanners.

No longer now he gambols in the orchards in the spring;
No longer do I lead him through the village on a string;
No longer in the mornings does the neighbourhood rejoice
To his hippopotamusically modulated voice.

I had a hippopotamus; but nothing upon earth
Is constant in its happiness or lasting in its mirth;
No joy that life can give me can be strong enough to smother
My sorrow for that might-have-been-a-hippopotamother.

PATRICK BARRINGTON

## Johnny Crow's Garden

Johnny Crow
Would dig and sow
Till he made a little Garden.

And the Lion
Had a green and yellow Tie on
In Johnny Crow's Garden.

And the Rat
Wore a Feather in his Hat
But the Bear
Had nothing to wear
In Johnny Crow's Garden.

So the Ape
Took his Measure with a Tape
In Johnny Crow's Garden.

Then the Crane
Was caught in the Rain
In Johnny Crow's Garden.

And the Beaver
Was afraid he had a Fever
But the Goat
Said:
'It's nothing but his Throat'
In Johnny Crow's Garden.

And the Pig
Danced a Jig
In Johnny Crow's Garden.

Then the Stork
Gave a Philosophic Talk
Till the Hippopotami
Said: 'Ask no further "What am I?" '
While the Elephant
Said something quite irrelevant
In Johnny Crow's Garden.

And the Goose –
Well,
The Goose *was* a Goose
In Johnny Crow's Garden.

And the Mouse
Built himself a little House
Where the Cat
Sat down beside the Mat
In Johnny Crow's Garden.

And the Whale
Told a very long Tale
In Johnny Crow's Garden.

And the Owl
Was a funny old Fowl
And the Fox
Put them all in the Stocks
In Johnny Crow's Garden.

But Johnny Crow
He let them go
And they all sat down
To their dinner in a row
In Johnny Crow's Garden!

*Written and illustrated by*
L. LESLIE BROOKE

# Pooh and Piglet Go Hunting

The Piglet lived in a very grand house in the middle of a beech tree, and the beech tree was in the middle of the forest, and the Piglet lived in the middle of the house. Next to his house was a piece of broken board which had: 'TRES-PASSERS W' on it. When Christopher Robin asked the Piglet what it meant, he said it was his grandfather's name, and had been in the family for a long time. Christopher Robin said you *couldn't* be called Trespassers W, and Piglet said yes, you could, because his grandfather was, and it was short for Trespassers Will, which was short for Trespassers William. And his grandfather had had two names in case he lost one – Trespassers after an uncle, and William after Trespassers.

'I've got two names,' said Christopher Robin carelessly.

'Well, there you are, that proves it,' said Piglet.

One fine winter's day when Piglet was brushing away the snow in front of his house, he happened to look up, and there was Winnie-the-Pooh. Pooh was walking round and round in a circle, thinking of something else, and when Piglet called to him, he just went on walking.

'Hallo!' said Piglet, 'what are *you* doing?'

'Hunting,' said Pooh.

'Hunting what?'

'Tracking something,' said Winnie-the-Pooh very mysteriously.

'Tracking what?' said Piglet, coming closer.

'That's just what I ask myself. I ask myself, What?'

'What do you think you'll answer?'

'I shall have to wait until I catch up with it,' said Winnie-the-Pooh. 'Now, look there.' He pointed to the ground in front of him. 'What do you see there?'

'Tracks,' said Piglet. 'Paw-marks.' He gave a little squeak of excitement. 'Oh, Pooh! Do you think it's a – a – a Woozle?'

'It may be,' said Pooh. 'Sometimes it is, and sometimes it isn't. You never can tell with paw-marks.'

With these few words he went on tracking, and Piglet, after watching him for a minute or two, ran after him. Winnie-the-Pooh had come to a sudden stop, and was bending over the tracks in a puzzled sort of way.

'What's the matter?' asked Piglet.

'It's a very funny thing,' said Bear, 'but there seem to be *two* animals now. This – whatever-it-was – has been joined by another – whatever-it-is – and the two of them are now proceeding in company. Would you mind coming with me, Piglet, in case they turn out to be Hostile Animals?'

Piglet scratched his ear in a nice sort of way, and said that he had nothing to do until Friday, and would be delighted to come, in case it really *was* a Woozle.

'You mean, in case it really is two Woozles,' said Winnie-the-Pooh, and Piglet said that anyhow he had nothing to do until Friday. So off they went together.

There was a small spinney of larch trees just here, and it seemed as if the two Woozles, if that is what they were, had been going round this spinney; so round this spinney

went Pooh and Piglet after them; Piglet passing the time
by telling Pooh what his Grandfather Trespassers W had
done to Remove Stiffness after Tracking, and how his
Grandfather Trespassers W had suffered in his later years
from Shortness of Breath, and other matters of interest, and
Pooh wondering what a Grandfather was like, and if perhaps this was Two Grandfathers they were after now, and,
if so, whether he would be allowed to take one home and
keep it, and what Christopher Robin would say. And still
the tracks went on in front of them . . .

Suddenly Winnie-the-Pooh stopped, and pointed excitedly in front of him. '*Look!*'

'*What?*' said Piglet, with a jump. And then, to show that he hadn't been frightened, he jumped up and down once or twice more in an exercising sort of way.

'The tracks!' said Pooh. '*A third animal has joined the other two!*'

'Pooh!' cried Piglet. 'Do you think it is another Woozle?'

'No,' said Pooh, 'because it makes different marks. It is either Two Woozles and one, as it might be, Wizzle, or Two as it might be, Wizzles and one, if so it is, Woozle. Let us continue to follow them.'

So they went on, feeling just a little anxious now, in case the three animals in front of them were of Hostile Intent. And Piglet wished very much that his Grandfather T. W. were there, instead of elsewhere, and Pooh thought how nice it would be if they met Christopher Robin suddenly but quite accidentally, and only because he liked Christopher Robin so much. And then, all of a sudden, Winnie-the-Pooh stopped again, and licked the tip of his nose in a cooling manner, for he was feeling more hot and anxious than ever in his life before. *There were four animals in front of them!*

'Do you see, Piglet? Look at their tracks! Three, as it were, Woozles, and one, as it was, Wizzle. *Another Woozle has joined them!*'

And so it seemed to be. There were the tracks; crossing over each other here, getting muddled up with each other there; but, quite plainly every now and then, the tracks of four sets of paws.

'I *think*,' said Piglet, when he had licked the tip of his nose too, and found it brought very little comfort, 'I *think* that I have just remembered something. I have just remembered something that I forgot to do yesterday and shan't be able to do tomorrow. So I suppose I really ought to go back and do it now.'

'We'll do it this afternoon, and I'll come with you,' said Pooh.

'It isn't the sort of thing you can do in the afternoon,' said Piglet quickly. 'It's a very particular morning thing, that has to be done in the morning, and, if possible, between the hours of – What would you say the time was?'

'About twelve,' said Winnie-the-Pooh, looking at the sun.

'Between, as I was saying, the hours of twelve and twelve-five. So, really, dear old Pooh, if you'll excuse me – *What's that?*'

Pooh looked up at the sky, and then, as he heard the whistle again, he looked up into the branches of a big oak tree, and then he saw a friend of his.

'It's Christopher Robin,' he said.

'Ah, then you'll be all right,' said Piglet. 'You'll be quite safe with *him*. Goodbye,' and he trotted off home as quickly as he could, very glad to be Out of All Danger again.

Christopher Robin came slowly down his tree.

'Silly old Bear,' he said, 'what *were* you doing? First you went round the spinney twice by yourself, and then Piglet ran after you and you went round again together, and then you were going round a fourth time –'

'Wait a moment,' said Winnie-the-Pooh, holding up his paw.

He sat down and thought, in the most thoughtful way he could think. Then he fitted his paw into one of the Tracks . . . and then he scratched his nose twice, and stood up.

'Yes,' said Winnie-the-Pooh.

'I see now,' said Winnie-the-Pooh.

'I have been Foolish and Deluded,' said he, 'and I am a Bear of No Brain at All.'

'You're the Best Bear in All the World,' said Christopher Robin soothingly.

'Am I?' said Pooh hopefully. And then he brightened up suddenly.

'Anyhow,' he said, 'it is nearly Luncheon Time.'

So he went home for it.

A. A. MILNE
*Illustrated by* E. H. SHEPARD

## Us Two

Wherever I am, there's always Pooh,
There's always Pooh and Me.
Whatever I do, he wants to do,
'Where are you going today?' says Pooh:
'Well, that's very odd 'cos I was too.
Let's go together,' says Pooh, says he.
'Let's go together,' says Pooh.

'What's twice eleven?' I said to Pooh.
('Twice what?' said Pooh to Me.)
'I *think* it ought to be twenty-two.'
'Just what I think myself,' said Pooh.
'It wasn't an easy sum to do,
But that's what it is,' said Pooh, said he.
'That's what it is,' said Pooh.

'Let's look for dragons,' I said to Pooh.
'Yes, let's,' said Pooh to Me.
We crossed the river and found a few –
'Yes, those are dragons all right,' said Pooh.
'As soon as I saw their beaks I knew.
That's what they are,' said Pooh, said he.
'That's what they are,' said Pooh.

'Let's frighten the dragons,' I said to Pooh.
'That's right,' said Pooh to Me.
'*I'm* not afraid,' I said to Pooh,
And I held his paw and I shouted 'Shoo!
Silly old dragons!' – and off they flew.
'I wasn't afraid,' said Pooh, said he,
'I'm *never* afraid with you.'

So wherever I am, there's always Pooh,
There's always Pooh and Me.
'What would I do?' I said to Pooh,
'If it wasn't for you,' and Pooh said: 'True,
It isn't much fun for One, but Two
Can stick together,' says Pooh, says he.
'That's how it is,' says Pooh.

A. A. MILNE

# Nicholas Nye

Thistle and darnel and dock grew there,
   And a bush, in the corner, of may;
On the orchard wall I used to sprawl
   In the blazing heat of the day:
Half asleep and half awake,
   While the birds went twittering by,
And nobody there my lone to share
    But Nicholas Nye.

Nicholas Nye was lean and grey,
   Lame of leg and old,
More than a score of donkey's years
   He had seen since he was foaled;
He munched the thistles, purple and spiked,
   Would sometimes stoop and sigh,
And turn his head, as if he said,
    'Poor Nicholas Nye!'

Alone with his shadow he'd drowse in the meadow,
    Lazily swinging his tail;
At break of day he used to bray –
    Not much too hearty and hale.
But a wonderful gumption was under his skin,
    And a clear calm light in his eye;
And once in a while he would smile a smile,
        Would Nicholas Nye.

Seem to be smiling at me, he would,
    From his bush, in the corner, of may –
Bony and ownerless, widowed and worn,
    Knobble-kneed, lonely, and grey;
And over the grass would seem to pass,
    'Neath the deep dark blue of the sky,
Something much better than words between me
        And Nicholas Nye.

But dusk would come in the apple boughs,
    The green of the glow-worm shine,
The birds in nest would crouch to rest,
    And home I'd trudge to mine;
And there, in the moonlight, dark with dew,
    Asking not wherefore nor why,
Would brood like a ghost, and as still as a post,
        Old Nicholas Nye.

WALTER DE LA MARE

# Cows

Half the time they munched the grass, and all the time
  they lay
Down in the water-meadows, the lazy month of May,
          A-chewing,
          A-mooing,
    To pass the hours away.

      'Nice weather,' said the brown cow.
        'Ah,' said the white.
      'Grass is very tasty.'
        'Grass is all right.'

# COWS

Half the time they munched the grass, and all the time
  they lay
Down in the water-meadows, the lazy month of May,
        A-chewing,
        A-mooing,
    To pass the hours away.

     'Rain coming,' said the brown cow.
      'Ah,' said the white.
    'Flies is very tiresome.'
     'Flies bite.'

Half the time they munched the grass, and all the time
  they lay
Down in the water-meadows, the lazy month of May,
        A-chewing,
        A-mooing,
    To pass the hours away.

     'Time to go,' said the brown cow.
      'Ah,' said the white.
    'Nice chat.' 'Very pleasant.'
     'Night.' 'Night.'

Half the time they munched the grass, and all the time
  they lay
Down in the water-meadows, the lazy month of May,
        A-chewing,
        A-mooing,
    To pass the hours away.

JAMES REEVES

# The Cat That Walked by Himself

Hear and attend and listen; for this befell and behappened and became and was, O my Best Beloved, when the Tame animals were wild. The Dog was wild, and the Horse was wild, and the Cow was wild, and the Sheep was wild, and the Pig was wild – as wild as wild could be – and they walked in the Wet Wild Woods by their wild lones. But the wildest of all the wild animals was the Cat. He walked by himself, and all places were alike to him.

Of course the Man was wild too. He was dreadfully wild. He didn't even begin to be tame till he met the Woman, and she told him that she did not like living in his Wild ways. She picked out a nice dry Cave, instead of a heap of wet leaves, to lie down in; and she strewed clean sand on the floor; and she lit a nice fire of wood at the back of the Cave; and she hung a dried wild-horse skin, tail-down, across the opening of the Cave; and she said, 'Wipe your feet, dear, when you come in, and now we'll keep house.'

That night, Best Beloved, they ate wild sheep roasted on the hot stones, and flavoured with wild garlic and wild pepper; and wild duck stuffed with wild rice and wild fenugreek and wild coriander; and marrow-bones of wild oxen; and wild cherries, and wild grenadillas. Then the Man went to sleep in front of the fire ever so happy; but the Woman sat up, combing her hair. She took the bone of the shoulder of mutton – the big flat blade-bone – and she looked at the wonderful marks on it, and she threw more wood on the fire, and she made a Magic. She made the First Singing Magic in the world.

Out in the Wet Wild Woods all the wild animals gathered together where they could see the light of the fire a long way off, and they wondered what it meant.

Then Wild Horse stamped with his wild foot and said, 'O my Friends and O my Enemies, why have the Man and the Woman made that great light in that great Cave, and what harm will it do us?'

Wild Dog lifted up his wild nose and smelled the smell of the roast mutton, and said, 'I will go up and see and look, and say; for I think it is good. Cat, come with me.'

'Nenni!' said the Cat. 'I am the Cat who walks by himself, and all places are alike to me. I will not come.'

'Then we can never be friends again,' said Wild Dog, and he trotted off to the Cave. But when he had gone a little way the Cat said to himself, 'All places are alike to me. Why should I not go too and see and look and come away at my own liking?' So he slipped after Wild Dog softly, very softly, and hid himself where he could hear everything.

When Wild Dog reached the mouth of the Cave he lifted up the dried horse-skin with his nose and sniffed the beautiful smell of the roast mutton, and the Woman, looking at the blade-bone, heard him, and laughed, and said, 'Here comes the first. Wild Thing out of the Wild Woods, what do you want?'

Wild Dog said, 'O my Enemy and Wife of my Enemy, what is this that smells so good in the Wild Woods?'

Then the Woman picked up a roasted mutton-bone and threw it to Wild Dog, and said, 'Wild Thing out of the Wild Woods, taste and try.' Wild Dog gnawed the bone, and it was more delicious than anything he had ever tasted, and he said, 'O my Enemy and Wife of my Enemy, give me another.'

The Woman said, 'Wild Thing out of the Wild Woods, help my Man to hunt through the day and guard this Cave at night and I will give you as many roast bones as you need.'

'Ah!' said the Cat, listening. 'This is a very wise Woman, but she is not so wise as I am.'

Wild Dog crawled into the Cave and laid his head on the Woman's lap, and said, 'O my Friend and Wife of my Friend, I will help your Man to hunt through the day, and at night I will guard your Cave.'

'Ah!' said the Cat, listening. 'That is a very foolish Dog.' And he went back through the Wet Wild Woods waving his wild tail, and walking by his wild lone. But he never told anybody.

When the Man waked up he said, 'What is Wild Dog doing here?' and the Woman said, 'His name is not Wild Dog any more, but the First Friend, because he will be our friend for always and always and always. Take him with you when you go hunting.'

Next night the Woman cut great green armfuls of fresh grass from the water-meadows, and dried it before the fire, so that it smelt like new-mown hay, and she sat at the mouth of the Cave and plaited a halter out of horse-hide, and she looked at the shoulder-of-mutton bone – at the big broad blade-bone – and she made a Magic. She made the Second Singing Magic in the world.

Out in the Wild Woods all the wild animals wondered what had happened to Wild Dog, and at last Wild Horse stamped with his foot and said, 'I will go and see and say why Wild Dog has not returned. Cat, come with me.'

'Nenni!' said the Cat. 'I am the Cat who walks by himself, and all places are alike to me. I will not come.' But all the same he followed Wild Horse softly, very softly, and hid himself where he could hear everything.

When the Woman heard Wild Horse, tripping and stumbling on his long mane, she laughed and said, 'Here comes the second Wild Thing out of the Wild Woods, what do you want?'

Wild Horse said, 'O my Enemy and Wife of my Enemy, where is Wild Dog?'

The Woman laughed, and picked up the blade-bone and looked at it, and said, 'Wild Thing out of the Wild Woods, you did not come here for Wild Dog, but for the sake of this good grass.'

And Wild Horse, tripping and stumbling on his long mane, said, 'That is true; give it me to eat.'

The Woman said, 'Wild Thing out of the Wild Woods, bend your head and wear what I give you, and you shall eat the wonderful grass three times a day.'

'Ah!' said the Cat, listening. 'This is a clever Woman, but she is not so clever as I am.'

Wild Horse bent his wild head, and the Woman slipped the plaited-hide halter over it, and Wild Horse breathed on the Woman's feet and said, 'O my Mistress, and Wife of my Master, I will be your servant for the sake of the wonderful grass.'

'Ah!' said the Cat, listening. 'That is a very foolish Horse.'

And he went back through the Wet Wild Woods, waving his wild tail and walking by his wild lone. But he never told anybody.

When the Man and the Dog came back from hunting, the Man said, 'What is Wild Horse doing here?' And the Woman said, 'His name is not Wild Horse any more, but the First Servant, because he will carry us from place to place for always and always and always. Ride on his back when you go hunting.'

Next day, holding her wild head high that her wild horns should not catch in the wild trees, Wild Cow came up to the Cave, and the Cat followed, and hid himself just the same as before; and everything happened just the same as before; and the Cat said the same things as before; and when Wild Cow had promised to give her milk to the Woman every day in exchange for the wonderful grass, the Cat went back through the Wet Wild Woods waving his wild tail and walking by his wild lone, just the same as before. But he never told anybody. And when the Man and the Horse and the Dog came home from hunting and asked the same questions same as before, the Woman said, 'Her name is not Wild Cow any more, but the Giver of Good Food. She will give us the warm white milk for always and always and always, and I will take care of her while you and the First Friend and the First Servant go hunting.'

Next day the Cat waited to see if any other Wild Thing would go up to the Cave, but no one moved in the Wet Wild Woods, so the Cat walked there by himself; and he saw the Woman milking the Cow, and he saw the light of the fire in the Cave, and he smelt the smell of the warm white milk.

Cat said, 'O my Enemy and Wife of my Enemy, where did Wild Cow go?'

The Woman laughed and said, 'Wild Thing out of the Wild Woods, go back to the Woods again, for I have braided up my hair, and I have put away the magic blade-bone, and we have no more need of either friends or servants in our Cave.'

Cat said, 'I am not a friend, and I am not a servant. I am the Cat who walks by himself, and I wish to come into your Cave.'

Woman said, 'Then why did you not come with First Friend on the first night?'

Cat grew very angry and said, 'Has Wild Dog told tales of me?'

Then the Woman laughed and said, 'You are the Cat who walks by himself, and all places are alike to you. You are neither a friend nor a servant. You have said it yourself. Go away and walk by yourself in all places alike.'

Then Cat pretended to be sorry and said, 'Must I never come into the Cave? Must I never sit by the warm fire? Must I never drink the warm white milk? You are very wise and very beautiful. You should not be cruel even to a Cat.'

Woman said, 'I knew I was wise, but I did not know I was beautiful. So I will make a bargain with you. If ever I say one word in your praise, you may come into the Cave.'

'And if you say two words in my praise?' said the Cat.

'I never shall,' said the Woman, 'but if I say two words in your praise, you may sit by the fire in the Cave.'

'And if you say three words?' said the Cat.

'I never shall,' said the Woman, 'but if I say three words

in your praise, you may drink the warm white milk three times a day for always and always and always.'

Then the Cat arched his back and said, 'Now let the Curtain at the mouth of the Cave, and the Fire at the back of the Cave, and the Milk-pots that stand beside the Fire, remember what my Enemy and the Wife of my Enemy has said.' And he went away through the Wet Wild Woods waving his wild tail and walking by his wild lone.

That night when the Man and the Horse and the Dog came home from hunting, the Woman did not tell them of the bargain she had made with the Cat, because she was afraid that they might not like it. Cat went far and far away and hid himself in the Wet Wild Woods by his wild lone for a long time till the Woman forgot all about him. Only the Bat – the little upside-down Bat – that hung inside the Cave knew where Cat hid; and every evening Bat would fly to Cat with news of what was happening.

One evening Bat said, 'There is a Baby in the Cave. He is new and pink and fat, and the Woman is very fond of him.'

'Ah,' said the Cat, listening, 'but what is the Baby fond of?'

'He is fond of things that are soft and tickle,' said the Bat. 'He is fond of warm things to hold in his arms when he goes to sleep. He is fond of being played with. He is fond of all those things.'

'Ah,' said the Cat, listening, 'then my time has come.'

Next night Cat walked through the Wet Wild Woods and hid very near the Cave till morning-time, and Man and Dog and Horse went hunting. The Woman was busy cooking that morning, and the Baby cried and interrupted.

So she carried him outside the Cave and gave him a handful of pebbles to play with. But still the Baby cried.

Then the Cat put out his paddy paw and patted the Baby on the cheek, and it cooed: and the Cat rubbed against its fat knees and tickled it under its fat chin with his tail. And the Baby laughed; and the Woman heard him and smiled.

Then the Bat – the little upside-down Bat – that hung in the mouth of the Cave said, 'O my Hostess and Wife of my Host and Mother of my Host's Son, a Wild Thing from the Wild Woods is most beautifully playing with your Baby.'

'A blessing on that Wild Thing whoever he may be,' said the Woman, straightening her back, 'for I was a busy woman this morning and he has done me a service.'

That very minute and second, Best Beloved, the dried horse-skin Curtain that was stretched tail-down at the mouth of the Cave fell down – *woosh*! – because it remembered the bargain she had made with the Cat; and when the Woman went to pick it up – lo and behold! – the Cat was sitting quite comfy inside the Cave.

'O my Enemy and Wife of my Enemy and Mother of my Enemy,' said the Cat, 'it is I: for you have spoken a word in my praise, and now I can sit within the Cave for always and always and always. But still I am the Cat who walks by himself, and all places are alike to me.'

The Woman was very angry, and shut her lips tight and took up her spinning-wheel and began to spin.

But the Baby cried because the Cat had gone away, and the Woman could not hush it, for it struggled and kicked and grew black in the face.

'O my Enemy and Wife of my Enemy and Mother of

my Enemy,' said the Cat, 'take a strand of the thread that you are spinning and tie it to your spinning-whorl and drag it along the floor, and I will show you a Magic that shall make your Baby laugh as loudly as he is now crying.'

'I will do so,' said the Woman, 'because I am at my wits' end; but I will not thank you for it.'

She tied the thread to the little clay spindle-whorl and drew it across the floor, and the Cat ran after it and patted it with his paws and rolled head over heels, and tossed it backward over his shoulder and chased it between his hind-legs and pretended to lose it, and pounced down upon it again, till the Baby laughed as loudly as it had been crying, and scrambled after the Cat and frolicked all over the Cave till it grew tired and settled down to sleep with the Cat in its arms.

'Now,' said Cat, 'I will sing the Baby a song that shall keep him asleep for an hour.' And he began to purr, loud and low, low and loud, till the Baby fell fast asleep. The Woman smiled as she looked down upon the two of them, and said, 'That was wonderfully done. No question but you are clever, O Cat.'

That very minute and second, Best Beloved, the smoke of the Fire at the back of the Cave came down in clouds from the roof – *puff*! – because it remembered the bargain she had made with the Cat; and when it had cleared away – lo and behold! – the Cat was sitting quite comfy close to the fire.

'O my Enemy and Wife of my Enemy and Mother of my Enemy,' said the Cat, 'it is I: for you have spoken a second word in my praise, and now I can sit by the warm fire at the back of the Cave for always and always and always. But still I am the Cat who walks by himself, and all places are alike to me.'

Then the Woman was very very angry, and let down her hair and put some more wood on the fire and brought out the broad blade-bone of the shoulder of mutton and began to make a Magic that should prevent her from saying a third word in praise of the Cat. It was not a Singing Magic, Best Beloved, it was a Still Magic; and by and by the Cave grew so still that a little wee-wee mouse crept out of a corner and ran across the floor.

'O my Enemy and Wife of my Enemy and Mother of my Enemy,' said the Cat, 'is that little mouse part of your Magic?'

'Ouh! Chee! No indeed!' said the Woman, and she dropped the blade-bone and jumped upon the footstool in front of the fire and braided up her hair very quick for fear that the mouse should run up it.

'Ah,' said the Cat, watching, 'then the mouse will do me no harm if I eat it?'

'No,' said the Woman, braiding up her hair, 'eat it quickly and I will ever be grateful to you.'

Cat made one jump and caught the little mouse, and the Woman said, 'A hundred thanks. Even the First Friend is not quick enough to catch little mice as you have done. You must be very wise.'

That very moment and second, O Best Beloved, the Milk-pot that stood by the fire cracked in two pieces – *ffft*! – because it remembered the bargain she had made with the Cat; and when the Woman jumped down from the foot-stool – lo and behold! – the Cat was lapping up the warm white milk that lay in one of the broken pieces.

'O my Enemy and Wife of my Enemy and Mother of my Enemy,' said the Cat, 'it is I: for you have spoken three words in my praise, and now I can drink the warm white milk three times a day for always and always and always. But *still* I am the Cat who walks by himself, and all places are alike to me.'

Then the Woman laughed and set the Cat a bowl of the warm white milk and said, 'O Cat, you are as clever as a man, but remember that your bargain was not made with the Man or the Dog, and I do not know what they will do when they come home.'

'What is that to me?' said the Cat. 'If I have my place in the Cave by the fire and my warm white milk three times a day I do not care what the Man or the Dog can do.'

That evening when the Man and the Dog came into the Cave, the Woman told them all the story of the bargain, while the Cat sat by the fire and smiled. Then the Man said, 'Yes, but he has not made a bargain with *me* or with all proper Men after me.' Then he took off his two leather boots and he took up his little stone axe (that makes three) and he fetched a piece of wood and a hatchet (that is five altogether), and he set them out in a row and he said, 'Now we will make *our* bargain. If you do not catch mice when you are in the Cave for always and always and always, I will throw these five things at you whenever I see you, and so shall all proper Men do after me.'

'Ah,' said the Woman, listening 'this is a very clever Cat, but he is not so clever as my Man.'

The Cat counted the five things (and they looked very knobby) and he said, 'I will catch mice when I am in the

Cave for always and always and always; but *still* I am the Cat who walks by himself, and all places are alike to me.'

'Not when I am near,' said the Man. 'If you had not said that last I would have put all these things away for always and always and always; but now I am going to throw my two boots and my little stone axe (that makes three) at you whenever I meet you. And so shall all proper Men do after me!'

Then the Dog said, 'Wait a minute. He has not made a bargain with *me* or with all proper Dogs after me.' And he showed his teeth and said, 'If you are not kind to the Baby while I am in the Cave for always and always and always, I will hunt you till I catch you, and when I catch you I will bite you. And so shall all proper Dogs do after me.'

'Ah,' said the Woman, listening, 'this is a very clever Cat, but he is not so clever as the Dog.'

Cat counted the Dog's teeth (and they looked very pointed) and he said, 'I will be kind to the Baby while I am in the Cave, as long as he does not pull my tail too hard, for always and always and always. But *still* I am the Cat that walks by himself, and all places are alike to me.'

'Not when I am near,' said the Dog. 'If you had not said that last I would have shut my mouth for always and always and always; but *now* I am going to hunt you up a tree whenever I meet you. And so shall all proper Dogs do after me.'

Then the Man threw his two boots and his little stone axe (that makes three) at the Cat, and the Cat ran out of the Cave and the Dog chased him up a tree; and from that day to this, Best Beloved, three proper Men out of five will always throw things at a Cat whenever they meet him, and all proper Dogs will chase him up a tree. But the Cat keeps his side of the bargain too. He will kill mice, and he will be kind to Babies when he is in the house, just as long as they do not pull his tail too hard. But when he has done that, and between times, and when the moon gets up and night comes, he is the Cat that walks by himself, and all places are alike to him. Then he goes out to the Wet Wild Woods or up the Wet Wild Trees or on the Wet Wild Roofs, waving his wild tail and walking by his wild lone.

*Written and illustrated by* RUDYARD KIPLING

# W

The King sent for his wise men all
   To find a rhyme for W;
When they had thought a good long time
But could not think of a single rhyme,
   'I'm sorry,' said he, 'to trouble you.'

JAMES REEVES

# Praying Lion

A missionary was walking through the bush one day when he came face to face with a prowling lion. Man and beast stopped dead in their tracks and stared at one another, each waiting for the other to make the first move.

The missionary, however, had been told that the best way of dealing with wild animals was to look hard and unblinkingly at them, eye to eye. So, courageously – for he felt frightened out of his skin – he went on staring at the lion.

After a few minutes of this, the lion put its front paws together and bowed its head.

The missionary, relieved and thinking danger was past, put his hands together, too, closed his eyes and began to give thanks for his deliverance.

It was then that he heard the lion say, 'I don't know what you're doing, but I'm saying grace.'

AIDAN CHAMBERS

## 'Peter Piper picked a peck of pickled pepper'

Peter Piper picked a peck of pickled pepper;
A peck of pickled pepper Peter Piper picked.
If Peter Piper picked a peck of pickled pepper,
Where's the peck of pickled pepper Peter Piper picked?

ANON.

*Illustrated by* RAYMOND BRIGGS

# 'Betty Botter bought some butter'

Betty Botter bought some butter,
But, she said, the butter's bitter;
If I put it in my batter
It will make my batter bitter,
But a bit of better butter,
That would make my batter better.
So she bought a bit of butter
Better than her bitter butter,
And she put it in her batter
And the batter was not bitter.
So 'twas better Betty Botter
Bought a bit of better butter.

ANON.

# Tikki Tikki Tembo

Once upon a time, a long, long time ago, it was the custom of all the fathers and mothers in China to give their first and honoured sons great long names. But second sons were given hardly any name at all.

In a small mountain village there lived a mother who had two little sons. Her second son she called Chang, which meant 'little or nothing'. But her first and honoured son she called Tikki tikki tembo-no sa rembo-chari bari ruchi-pip peri pembo, which meant 'the most wonderful thing in the whole wide world'!

Every morning the mother went to wash in a little stream near her home. The two boys always went chattering along with her. On the bank was an old well.

'Don't go near the well,' warned the mother, 'or you will surely fall in.'

The boys did not always mind their mother, and one day they were playing beside the well and on the well when Chang fell in! Tikki tikki tembo-no sa rembo-chari bari ruchi-pip peri pembo ran as fast as his little legs could carry him to his mother and said,

'Most Honourable Mother, Chang has fallen in the well!'

'The water roars, "Little Blossom", I cannot hear you,' said the mother.

Then Tikki tikki tembo-no sa rembo-chari bari ruchi-pip peri pembo raised his voice and cried,

'Oh, most Honourable One, Chang has fallen in the well!'

'That troublesome boy,' answered the mother. 'Run and get the Old Man With The Ladder to fish him out.'

Then Tikki tikki tembo-no sa rembo-chari bari ruchi-pip peri pembo ran as fast as his little legs could carry him to the Old Man With The Ladder and said,

'Old Man With The Ladder, Chang has fallen into the well. Will you come and fish him out?'

'So,' said the Old Man With The Ladder, 'Chang has fallen into the well.'

And he ran as fast as his old legs could carry him. Step over step, step over step he went into the well, picked up little Chang, and step over step, step over step brought him out of the well. He pumped the water out of him and pushed the air into him, and pumped the water out of him and pushed the air into him, and soon Chang was just as good as ever!

Now, for several months the boys did not go near the well. But after the Festival of the Eighth Moon they ran to the well to eat their rice cakes. They ate near the well, they played around the well, they walked on the well and Tikki tikki tembo-no sa rembo-chari bari ruchi-pip peri pembo fell into the well!

Chang ran as fast as his little legs could carry him to his mother and said, 'Oh, Most Honourable Mother, Tikki tikki tembo-no sa rembo-chari bari ruchi-pip peri pembo has fallen into the well!'

'The water roars, "Little One", I cannot hear you.'

So little Chang took a deep breath. 'Oh, Mother, Most Honourable,' he panted, 'Tikki tikki tembo-no sa rembo-chari bari ruchi-pip peri pembo has fallen into the well!'

'Tiresome Child, what are you trying to say?' said his mother.

'Honourable Mother! Chari bari rembo tikki tikki,' he gasped, 'pip pip has fallen into the well!'

'Unfortunate Son, surely the evil spirits have bewitched your tongue. Speak your brother's name with reverence.'

Poor little Chang was all out of breath from saying that great long name, and he didn't think he could say it one more time. But then he thought of his brother in the old well. Chang bowed his little head clear to the sand, took a deep breath and slowly, very slowly, said, 'Most Honourable Mother, Tikki tikki – tembo-no – sa rembo-chari bari – ruchi-pip – peri pembo is at the bottom of the well.'

'Oh, not my first and honoured son, heir to all I possess! Run quickly and tell the Old Man With The Ladder that your brother has fallen into the well.'

So Chang ran as fast as his little legs would carry him to the Old Man With The Ladder. Under a tree the Old Man With The Ladder sat bowed and silent. 'Old Man, Old Man,' shouted Chang. 'Come right away! Tikki tikki tembo-no sa rembo-chari bari ruchi-pip peri pembo has fallen into the stone well!'

But there was no answer. Puzzled, he waited. Then with the very last bit of breath he shouted, 'Old Man With The Ladder, Tikki tikki tembo-no sa rembo-chari bari ruchi-pip peri pembo is at the bottom of the well.'

'Miserable child, you disturb my dream. I had floated into a purple mist and found my youth again. There were glittering gateways and jewelled blossoms. If I close my eyes, perhaps I will again return.'

Poor little Chang was frightened. How could he say that great long name again? 'Please, Old Man With The Ladder, please help my brother out of the cold well.'

'So,' said the Old Man With The Ladder, 'your mother's "Precious Pearl" has fallen into the well!' And the Old Man With The Ladder hurried as fast as his old legs could carry him. Step over step, step over step he went into the well, and step over step, step over step out of the well with the little boy in his arms. Then he pumped the water out of him and pushed the air into him, and pumped the water out of him and pushed the air into him. But little Tikki

tikki tembo-no sa rembo-chari bari ruchi-pip peri pembo had been in the water so long, all because of his great long name, that the moon rose many times before he was quite the same again.

And from that day to this the Chinese have always thought it wise to give all their children little, short names instead of great long names.

ARLENE MOSEL

# Theseus and the Minotaur

Long ago there ruled a great king in Athens called Aegeus, and his son, Theseus, was a hero who had done many brave and mighty deeds.

Now the whole country was happy and at peace except for one great sorrow. Minos, king of Crete, had fought against the Athenians and had conquered them; and before returning to Crete he had made a hard and cruel peace. Each year the Athenians were forced to send seven young men and seven maidens to be sacrificed to the Minotaur. This was a monster who lived in the labyrinth, a winding path among rocks and caves. So each spring seven youths and maidens, chosen by lot, journeyed in a ship with black sails to the shores of Crete, to be torn to pieces by the savage Minotaur.

One spring, when the herald from King Minos arrived, Theseus determined to make an end of the beast and rid his father's people of this horrible evil. He went and told Aegeus that when the black-sailed ship set out on the morrow he would go too and slay the Minotaur.

'But how will you slay him, my son?' said Aegeus. 'For you must leave your club and your shield behind, and be cast to the monster, defenceless and naked like the rest.'

And Theseus said, 'Are there no stones in that labyrinth; and have I not fists and teeth?'

Then Aegeus clung to his knees; but he would not hear; and at last he let him go, weeping bitterly, and said only this one word:

'Promise me but this, if you return in peace, though that may hardly be, take down the black sail of the ship (for I shall watch for it all day upon the cliffs), and hoist instead a white sail, that I may know afar off that you are safe.'

And Theseus promised, and went out, and to the market-place where the herald stood, while they drew lots for the youths and maidens, who were to sail in that doleful crew. And the people stood wailing and weeping, as the lot fell on this one and on that; but Theseus strode into the midst, and cried:

'Here is a youth who needs no lot. I myself will be one of the seven.'

And the herald asked in wonder, 'Fair youth, know you whither you are going?'

And Theseus said, 'I know. Let us go down to the black-sailed ship.'

So they went down to the black-sailed ship, seven maidens and seven youths, and Theseus before them all, and the people following them lamenting. But Theseus whispered to his companions, 'Have hope, for the monster is not immortal.' Then their hearts were comforted a little; but they wept as they went on board, and the cliffs of Sunium rang, and all the isles of the Aegean Sea, with the voice of their lamentation, as they sailed on towards their deaths in Crete.

And at last they came to Crete, and to Cnossus, beneath the peaks of Ida, and to the palace of Minos the great king, to whom Zeus himself taught laws. So he was the wisest of all mortal kings, and conquered all the Aegean isles; and his ships were as many as the sea-gulls, and his palace like a marble hill.

But Theseus stood before Minos, and they looked each other in the face. And Minos bade take them to prison, and cast them to the monster one by one. Then Theseus cried:

'A boon, O Minos! Let me be thrown first to the beast. For I came hither for that very purpose, of my own will, and not by lot.'

'Who art thou, then, brave youth?'

'I am the son of him whom of all men thou hatest most, Aegeus, the king of Athens, and I am come here to end this matter.'

And Minos pondered awhile, looking steadfastly at him, and he answered at last mildly:

'Go back in peace, my son. It is a pity that one so brave should die.'

But Theseus said, 'I have sworn that I will not go back till I have seen the monster face to face.'

And at that Minos frowned, and said, 'Then thou shalt see him; take the madman away.'

And they led Theseus away into prison, with the other youths and maids.

But Ariadne, Minos' daughter, saw him as she came out of her white stone hall; and she loved him for his courage and his majesty, and said, 'Shame that such a youth should die!' And by night she went down to the prison, and told him all her heart, and said:

'Flee down to your ship at once, for I have bribed the guards before the door. Flee, you and all your friends, and go back in peace to Greece; and take me, take me with you! for I dare not stay after you are gone; for my father will kill me miserably, if he knows what I have done.'

And Theseus stood silent awhile; for he was astonished and confounded by her beauty; but at last he said, 'I cannot go home in peace till I have seen and slain this Minotaur, and avenged the deaths of the youths and maidens, and put an end to the terrors of my land.'

'And will you kill the Minotaur? How, then?'

'I know not, nor do I care: but he must be strong if he be too strong for me.'

Then she loved him all the more, and said, 'But when you have killed him, how will you find your way out of the labyrinth?'

'I know not, neither do I care; but it must be a strange road, if I do not find it out before I have eaten up the monster's carcase.'

Then she loved him all the more, and said:

'Fair youth, you are too bold; but I can help you, weak as I am. I will give you a sword, and with that perhaps you may slay the beast; and a clue of thread, and by that, perhaps, you may find your way out again. Only promise me that if you escape safe you will take me home with you to Greece; for my father will surely kill me, if he knows what I have done.'

Then Theseus laughed and said, 'Am I not safe enough now?' And he hid the sword in his bosom, and rolled up the clue in his hand; and then he swore to Ariadne, and fell down before her and kissed her hands and her feet; and she wept over him a long while, and then went away; and Theseus lay down and slept sweetly.

★

When the evening came, the guards came in and led him away to the labyrinth.

And he went down into that doleful gulf, through winding paths among the rocks, under caverns, and arches, and galleries, and over heaps of fallen stone. And he turned on the left hand, and on the right hand, and went up and down, till his head was dizzy; but all the while he held his clue. For when he went in he had fastened it to a stone, and left it to unroll out of his hand as he went on; and it lasted him till he met the Minotaur, in a narrow chasm between black cliffs.

And when he saw him he stopped awhile, for he had never seen so strange a beast. His body was a man's; but his head was the head of a bull, and his teeth were the teeth of a lion, and with them he tore his prey. And when he saw Theseus he roared, and put his head down, and rushed right at him.

But Theseus stept aside nimbly, and as he passed by, cut him in the knee; and ere he could turn in the narrow path, he followed him, and stabbed him again and again from behind, till the monster fled bellowing wildly; for he never before had felt a wound. And Theseus followed him at full speed, holding the clue of thread in his left hand.

Then on, through cavern after cavern, under dark ribs of sounding stone, and up rough glens and torrent-beds, among the sunless roots of Ida, and to the edge of the eternal snow, went they, the hunter and the hunted, while the hills bellowed to the monster's bellow.

And at last Theseus came up with him, where he lay panting on a slab among the snows, and caught him by the horns, and forced his head back, and drove the keen sword through his throat.

Then he turned, and went back limping and weary, feeling his way down by the clue of thread till he came to the mouth of that doleful place; and saw waiting for him, whom but Ariadne!

And he whispered, 'It is done!' and showed her the sword; and she laid her finger on her lips and led him to the prison, and opened the doors, and set all the prisoners free, while the guards lay sleeping heavily; for she had silenced them with wine.

Then they fled to their ship together, and leapt on board, and hoisted up the sail; and the night lay dark around them, so that they passed through Minos' ships, and escaped all safe to Naxos; and there Ariadne became Theseus' wife.

But that fair Ariadne never came to Athens with her husband. Some say that Theseus left her sleeping on Naxos among the Cyclades; and that Dionysus the wine-king found her, and took her up into the sky. And some say that Dionysus drove away Theseus, and took Ariadne from him by force; but however that may be, in his haste or in his grief, Theseus forgot to put up the white sail. Now Aegeus his father sat and watched on Sunium day after day, and strained his old eyes across the sea to see the ship afar. And when he saw the black sail, and not the white one, he gave up Theseus for dead, and in his grief he fell into the sea, and died; so it is called the Aegean to this day.

And now Theseus was king of Athens, and he guarded it and ruled it well.

CHARLES KINGSLEY

# It's Spring, It's Spring

It's spring, it's spring —

when everyone sits round a roaring fire
telling ghost stories!

It's spring, it's spring —

when everyone sneaks into everyone else's yard
and bashes up their snowman!

It's spring, it's spring —

when the last dead leaves fall from the trees
and Granny falls off your toboggan!

It's spring, it's spring —

when you'd give your right arm
for a steaming hot bowl of soup!

It's spring, it's spring —

when you'd give your right leg
not to be made to wash up after Christmas dinner!

It's spring, it's spring —

*isn't it?*

KIT WRIGHT
*Illustrated by* POSY SIMMONDS

# A Morning Song
### (For the First Day of Spring)

Morning has broken
Like the first morning,
Blackbird has spoken
   Like the first bird.
Praise for the singing!
Praise for the morning!
Praise for them, springing
   From the first Word.

Sweet the rain's new fall
Sunlit from heaven,
Like the first dewfall
   In the first hour.
Praise for the sweetness
Of the wet garden,
Spring in completeness
   From the first shower.

Mine is the sunlight!
Mine is the morning
Born of the one light
   Eden saw play.
Praise with elation,
Praise every morning
Spring's re-creation
   Of the First Day!

ELEANOR FARJEON

# Tim Rabbit

The wind howled and the rain poured down in torrents. A young rabbit hurried along with his eyes half shut and his head bent as he forced his way against the gale. He tore his trousers on a bramble and left a piece of his coat on a gorse-bush. He bumped his nose and scratched his chin, but he didn't stop to rub himself. He hurried and scurried towards the snug little house on the common, where his mother was making bread.

At last he saw the open door, he smelled the warm smell of baking, and in he rushed without wiping his feet on the little brown doormat.

'What's the matter, Tim?' asked Mrs Rabbit as she shut the oven door. 'Whatever has happened?' She looked anxiously at Tim who lay panting on the floor.

'Something came after me,' cried Tim, breathlessly.

'Something came after you?' echoed Mrs Rabbit. 'What was it like, my son?'

'It was very big and noisy,' replied Tim, with a shiver. 'It ran all round me, and tried to pull the coat off my back, and it snatched at my trousers.' He gave a sob, and his mother stroked his head.

'What did it say?' she asked. 'Did it speak or growl?'

'It called, "Whoo-oo-oo. Whoo-oo-oo. Whoo-oo-oo,"' whimpered the little rabbit.

'That was only the wind, my son,' said Mrs Rabbit, with a laugh. 'Never fear the wind, for he is a friend.' She gave the little rabbit a crust of new bread, and he was comforted.

The next day, when Tim Rabbit was nibbling a morsel of sweet grass under the hedge, the sky darkened, and a hailstorm swept across the sky, with stinging hailstones. They bounced on the small rabbit and frightened him out of his wits. Off he ran, helter-skelter, with his white tail bobbing, and his eyes wide with fear. He lost his pocket handkerchief and left his scarf in a thicket, but he hadn't time to pick them up, he was in such a hurry.

He raced and he tore towards the snug little house on the common, where his mother was tossing pancakes and catching them in her tiny stone frying-pan.

At last he reached the door, and in he raced without stopping to smooth his rough untidy hair.

'What's the matter, Tim?' asked Mrs Rabbit as she put down her frying-pan. 'Whatever is the matter?'

'Something came after me,' exclaimed Tim, hiding behind her skirts.

'Something came after you?' cried Mrs Rabbit. 'What was it like?'

'It was big and dark,' said Tim. 'It threw hard stones at me, and hit my nose and back and ears. It must have a hundred paws, to throw so many stones, and every time it hit me and hurt me.'

'What did it say?' asked Mrs Rabbit, lifting her son from the floor, and straightening his ruffled hair.

'It shouted, "Whissh-ssh-ssh! Whissh-ssh-ssh!"' sobbed the little rabbit.

'That was only a hailstorm, Tim,' explained Mrs Rabbit. 'Never heed a hailstorm, for it clears the air, and makes all fresh for us rabbits.' She gave the little rabbit a curly yellow pancake with some sugar on the top, and he forgot his troubles.

The next day, when Tim was tasting an early primrose, the first he had seen in his short life, he had another fright. A thunderstorm broke out of the sky, with lightning which flashed around him, and peals of roaring thunder which echoed from the hills.

Tim scampered home as fast as his legs could carry him, to the warm little house on the common, where his mother was toasting currant teacakes in front of the wood fire.

At last he came to the door, and the smell of the teacakes made his whiskers twitch. He rushed inside, without stopping to shake the wet from his coat.

'What's the matter, Tim?' cried Mrs Rabbit, as he

stumbled into a chair. She dropped her toasting-fork and leaned over him. 'What's the matter, my son?'

'Something came after me,' whispered Tim, shuddering.

'Something came after you?' echoed his mother. 'What was it like?'

'It was very big and high,' cried Tim. 'It stuck bright swords at me, and flashed lights in my eyes.'

'What did it say?' asked Mrs Rabbit softly.

'It roared "Roo-oo-oo-oo-oo-oo-oo!"' wept the little rabbit.

'That was only a thunderstorm, my son,' replied Mrs Rabbit, soothingly. 'Never mind the thunder and lightning. They never harmed a rabbit yet.' She gave him a large teacake, and he sat by the fire munching it, with his troubles forgotten.

But there came a day when Tim Rabbit sat dozing in a clump of ferns, half asleep, and comfortable. A gust of wind brought a queer scent to his nostrils and he awoke suddenly. He stared round and saw a strange animal bounding towards him with joyous leaps. It wasn't a lamb, nor a foal, nor a calf, nor even a pigling. It looked so playful and danced along so merrily on its four hairy legs that Tim wanted to play Catch and Hide-and-seek.

What a jolly creature it was! How curly was its hair and its long waving tail! It hadn't seen Tim, for the ferns covered him, but he was prepared to run out and meet it. He would have invited it home with him if a storm hadn't suddenly swept down from a dark cloud which hung in the sky.

'Beware! Beware!' howled the wind fiercely, and it blew Tim's fur the wrong way, until he was uncomfortable and cold.

'Shoo! Shoo!' sighed the trees, waving their branches and crackling their twigs at him, like tiny wooden fingers.

'Run! Run!' cried the bushes, snapping and rustling their spiky boughs, with the prickly thorns.

'Be off! Be off!' roared the thunder, banging its drum inside the black cloud.

The lightning flashed and showed him the sharp teeth of the merry dancing animal. The hailstones rattled down and hit foolish Tim's nose, so that he turned and ran, leaving the creature to play by itself in the wet field.

He scuttled towards the safe little house on the common, where his mother was making crab-apple tart. He ran in at the door, and flopped down on the oak bench.

'What's the matter, Tim?' asked his mother, dropping her rolling-pin and scattering the bowl of crab-apples. 'Whatever is the matter, my son?'

'Mother, I saw an animal. It was not a lamb, nor a foal, nor a calf, nor a pigling, but a lovely jumping animal. I was going to play with it, but the wind blew me, and the hailstones hit me, and the thunder scolded me, and they all drove me home.'

'What was it like, my son?' asked Mrs Rabbit, as she wiped the floor, and picked up her crab-apples.

'It was white, with kind eyes, and long ears and shining teeth, Mother, and its paws danced and pattered.'

'What did it say, Tim?' cried Mrs Rabbit, faintly.

'It said, "Bow-wow! Bow-wow!"'

'That was a dog, Tim,' whispered Mrs Rabbit, in a frightened tone. 'Beware of a dog! He would have killed you with his sharp teeth and pattering paws.'

So the little rabbit sat on his stool in the chimney corner, warming his toes by the fire, whilst he learned his first lesson:

> *'Crouch among the heather,*
> *Never mind the weather,*
> *Forget it altogether.*
> *Run from a dog, a man, and a gun,*
> *Or your happy young life will soon be undone.'*

ALISON UTTLEY

*Illustrated by* MARGARET GORDON

# Written in March

> The cock is crowing,
> The stream is flowing,
> Small birds twitter,
> The lake doth glitter,
> The green fields sleep in the sun;
> The oldest and youngest
> Are at work with the strongest;
> The cattle are grazing,
> Their heads never raising;
> There are forty feeding like one!

Like an army defeated
The snow hath retreated,
And now doth fare ill
On the top of the bare hill;
The ploughboy is whooping – anon – anon:
There's joy in the mountains;
There's life in the fountains;
Small clouds are sailing,
Blue sky prevailing;
The rain is over and gone!

WILLIAM WORDSWORTH

361

# Spells

I dance and dance without any feet –
This is the spell of the ripening wheat.

With never a tongue I've a tale to tell –
This is the meadow-grasses' spell.

I give you health without any fee –
This is the spell of the apple tree.

I rhyme and riddle without any book –
This is the spell of the bubbling brook.

Without any legs I run for ever –
This is the spell of the mighty river.

I fall for ever and not at all –
This is the spell of the waterfall.

Without a voice I roar aloud –
This is the spell of the thunder-cloud.

No button or seam has my white coat –
This is the spell of the leaping goat.

I can cheat strangers with never a word –
This is the spell of the cuckoo-bird.

SPELLS

We have tongues in plenty but speak no names –
This is the spell of the fiery flames.

The creaking door has a spell to riddle –
I play a tune without any fiddle.

JAMES REEVES


# Old Shellover

'Come!' said Old Shellover.
'What?' says Creep.
'The horny old Gardener's fast asleep;
The fat cock Thrush
To his nest has gone,
And the dew shines bright
In the rising Moon;
Old Sallie Worm from her hole doth peep;
Come!' said old Shellover.
'Ay!' said Creep.

WALTER DE LA MARE

# Guess

That last day of October a freak storm hit the suburb of Woodley Park. Slates rattled off roofs, dustbins chased dustbin lids along the streets, hoardings were slammed down, and at midnight there was a huge sound like a giant breaking his kindling wood, and then an almighty crash, and then briefly the sound of the same giant crunching his toast.

Then only the wind, which died surprisingly soon.

In the morning everyone could see that the last forest tree of Grove Road – of the whole suburb – had fallen, crashing down on to Grove Road Primary School. No lives had been lost, since the caretaker did not live on the premises; but the school hamster had later to be treated for shock. The school buildings were wrecked.

Everyone went to stare, especially, of course, the children of the school. They included Netty and Sid Barr.

The fallen tree was an awesome sight, partly because of its size and partly because of its evident great age. Someone in the crowd said that the acorn that grew into *that* must have been planted centuries ago.

As well as the confusion of fallen timber on the road and on the school premises, there was an extraordinary spatter of school every where: slates off the roof, bricks from the broken walls, glass from the windows, and the contents of classrooms, cloakrooms and storerooms – books and collages and clay and paints and nature tables and a queer mixture of clothing, both dingy and weird, which meant that the contents of the Lost Property cupboard and the dressing-up cupboard had been whirled together and tossed outside. Any passer-by could have taken his pick, free of charge. Netty Barr, who had been meaning to claim her gym-shoes from Lost Property, decided that they had gone for good now. This was like the end of the world – a school world.

Council workmen arrived with gear to cut, saw and haul timber. Fat old Mr Brown from the end of the Barrs' road told the foreman that they ought to have taken the tree down long ago. Perhaps he was right. In spite of last season's leaves and next year's buds, the trunk of the tree was quite hollow: a cross-section revealed a rim of wood the width of a man's hand, encircling a space large enough for a child or a smallish adult. As soon as the workmen's backs were turned, Sid Barr crept in. He then managed to get stuck and had to be pulled out by Netty. An untidy young woman nearby was convulsed with silent laughter at the incident.

'You didn't stay inside for a hundred years,' she said to Sid.

'That smelt funny,' said Sid. 'Rotty.' Netty banged his clothes for him: the smell clung.

'Remember that day last summer, Net? After the picnic? When I got stuck inside that great old tree in Epping Forest?' Sid liked to recall near-disasters.

'Epping Forest?' said the young woman, sharply interested. But no one else was.

Meanwhile the headmaster had arrived, and that meant all fun was over. School would go on, after all, even if not

in these school buildings for the time being. The pupils of
Grove Road were marshalled and then sent off in groups
to various other schools in the neighbourhood. Netty and
Sid Barr, with others, went to Stokeside School: Netty in
the top class, Sid in a lower one.

There was a good deal of upheaval in Netty's new classroom before everyone had somewhere to sit. Netty was the
next-to-last to find a place; the last was a thin, pale girl
who chose to sit next to Netty. Netty assumed that she
was a Stokesider; yet there was something familiar about
her, too. Perhaps she'd just seen her about. The girl had
dark, lank hair gathered into a pony-tail of sorts, and a
pale pointed face with greyish-green eyes. She wore a dingy
green dress that looked ready for a jumble sale, and gym-
shoes.

Netty studied her sideways. At last, 'You been at Stokeside
long?' Netty asked.

The other girl shook her head and glanced at the teacher,
who was talking. She didn't seem to want to talk; but Netty
did.

'A tree fell on our school,' whispered Netty. The other
girl laughed silently, although Netty could see nothing to
laugh about. She did see something, however: this girl bore
a striking resemblance to the young woman who had
watched Sid being pulled from the hollow tree-trunk. The
silent laughter clinched the resemblance.

Of course, this girl was much, much younger. Of course.

'How old are you?' whispered Netty.

The girl said a monosyllable, still looking amused.

'What did you say?'

Clearly now: 'Guess.'

Netty was furious: 'I'm just eleven,' she said coldly.

'So am I,' said the other girl.

Netty felt tempted to say 'Liar'; but instead she asked, 'Have you an elder sister?'

'No.'

'What's your name?'

Again that irritating monosyllable. Netty refused to acknowledge it. 'Did you say Jess?' she asked.

'Yes. Jess.'

In spite of what she felt, Netty decided not to argue about that Jess, but went on: 'Jess what?'

The girl looked blank.

'I'm Netty Barr: you're Jess Something – Jess what?'

This time they were getting somewhere: after a tiny hesitation, the girl said, 'Oakes'.

'Jess Oakes. Jessy Oakes.' But whichever way you said it, Netty decided, it didn't sound quite right; and that was because Jess Oakes herself didn't seem quite right. Netty wished now that she weren't sitting next to her.

At playtime Netty went out into the playground; Jess Oakes followed her closely. Netty didn't like that. Unmistakably, Jess Oakes wanted to stick with her. Why? She hadn't wanted to answer Netty's questions; she hadn't been really friendly. But she clung to Netty. Netty didn't like it – didn't like *her*.

Netty managed to shake Jess Oakes off, but then saw her talking with Sid on the other side of the playground. That made her uneasy. But Jess Oakes did not reappear in the classroom after playtime: Netty felt relieved, although she wondered. The teacher made no remark.

Netty went cheerfully home to tea, a little after Sid.

And there was Jess Oakes sitting with Sid in front of the television set. Netty went into the kitchen, to her mother.

'Here you are,' said Mrs Barr. 'You can take all the teas in.' She was loading a tray.

'When did *she* come?' asked Netty.

'With Sid. Sid said she was your friend.' Netty said nothing. 'She's a lot older than you are, Netty.'

'She's exactly my age. So she says.'

'Well, I suppose with that face and that figure – or that no-figure – she could be any age. Any age.'

'Yes.'

Mrs Barr looked thoughtfully at Netty, put down the breadknife she still held, and with decision set her hands on her hips: 'Netty!'

'Yes?'

'I don't care what age she is, I like your friends better washed than that.'

Netty gaped at her mother.

'She smells,' said Mrs Barr. 'I don't say it's unwashed body, I don't say it's unwashed clothes – although I don't think much of hers. All I know is she smells nasty.'

'Rotty,' said Netty under her breath.

'Don't bring her again,' said Mrs Barr crisply.

Netty took the tea-tray in to the other two. In the semi-dark they all munched and sipped while they watched the TV serial. But Netty was watching Jess Oakes: the girl only seemed to munch and sip; she ate nothing, drank nothing.

A friend called for Sid, and he went out. Mrs Barr looked in to ask if the girls wanted more tea; Netty said no. When her mother had gone, Netty turned off the television and switched on the light. She faced Jess Oakes: 'What do you want?'

The girl's green glance slid away from Netty. 'No harm. To know something.'

'What?'

'The way home.'

Netty did not ask where she had been living, or why she was lost, or any other commonsense questions. They weren't the right questions, she knew. She just said savagely: 'I wish I knew what was going on inside your head, Jess Oakes.'

Jess Oakes laughed almost aloud, as though Netty had said something really amusing. She reached out her hand and touched Netty, for the first time: her touch was cool, damp. 'You shall,' she said. 'You shall.'

And where was Netty now? If she were asleep and dreaming, the falling asleep had been very sudden, at the merest touch of a cool, damp hand. But certainly Netty must be dreaming . . .

She dreamt that she was in a strange room filled with a greenish light that seemed partly to come in through two windows, of curious shape, set together rather low down at one side. The walls and ceilings of this chamber were continuous, as in a dome; all curved. There was nothing inside the dome-shaped chamber except the greenish light, of a curious intensity; and Netty. For some reason Netty wanted to look out of the two windows, but she knew that before she could do that, something was required of her. In her dreaming state, she was not at first sure what this was, except that it was tall – very tall – and green. Of course, green: green in spring and summer, and softly singing to itself with leaves; in autumn, yellow and brown and red, and its leaves falling. In winter, leafless. A tree, a forest tree, a tree of the Forest, a tree of Epping Forest. A tree – a hundred trees − a thousand trees − a choice of all the trees of Epping Forest. She had been to the Forest; she was older than Sid, and therefore she knew the direction in which the Forest lay, the direction in which one would have to go to reach the Forest. Her knowledge of the Forest and its whereabouts was in the green-glowing room, and it passed from her in that room, and became someone else's knowledge too ...

Now Netty knew that she was free to look out of the windows of the room. Their frames were curiously curved; there was not glass in them, but some other greenish-grey substance. She approached the windows; she looked through them; and she saw into the Barrs' sitting-room, and she saw Netty Barr sitting in her chair by the television set, huddled in sudden sleep.

She saw herself apart from herself, and she cried out in terror, so that she woke, and she was sitting in her chair, and the girl who called herself Jess Oakes was staring at her with her grey-green eyes, smiling.

'Thank you,' said Jess Oakes. 'Now I know all I need to know.' She got up, unmistakably to go. 'Goodbye.'

She went out of the sitting-room, leaving the door open; Netty heard her go out of the front door, leaving that open too. The doors began to bang in a wind that had risen. The front gate banged as well.

Mrs Barr came crossly out of the kitchen to complain. She saw that Netty was alone in the sitting-room. 'Has she gone, then?'

Netty nodded, dumb.

They went into the hall together. Scattered along the hall were pieces of clothing: one gym-shoe by the sitting-room

370

door, another by the coat-hooks; a dingy green dress, looking like something out of a dressing-up box, by the open
front door . . .

Mrs Barr ran to the front gate and looked up and down
the road. No one; just old Mr Brown on the lookout, as
usual. Mrs Barr called to him: 'Have you seen anyone?'

'No. Who should I have seen?'

Mrs Barr came back, shaken. 'She can't have gone stark
naked,' she said. Then, as an afterthought, 'She can't have
gone, anyway.' Then, again, 'But she has gone.'

Netty was looking at the gym-shoes in the hall. She could
see inside one of them; and she could see a name printed
there. It would not be JESS OAKES; it would be some other
name. Now she would find out the true identity of the girl
with the greenish eyes. She stooped, picked up the shoe,
read the name: NETTY BARR.

'Those are the gym-shoes you lost at school,' said Mrs
Barr. 'How did she get hold of them? Why was she wearing
them? What kind of a girl or a woman was she, with that
smell on her? Where did she come from? And where's she
gone? Netty, you bad girl, what kind of a friend was she?'

'She wasn't my friend,' said Netty.

'What was she then? And where's she gone – *where's she
gone*?'

'I don't know,' said Netty. 'But guess.'

PHILIPPA PEARCE

# The Wind in a Frolic

The wind one morning sprang up from sleep,
Saying, 'Now for a frolic! now for a leap!
Now for a madcap galloping chase!
I'll make a commotion in every place!'

So it swept with a bustle right through a great town,
Cracking the signs and scattering down
Shutters; and whisking with merciless squalls,
Old women's bonnets and gingerbread stalls.

There never was heard a much lustier shout,
As the apples and oranges trundled about;
And the urchins that stand, with their thievish eyes
For ever on watch, ran off each with a prize.

Then away to the fields it went blustering and humming,
And the cattle all wondered what monster was coming.
It plucked by the tails the grave matronly cows,
And tossed the colts' manes all over their brows;
Till, offended at such an unusual salute,
They all turned their backs and stood sulky and mute.

So on it went, capering and playing its pranks –
Whistling with reeds on the broad river's banks,
Puffing the birds as they sat on the spray,
Or the traveller grave on the King's highway.
It was not too nice to hustle the bags
Of the beggar, and flutter his dirty rags;
'Twas so bold that it feared not to play its joke
With the doctor's wig or the gentleman's cloak.

Through the forest it roared, and cried gaily, 'Now,
You sturdy old oaks, I'll make you bow!'
And it made them bow without more ado,
For it cracked their great branches through and through.

Then it rushed like a monster on cottage and farm,
Striking their dwellers with sudden alarm;
And they ran out like bees in a mid-summer swarm:
There were dames with their kerchiefs tied over their caps,
To see if their poultry were free from mishaps;
The turkeys they gobbled, the geese screamed aloud,
And the hens crept to roost in a terrified crowd;
There was rearing of ladders, and logs were laid on,
Where the thatch from the roof threatened soon to be gone.

But the wind had swept on, and had met in a lane
With a schoolboy, who panted and struggled in vain;
For it tossed him and twirled him, then passed – and he stood
With his hat in a pool, and his shoes in the mud!

Then away went the wind in its holiday glee,
And now it was far on the billowy sea:
And the lordly ships felt its staggering blow,
And the little boats darted to and fro.

But, lo! it was night, and it sank to rest
On the sea-bird's rock in the gleaming west,
Laughing to think, in its frolicsome fun,
How little of mischief it really had done.

WILLIAM HOWITT
*Illustrated by* PEGGY FORTNUM

# Three Raindrops

A raindrop was falling out of a cloud, and it said to the raindrop next to it: 'I'm the biggest and best raindrop in the whole sky!'

'You are indeed a fine raindrop,' said the second, 'but you are not nearly so beautifully shaped as I am. And in my opinion it's shape that counts, and *I* am therefore the best raindrop in the whole sky.'

The first raindrop replied: 'Let us settle this matter once and for all.' So they asked a third raindrop to decide between them.

But the third raindrop said: 'What nonsense you're both talking! *You* may be a big raindrop, and *you* are certainly well shaped, but, as everybody knows, it's purity that really counts, and I am purer than either of you. *I* am therefore the best raindrop in the whole sky!'

Well, before either of the other raindrops could reply, they all three hit the ground and became part of a very muddy puddle.

TERRY JONES

# Index of Titles

Adventures of Isabel, The, 138
Alarm Cock, The, 115
Bad Report – Good Manners, 202
'Betty Botter bought some butter', 339
Big Sister and Little Sister, 103
Blind Alley, 163
Boredom, 154
Calico Pie, 265
Camel, The, 292
Cat That Walked by Himself, The, 323
Constant Tin Soldier, The, 32
Coronation Mob, The, 165
Cow, The, 291
Cows, 321
Crocodile, The, 301
Daddy Fell into the Pond, 184
Dark House, The, 163
Dear Bren, 231
'Did you ever see a lassie', 24
Dinner Lady Who Made Magic, The, 219
Dutch Cheese, The, 253
Fairies, The, 262
First Day at School, 201
Fishy Tale, A, 176
'Five little monkeys walked along the shore', 100
Fool of the World and the Flying Ship, The, 186
'Four stiff-standers', 151
Freddie, the Toothbrush Cheat, 246
From a Railway Carriage, 107
'From Wibbleton to Wobbleton', 88
Giacco and His Bean, 108
Golden Touch, The, 63
Granny, 149
Growing, 86
Growing Tale, A, 84
Gruesome, 87

Guess, 364
Hare and Tortoise, 293
Hero of Haarlem, The, 39
Horrible Story, The, 130
I Had a Hippopotamus, 306
I Saw a Jolly Hunter, 152
If All the Seas, 278
'If you don't put your shoes on . . .' 212
If You Should Meet a Crocodile, 302
It's Spring, It's Spring, 352
'Jelly on a plate', 141
Johnny Crow's Garden, 308
Juba: A Chant, 200
Jumblies, The, 44
'Last one into bed', 127
Lazy Tok, 17
'Little Arabella Miller', 140
Little Fan, 22
Little Girl Who Got Out of Bed the Wrong Side, The, 112
Monkey and the Crocodile, The, 297
Morning Song, A, 354
'Moses supposes his toeses are roses', 38
Mrs Simkin's Bathtub, 48
My Sister Jane, 28
Nicholas Nye, 319
Night, 137
'Now I'll tell you a story', 99
'Old Mother Twitchett', 149
'Old Roger is dead', 101
Old Shellover, 363
Old Woman and Her Pig, The, 80
'One finger, one thumb, keep moving', 303
Owl and the Pussy-cat, The, 251
Parrot Pirate Princess, The, 279
Paul's Tale, 89
'Peter hammers with one hammer', 304

'Peter Piper picked a peck of pickled pepper', 338
Pig Tale, 83
'Piggy on the Railway', 106
Pooh and Piglet Go Hunting, 312
Praying Lion, 337
Questions, 62
Rat Princess, The, 25
Row, Row, Row Your Boat, 153
Send Three and Fourpence We are Going to a Dance, 203
'She sells sea-shells on the sea shore', 43
Silver Fish, The, 183
Small Brown Mouse, The, 53
Snake in the Grass, 236
Snooks Family, The, 125
Spells, 362
Story of Giant Kippernose, The, 71
Teeny-weeny Tale, A, 161
'There were ten in the bed', 114

Theseus and the Minotaur, 345
Thought, A, 102
Three Raindrops, 375
Tikki, Tikki, Tembo, 340
Tim Rabbit, 355
Turtle Soup, 230
'Two legs sat upon three legs', 150
Two Octopuses, 303
Uninvited Ghosts, 155
Us Two, 317
W, 336
Well Bread, 185
Well of the World's End, The, 268
What Did You Put in Your Pocket?, 214
Where Arthur Sleeps, 142
Wind in a Frolic, The, 372
Witches' Call, The, 276
Written in March, 360
Yellow Ribbon, The, 30
You Tell Me, 245

# Index of Authors

AESOP
Hare and Tortoise, 293
AIKEN, Joan
The Alarm Cock, 115
The Parrot Pirate Princess, 279
AINSWORTH, Ruth
The Little Girl Who Got Out of Bed the
Wrong Side, 112
ALLEN, Linda
Mrs Simkin's Bathtub, 48
ALLINGHAM, William
The Fairies, 262
ANDERSEN, Hans
The Constant Tin Soldier, 32
ASHLEY, Bernard
Dear Bren, 231
BARRINGTON, Patrick
I Had a Hippopotamus, 306
BLAKE, William
Night, 137
BOTSFORD, Florence
Giacco and His Bean, 108
BROOKE, L. Leslie
Johnny Crow's Garden, 308
CARROLL, Lewis
The Crocodile, 301
Turtle Soup, 230
CAUSLEY, Charles
I Saw a Jolly Hunter, 152
CHAMBERS, Aidan
Pig Tale, 83
Praying Lion, 337
CHARLIP, Remy
Two Octopuses, 303
CRAIG, Wendy
Freddie, the Toothbrush Cheat, 246
CRESSWELL, Helen
Snake in the Grass, 236

CUNLIFFE, John
The Story of Giant Kippernose, 71
DE LA MARE, Walter
The Dutch Cheese, 253
Nicholas Nye, 319
Old Shellover, 363
DODGE, Mary Mapes
The Hero of Haarlem, 39
EDWARDS, Dorothy
The Dinner Lady Who Made Magic, 219
FARJEON, Eleanor
Blind Alley, 163
Boredom, 154
A Morning Song, 354
FATCHEN, Max
Growing, 86
GALDONE, Paul
The Monkey and the Crocodile, 297
HOWITT, William
The Wind in a Frolic, 372
HUGHES, Ted
My Sister Jane, 28
JONES, Gwyn
Where Arthur Sleeps, 142
JONES, Terry
Three Raindrops, 375
KEMP, Gene
A Fishy Tale, 176
KINGSLEY, Charles
Theseus and the Minotaur, 345
KIPLING, Rudyard
The Cat That Walked by Himself, 323
LEACH, Maria
The Yellow Ribbon, 30
LEAR, Edward
Calico Pie, 265
The Jumblies, 44
The Owl and the Pussy-cat, 251

# INDEX OF AUTHORS

LIVELY, Penelope
  Uninvited Ghosts, 155
MCGOUGH, Roger
  First Day at School, 201
  Gruesome, 87
MCNEILL, Janet
  The Small Brown Mouse, 53
MAHY, Margaret
  The Horrible Story, 130
MARK, Jan
  The Coronation Mob, 165
  Send Three and Fourpence We are
    Going to a Dance, 203
MILLIGAN, Spike
  Bad Report – Good Manners, 202
  Granny, 149
  Well Bread, 185
MILNE, A. A.
  Pooh and Piglet Go Hunting, 312
  A Thought, 102
  Us Two, 317
MONTGOMERIE, Norah
  A Growing Tale, 84
  The Rat Princess, 25
  A Teeny-weeny Tale, 161
MOSEL, Arlene
  Tikki Tikki Tembo, 340
NASH, Ogden
  The Adventures of Isabel, 138
  The Camel, 292
  The Cow, 291
NORTON, Mary
  Paul's Tale, 89
NOYES, Alfred
  Daddy Fell into the Pond, 184
PEARCE, Philippa
  Guess, 364

RANSOME, Arthur
  The Fool of the World and the Flying
    Ship, 186
REEVES, James
  Cows, 321
  Little Fan, 22
  Spells, 362
  W, 336
  The Well of the World's End, 268
ROSEN, Michael
  'If you don't put your shoes on . . .', 212
  'Last one into bed', 127
  You Tell Me, 245
SANSOM, Clive
  The Witches' Call, 276
SCHENK DE REGNIERS, Beatrice
  What Did You Put in Your Pocket?, 214
SILVERSTEIN, Shel
  The Silver Fish, 183
SKIPPER, Mervyn
  Lazy Tok, 17
STEVENSON, Robert Louis
  From a Railway Carriage, 107
UTTLEY, Alison
  Tim Rabbit, 355
WILLIAMS, Harcourt
  The Snooks Family, 125
WILSON, Raymond
  Questions, 62
WORDSWORTH, William
  Written in March, 360
WRIGHT, Kit
  It's Spring, It's Spring, 352
WYATT, Honor
  The Golden Touch, 63
ZOLOTOW, Charlotte
  Big Sister and Little Sister, 103

# Index of First Lines of Verse

A millionbillionwillion miles from home, 201

And I say nothing – no, not a word, 28

Beautiful soup, so rich and green, 230

Betty Botter bought some butter, 339

Calico Pie, 265

'Come!' said Old Shellover, 363

Come, witches, come, on your hithering brooms!, 276

Did you ever see a lassie, 24

Everyone grumbled. The sky was grey, 184

Faster than fairies, faster than witches, 107

Five little monkeys walked along the shore, 100

Four stiff-standers, 151

From Wibbleton to Wobbleton is fifteen miles, 88

Half the time they munched the grass, and all the time they lay, 321

Here are the football results, 245

How doth the little crocodile, 301

I dance and dance without any feet, 362

'I don't like the look of little Fan, mother, 22

I had a hippopotamus; I kept him in a shed, 306

I often wonder, why, oh why, 62

I saw a jolly hunter, 152

I was sitting in the sitting room, 87

If all the seas were one sea, 278

If I were John and John were Me, 102

If you cast your bread on the waters, 185

If you don't put your shoes on before I count fifteen, 212

If you should meet a crocodile, 302

In a dark, dark wood, there was a dark, dark house, 163

Isabel met an enormous bear, 138

It's spring, it's spring, 352

Jelly on a plate, 141

Johnny Crow, 308

Juba this and juba that, 200

'Last one into bed, 127

Little Arabella Miller, 140

Morning has broken, 354

Moses supposes his toeses are roses, 38

My daddy said, 'My son, my son, 202

Now I'll tell you a story, and this story is new, 99

Oh dear! What shall I do?, 154

Old Mother Twitchett has but one eye, 149

Old Roger is dead and he lies in his grave, 101

One finger, one thumb, keep moving, 303

Peter hammers with one hammer, 304

Peter Piper picked a peck of pickled pepper, 338

Piggy on the railway, 106

Row, row, row your boat, 153

She sells sea-shells on the sea shore, 43

The camel has a single hump, 292

The cock is crowing, 360

The cow is of the bovine ilk, 291

The King sent for his wise men all, 336

The Owl and the Pussy-cat went to sea, 251

The sun descending in the west, 137

The wind one morning sprang up from sleep, 372

There were ten in the bed, 114

There's a turning I must pass, 163

They went to sea in a Sieve, they did, 44

Thistle and darnel and dock grew there, 319

Through every nook and every cranny, 149

Two legs sat upon three legs, 150

Up the airy mountain, 262

What did you put in your pocket, 214

When I grow up I'll be so kind, 86

Wherever I am, there's always Pooh, 317

While fishing in the blue lagoon, 183

# Index of Artists

Ambrus, Victor, 184

Ardizzone, Edward, 22

Bennett, Jill, 224, 227

Blake, Quentin, 138, 291, 292

Briggs, Raymond, 88, 106, 149, 150, 151, 338

Brooke, L. Leslie, 308, 310

Dyke, John, 28

Foreman, Michael, 128

Fortnum, Peggy, 372, 373

Gordon, Margaret, 355

Hughes, Shirley, 133

Hunter, Susan, 280, 288

Jaques, Faith, 56

Julian-Ottie, Vanessa, 3, 27, 38, 41, 43, 68, 80, 83, 84, 94, 97, 105, 107, 110, 112, 141, 147, 157, 159, 161, 164, 179, 180, 189, 191, 200, 231, 248, 255, 262, 263, 264, 271, 275, 276, 277, 299, 301, 302, 305, 306, 319, 321, 342, 350, 361

Kilroy, Sally, 24

Kipling, Rudyard, 327

Lear, Edward, 44, 251, 252, 265, 266, 267

McKee, David, 216

McNaughton, Colin, 20

Maitland, Antony, 35

Ormerod, Jan, 239

Parkins, David, 174, 203

Pieńkowski, Jan, 118, 124

Shepard, E. H., 314

Thompson, Ross, 29

Simmonds, Posy, 353

Wegner, Fritz, 71, 75, 78

# The Stories and Poems Classified

The following classified list has been included as a help to parents, teachers and librarians

## STORIES FOR THE YOUNGEST READERS

LAZY TOK by Mervyn Skipper    17

THE RAT PRINCESS by Norah Montgomerie    25

THE OLD WOMAN AND HER PIG    80

A GROWING TALE by Norah Montgomerie    84

BIG SISTER AND LITTLE SISTER by Charlotte Zolotow    103

GIACCO AND HIS BEAN by Florence Botsford    108

THE LITTLE GIRL WHO GOT OUT OF BED THE WRONG SIDE by Ruth Ainsworth    112

THE SNOOKS FAMILY by Harcourt Williams    125

TIKKI TIKKI TEMBO by Arlene Mosel    340

TIM RABBIT by Alison Uttley    355

## FOLKTALES (Traditional and Modern)

LAZY TOK (Borneo) by Mervyn Skipper    17

THE RAT PRINCESS (China) by Norah Montgomerie    25

THE CONSTANT TIN SOLDIER by Hans Andersen    32

THE STORY OF GIANT KIPPERNOSE by John Cunliffe    71

THE OLD WOMAN AND HER PIG    80

GIACCO AND HIS BEAN (Italy) by Florence Botsford    108

THE ALARM COCK by Joan Aiken    115

THE FOOL OF THE WORLD AND THE FLYING SHIP (Russia) by Arthur Ransome    186

THE DUTCH CHEESE by Walter de la Mare    253

# THE STORIES AND POEMS CLASSIFIED

THE WELL OF THE WORLD'S END by James Reeves 268

THE PARROT PIRATE PRINCESS by Joan Aiken 279

THE MONKEY AND THE CROCODILE (*India*) by Paul Galdone 297

TIKKI TIKKI TEMBO (*China*) by Arlene Mosel 340

THREE RAINDROPS by Terry Jones 375

## FABLES AND ANIMAL STORIES

THE SMALL BROWN MOUSE by Janet McNeill 53

PIG TALE retold by Aidan Chambers 83

HARE AND TORTOISE by Aesop 293

THE MONKEY AND THE CROCODILE by Paul Galdone 297

TWO OCTOPUSES by Remy Charlip 303

POOH AND PIGLET GO HUNTING by A. A. Milne 312

THE CAT THAT WALKED BY HIMSELF by Rudyard Kipling 323

PRAYING LION by Aidan Chambers 337

TIM RABBIT by Alison Uttley 355

## MYTHS AND LEGENDS

THE HERO OF HAARLEM (*Dutch*) by Mary Mapes Dodge 39

THE GOLDEN TOUCH (*Greek*) by Honor Wyatt 63

WHERE ARTHUR SLEEPS (*Welsh*) by Gwyn Jones 142

THESEUS AND THE MINOTAUR (*Greek*) by Charles Kingsley 345

## STORIES OF THE SUPERNATURAL

THE YELLOW RIBBON by Maria Leach 30

MRS SIMKIN'S BATHTUB by Linda Allen 48

UNINVITED GHOSTS by Penelope Lively 155

A TEENY-WEENY TALE by Norah Montgomerie 161

THE DARK HOUSE 163

GUESS by Philippa Pearce 364

## CONTEMPORARY STORIES

A GROWING TALE by Norah Montgomerie 84

PAUL'S TALE by Mary Norton 89

BIG SISTER AND LITTLE SISTER by Charlotte Zolotow 103

THE LITTLE GIRL WHO GOT OUT OF BED ON THE WRONG SIDE by Ruth
Ainsworth 112

# THE STORIES AND POEMS CLASSIFIED

THE HORRIBLE STORY by Margaret Mahy 130

THE CORONATION MOB by Jan Mark 165

A FISHY TALE told to Gene Kemp by John Sweet 176

SEND THREE AND FOURPENCE WE ARE GOING TO A DANCE by Jan
Mark 203

THE DINNER LADY WHO MADE MAGIC by Dorothy Edwards 219

DEAR BREN by Bernard Ashley 231

SNAKE IN THE GRASS by Helen Cresswell 236

FREDDIE, THE TOOTHBRUSH CHEAT by Wendy Craig 246

## POEMS

LITTLE FAN by James Reeves 22

MY SISTER JANE by Ted Hughes 28

QUESTIONS by Raymond Wilson 62

GROWING by Max Fatchen 86

GRUESOME by Roger McGough 87

A THOUGHT by A. A. Milne 102

FROM A RAILWAY CARRIAGE by R. L. Stevenson 107

LAST ONE INTO BED by Michael Rosen 127

NIGHT by William Blake 137

THE ADVENTURES OF ISABEL by Ogden Nash 138

BOREDOM by Eleanor Farjeon 154

BLIND ALLEY by Eleanor Farjeon 163

THE SILVER FISH by Shel Silverstein 183

DADDY FELL INTO THE POND by Alfred Noyes 184

FIRST DAY AT SCHOOL by Roger McGough 201

'IF YOU DON'T PUT YOUR SHOES ON ...' by Michael Rosen 212

YOU TELL ME by Michael Rosen 245

THE FAIRIES by William Allingham 262

THE WITCHES' CALL by Clive Sansom 276

I HAD A HIPPOPOTAMUS by Patrick Barrington 306

US TWO by A. A. Milne 317

NICHOLAS NYE by Walter de la Mare 319

COWS by James Reeves 321

W by James Reeves 336

IT'S SPRING, IT'S SPRING by Kit Wright 352

WRITTEN IN MARCH by William Wordsworth 360

# THE STORIES AND POEMS CLASSIFIED

SPELLS by James Reeves                                    362

OLD SHELLOVER by Walter de la Mare                        363

THE WIND IN A FROLIC by William Howitt                    372


## NONSENSE POEMS

THE JUMBLIES by Edward Lear                                44

GRANNY by Spike Milligan                                  149

I SAW A JOLLY HUNTER by Charles Causley                   152

WELL BREAD by Spike Milligan                              185

BAD REPORT — GOOD MANNERS by Spike Milligan               202

TURTLE SOUP by Lewis Carroll                              230

THE OWL AND THE PUSSY-CAT by Edward Lear                  251

CALICO PIE by Edward Lear                                 265

IF ALL THE SEAS                                           278

THE COW by Ogden Nash                                     291

THE CAMEL by Ogden Nash                                   292

THE CROCODILE by Lewis Carroll                            301

JOHNNY CROW'S GARDEN by L. Leslie Brooke                  308


## TONGUE TWISTERS

'MOSES SUPPOSES HIS TOESES ARE ROSES'                      38

'SHE SELLS SEA-SHELLS ON THE SEA SHORE'                    43

'FROM WIBBLETON TO WOBBLETON'                              88

'PETER PIPER PICKED A PECK OF PICKLED PEPPER'             338

'BETTY BOTTER BOUGHT SOME BUTTER'                         339


## RIDDLES

'OLD MOTHER TWITCHETT'                                    149

'TWO LEGS SAT UPON THREE LEGS'                            150

'FOUR STIFF-STANDERS'                                     151


## FINGER RHYMES

'NOW I'LL TELL YOU A STORY'                                99

'FIVE LITTLE MONKEYS WALKED ALONG THE SHORE'             100

'PIGGY ON THE RAILWAY'                                    106

'THERE WERE TEN IN THE BED' (with music)                 114

# THE STORIES AND POEMS CLASSIFIED

'LITTLE ARABELLA MILLER' (with music)                                    140
IF YOU SHOULD MEET A CROCODILE                                           302

## ACTION RHYMES

THE SNOOKS FAMILY by Harcourt Williams                                   125
'JELLY ON A PLATE'                                                        141
ROW, ROW, ROW YOUR BOAT (with music)                                     153
JUBA: A CHANT                                                            200
WHAT DID YOU PUT IN YOUR POCKET? by Beatrice Schenk de
    Regniers                                                            214
'ONE FINGER, ONE THUMB, KEEP MOVING' (with music)                       303
PETER HAMMERS WITH ONE HAMMER (with music)                              304

## SONGS AND CHANTS

'DID YOU EVER SEE A LASSIE' (with music)                                  24
'OLD ROGER IS DEAD' (with music)                                         101
THE DARK HOUSE                                                           163
A MORNING SONG by Eleanor Farjeon                                        354

# Acknowledgements

The editor and publishers gratefully acknowledge permission to reproduce copyright material in this book.

'The Alarm Cock' by Joan Aiken from *Tale of a One-Way Street* and 'The Parrot Pirate Princess' by Joan Aiken from *All and More*, reprinted by permission of Jonathan Cape Ltd; 'The Little Girl Who Got Out of Bed' by Ruth Ainsworth from *Three Bags Full*, reprinted by permission of William Heinemann Ltd; 'Mrs Simkin's Bathtub' by Linda Allen from *All the Year Round*, reprinted by permission of the author; illustration by Victor Ambrus for 'Daddy Fell into the Pond' from *Rhyme and Rhythm Blue Book* compiled by J. Gibson and R. Wilson, reproduced by permission of Macmillan, London and Basingstoke; illustration for 'Little Fan' by Edward Ardizzone, reproduced by permission of the Estate of Edward Ardizzone; 'Dear Bren' by Bernard Ashley from *I'm Trying to Tell You* (Kestrel Books) reprinted by permission of Penguin Books Ltd; 'I Had a Hippopotamus' by Patrick Barrington, published in *Punch*; illustrations by Jill Bennett for 'The Dinner Lady Who Made Magic' reproduced by permission of Jill Bennett; illustrations by Quentin Blake for 'The Adventures of Isabel', 'The Cow' and 'The Camel' © Quentin Blake 1979 from *Custard and Company*, reproduced by permission of Quentin Blake; Giacco and his Bean by Florence Botsford from *Picture Tales from the Italian*, reprinted by permission of J. B. Lippincott & Co; illustrations by Raymond Briggs for 'From Wibbleton', 'Old Mother Twitchett', 'Two legs sat upon three legs', 'Four stiff-standers' and 'Peter Piper' from the *Mother Goose Treasure*, reproduced by permission of Raymond Briggs and Hamish Hamilton Ltd; illustration by Raymond Briggs for 'Piggy on the Railway' from *This Little Puffin*, reproduced by permission of Penguin Books Ltd; 'Johnny Crow's Garden' by L. Leslie Brooke reprinted by permission of the Estate of L. Leslie Brooke and Frederick Warne Ltd; 'I Saw a Jolly Hunter' by Charles Causley from *Figgie Hobbin*, reprinted by permission of David Higham Ltd; 'Pig Tale' and 'Praying Lion' retold by Aidan Chambers in *Funny Folk: A Book of Comic Tales*, reprinted by permission of William Heinemann Ltd; 'Two Octopuses' from *Arm in Arm*, reprinted by permission of Remy Charlip; 'Freddie, the Toothbrush Cheat' by Wendy Craig from *Happy Endings*, reprinted by permission of Hutchinson Books Ltd; 'Snake in the Grass' by Helen Cresswell from *Baker's Dozen*, reprinted by permission of the author; 'The Story of Giant Kippernose' by John Cunliffe from *Giant Kippernose and Other Stories*, reprinted by permission of Andre Deutsch Ltd; 'The Dutch Cheese' from *Collected Stories for Children*, 'Old Shellover' and 'Nicholas Nye' by Walter de la Mare, reprinted by permission of the Literary Trustees of Walter de la Mare and The Society of Authors as their representative; 'The Dinner Lady Who Made Magic' by Dorothy Edwards,

# ACKNOWLEDGEMENTS

reprinted by permission of Deborah Rogers Ltd on behalf of the Estate of Dorothy Edwards; 'Blind Alley' and 'Boredom' by Eleanor Farjeon from *Silver Sand and Snow*, reprinted by permission of Michael Joseph Ltd and 'A Morning Song' by Eleanor Farjeon from *The Children's Bells*, reprinted by permission of Oxford University Press; 'Growing' by Max Fatchen from *Songs for My Dog and Other People* (Kestrel Books), reprinted by permission of Penguin Books Ltd; illustrations for 'The Wind in a Frolic' reproduced by permission of Peggy Fortnum; 'The Monkey and the Crocodile' by Paul Galdone, reprinted by permission of Worlds Work Ltd; illustration by Shirley Hughes for 'The Horrible Story' reproduced by permission of J. M. Dent & Sons Ltd; 'My Sister Jane' reprinted by permission of Faber & Faber Ltd from *Meet My Folks* by Ted Hughes; illustration for 'My Sister Jane' is reproduced from *Bulls Eyes* by permission of the Longman Group Ltd; illustrations by Susan Hunter for 'The Parrot Pirate Princess' in *Stories for Children* edited by Anne Wood, reproduced by permission of Hodder & Stoughton; 'Where Arthur Sleeps' from *Welsh Legends and Folk-Tales* retold by Gwyn Jones © Gwyn Jones 1955, reprinted by permission of Oxford University Press; 'Three Raindrops' by Terry Jones from *Fairy Tales*, reprinted by permission of Michael Joseph/Pavilion; 'A Fishy Tale or, How I Joined the Mixed Maggots and Bottom Feeders' reprinted by permission of Gene Kemp; 'The Cat That Walked by Himself' by Rudyard Kipling, reprinted by permission of The National Trust and Macmillan London Ltd; 'The Yellow Ribbon' by Maria Leach, reprinted by permission of World Publishing Co; 'Uninvited Ghosts' by Penelope Lively from *Big Dipper*, published by William Heinemann Ltd and reprinted by permission of A. P. Watt Ltd; 'First Day at School' by Roger McGough from *In the Glassroom*, reprinted by permission of Jonathan Cape Ltd; 'Gruesome' by Roger McGough from *You Tell Me*, reprinted by permission of A. D. Peters & Co Ltd; 'The Small Brown Mouse' by Janet McNeill reprinted by permission of Mrs Janet Alexander; 'The Horrible Story' by Margaret Mahy from *The Second Margaret Mahy Story Book*, reprinted by permission of the author and J. M. Dent & Sons Ltd; 'Send Three and Fourpence We are Going to a Dance' and 'The Coronation Mob' by Jan Mark from *Nothing to be Afraid of* (Kestrel Books), reprinted by permission of Penguin Books Ltd; 'Well Bread' and 'Bad Report – Good Manners' by Spike Milligan from *Unspun Socks from a Children's Laundry*, reprinted by permission of Michael Joseph Ltd; 'Pooh and Piglet Go Hunting' from *Winnie the Pooh* by A. A. Milne and 'A Thought' and 'Us Two' from *Now We Are Six* by A. A. Milne, reprinted by permission of Methuen Children's Books and McClelland & Stewart; 'The Rat Princess', 'A Growing Tale' and 'A Teeny-weeny Tale' by Norah Montgomerie and published by The Bodley Head are reprinted by permission of the author; 'Tikki Tikki Tembo' retold by Arlene Mosel, Copyright © 1968 by Arlene Mosel, reprinted by permission of Holt, Rinehart & Winston, Publishers; 'The Adventures of Isabel', 'The Cow' and 'The Camel' by Ogden Nash reprinted by permission of Curtis Brown, London and Curtis Brown, New York, on behalf of the Estate of Ogden Nash; 'Paul's Tale' by Mary Norton, reprinted by permission of Hughes Massie Ltd;

# ACKNOWLEDGEMENTS

'Daddy Fell into the Pond' by Alfred Noyes, reproduced by kind permission of the Trustees of the Alfred Noyes Estate; 'The Dark House' reprinted by permission of Oxford University Press from *The Lore and Language of Schoolchildren* by Iona and Peter Opie © Iona and Peter Opie 1959; illustrations by David Parkin for 'Send Three and Fourpence We are Going to a Dance', and 'The Coronation Mob' from *Nothing to Be Afraid Of*, reprinted by permission of Penguin Books Ltd; 'Guess' by Philippa Pearce from *The Shadow Cage* (Kestrel Books), reprinted by permission of Penguin Books Ltd; illustrations by Jan Pieńkowski for 'The Alarm Cock' reproduced by permission of Jonathan Cape Ltd; 'The Fool of the World and the Flying Ship' from *Old Peter's Russian Tales* by Arthur Ransome, reprinted by permission of Hamish Hamilton Ltd; 'Last One into Bed' and 'If you don't put your shoes on ...' by Michael Rosen from *You Can't Catch Me*, reprinted by permission of Andre Deutsch Ltd; 'You Tell Me' by Michael Rosen from *You Tell Me* (Kestrel Books), reprinted by permission of Penguin Books Ltd; 'What Did You Put in Your Pocket?' by Beatrice Schenk de Regniers from *Something Special*, reprinted by permission of Harcourt Brace Jovanovich Inc; line illustration by E. H. Shepard for 'Pooh and Piglet Go Hunting' copyright under the Berne convention, reproduced by permission of Curtis Brown, London and McClelland & Stewart; 'Lazy Tok' by Mervyn Skipper from *The Meeting Pool*, reprinted by permission of Angus & Robertson Ltd; 'Spells' and 'Little Fan' from *The Wandering Moon* by James Reeves, reprinted by permission of William Heinemann Ltd; the adaptation by James Reeves of Aesop's 'Hare and Tortoise' reprinted by permission of John Johnson Ltd; 'W' and 'Cows' from *The Blackbird in the Lilac* by James Reeves (1952) and 'The Well of the World's End' from *English Fables and Fairy Tales* retold by James Reeves (1954), reprinted by permission of Oxford University Press; 'The Witches' Call' by Clive Sansom from *The Golden Unicorn*, reprinted by permission of Methuen Children's Books; illustration by Posy Simmonds for 'It's Spring, It's Spring' from *Hot Dog and Other Poems*, reprinted by permission of Penguin Books Ltd; 'Tim Rabbit' reprinted by permission of Faber & Faber Ltd from *The Adventures of No Ordinary Rabbit* by Alison Uttley; illustrations by Fritz Wegner for 'The Story of Giant Kippernose' reproduced by permission of Andre Deutsch Ltd; 'The Snooks Family' by Harcourt Williams, taken from *Second Storytellers Choice* compiled by Eileen Colwell, reprinted by permission of The Bodley Head; 'Questions' by Raymond Wilson from *Rhyme and Rhythm Red Book* compiled by J. Gibson and R. Wilson, reprinted by permission of Macmillan, London and Basingstoke; 'It's Spring, It's Spring' by Kit Wright from *Hot Dog and Other Poems* (Kestrel Books), reprinted by permission of Penguin Books Ltd; 'Big Sister and Little Sister' by Charlotte Zolotow, reprinted by permission of Worlds Work Ltd.

Every effort has been made to trace copyright holders, but in a few cases this has proved impossible. The editor and publishers apologize for these unwilling cases of copyright transgression and would like to hear from any copyright holders not acknowledged.

*There are now more than 1,000 Puffin books
to choose from. A selection of anthologies appears
on the following pages.*

## THE GNOME FACTORY AND OTHER STORIES

*James Reeves*

The imagination of James Reeves's stories and the wit of Edward Ardizzone's drawings combine to make this enchanting collection.

## THE WILD RIDE AND OTHER SCOTTISH STORIES

*ed. Gordon Jarvie*

A spirited anthology of modern short stories from Scotland, ranging widely through ghost stories, adventure, drama and humour.

## GUARDIAN ANGELS

*ed. Stephanie Nettell*

An anthology of stories specially written to commemorate the prestigious Guardian Children's Books Award's 20th anniversary.

## TALES FOR THE TELLING

*Edna O'Brien*

A collection of heroic Irish tales to stir the imagination.

## STORIES FOR CHRISTMAS

*by Alison Uttley*

Chosen by Kathleen Lines

Blazing log fires, mince pies, red holly berries and the peal of church bells ringing out over snow-covered fields: the twelve stories in this collection capture the warmth and fun of Christmas as celebrated in the traditional country way that Alison Uttley knew and loved when she was a child.

## PUFFIN BOOK OF MODERN FAIRY STORIES

*Edited by Sara and Stephen Corrin*

Thirteen modern stories set firmly in a world of magic and enchantment, from A. A. Milne's deliciously funny 'Prince Rabbit' to the first part of Ted Hughes's magnificent modern myth 'The Iron Man'.

## STORIES FOR TENS AND OVER

*Edited by Sara and Stephen Corrin*

What's it like to lead a dog's life? Why did Lady Godiva ride naked through the streets of Coventry? Was it fun to live in Roman Britain? Dip into this selection of stories and you'll find all the answers and lots more to excite your imagination.

## COLLECTED STORIES FOR CHILDREN

*Walter de la Mare*

These sixteen strange tales offer, you might say, sixteen gateways into the country of Walter de la Mare, which is easy to enter, for it shares a border with fairytale, where witches, ogres and ghosts are regular citizens, and where everyone ready to risk it has a chance of a wish coming true.

## I'M TRYING TO TELL YOU

### Bernard Ashley

If you had a chance to talk about your school, what would you say . . . honestly?

Nerissa, Ray, Lyn and Prakash are all in the same class at Saffin Street School. Each of them has a story to tell about their school – sometimes dramatic, sometimes quiet, but always with a real sense of humour.

## GHOSTS THAT HAUNT YOU

### Edited by Aidan Chambers

Sometimes funny, sometimes horrifying, these ten ghost stories all involve young people in some way, and will keep readers of ten and over enthralled for hours.

## WITCH'S BREW

### Alfred Hitchcock

Witches sorceresses and a modern vampire feature in Alfred Hitchcock's cauldron of horrors. This heart-thumping collection of stories is guaranteed to give you the jitters.

## MR CORBETT'S GHOST AND STORIES

### Leon Garfield

Three chilling stories for those who like a shivery thrill.

## SWEETS FROM A STRANGER AND OTHER STRANGE TALES

### Nicholas Fisk

A collection of imaginative and macabre science fiction stories.

## WELSH LEGENDS AND FOLK TALES

*Gwyn Jones*

Heroic deeds and high adventure; some of the great stories from Welsh legend preserved in the *Mabinogion*, and retold to delight the reader of today.

## NOTHING TO BE AFRAID OF

*Jan Mark*

The characters in Jan Mark's stories are the sort of people who create their own imaginary world of horrors ... and then get trapped in it because these are the sort of horrors that won't go away. They follow you upstairs in the dark and slide under the bed, and there they stay ...

## ANIMAL STORIES

*Ruth Manning-Sanders*

True stories about such extraordinary animal characters as a tame gorilla that helped with the household chores, a fox that could fly, and a horse that made tea.

## WHAT THE NEIGHBOURS DID
### and Other Stories

*Philippa Pearce*

Gently humorous tales of 'ordinary' people's ordinary lives, told with the artistry and understanding of the author of *Tom's Midnight Garden*.

## THE SHADOW CAGE
### and Other Tales of the Supernatural
*Philippa Pearce*

The supernatural takes some unexpected forms in these ten eerie, gently menacing tales. Like all the best ghost stories, each one suggests more than it says as it unfolds quietly towards its chilling close.

## OLD PETER'S RUSSIAN TALES
*Arthur Ransome*

Firebirds and flying ships, step-mothers and -daughters, witches and princes. This is a brilliant collection of Russian fairy tales, told by one of our classic storytellers.

## MESSAGES
*Marjorie Darke*

A collection of shivery tales which you'd better not read alone . . .

## IMAGINE THAT!
*Sara and Stephen Corrin*

Fifteen fantastic tales, mostly traditional, from all over the world, including China and Asia.

## THE GHOST'S COMPANION
*ed. Peter Haining*

Thrilling ghost stories by well-known writers – and the incidents which first gave them the idea.

## WOOF!
### Allan Ahlberg

Eric is a perfectly ordinary boy. Perfectly ordinary that is, until the night when, safely tucked up in bed, he slowly but surely turns into a dog! Fritz Wagner's drawings illustrate this funny and exciting story superbly.

## VERA PRATT AND THE FALSE MOUSTACHES
### Brough Girling

There were times when Wally Pratt wished his mum was more ordinary and not the fanatic mechanic she was, but when he and his friends find themselves caught up in a real 'cops and robbers' affair, he is more than glad to have his mum, Vera, to help them.

## SADDLEBOTTOM
### Dick King-Smith

Hilarious adventures of a Wessex Saddleback pig whose white saddle is in the wrong place, to the chagrin of his mother.

## SLADE
### John Tully

Slade has a mission – to investigate life on Earth. When Eddie discovers the truth about Slade he gets a whole lot more adventure than he bargained for.

## A TASTE OF BLACKBERRIES
### Doris Buchanan Smith

The moving story about a young boy who has to come to terms with the tragic death of his best friend and the guilty feeling that he could somehow have saved him.

## COME BACK SOON
### *Judy Gardiner*

Val's family seem quite an odd bunch and their life is hectic but happy. But then Val's mother walks out on them and Val's carefree life is suddenly quite different. This is a moving but funny story.

## AMY'S EYES
### *Richard Kennedy*

When a doll changes into a man it means that anything might happen . . . and in this magical story all kinds of strange and wonderful things do happen to Amy and her sailor doll, the Captain. Together they set off on a fantastic journey on a quest for treasure more valuable than mere gold.

## ASTERCOTE
### *Penelope Lively*

Astercote village was destroyed by plague in the fourteenth century and Mair and her brother Peter find themselves caught up in a strange adventure when an ancient superstition is resurrected.

## THE HOUNDS OF THE MÓRRÍGAN
### *Pat O'Shea*

When the Great Queen Mórrígan, evil creature from the world of Irish mythology, returns to destroy the world, Pidge and Brigit are the children chosen to thwart her. How they go about it makes an hilarious, moving story, full of original and unforgettable characters.

## COME SING, JIMMY JO
### *Katherine Paterson*

An absorbing story about eleven-year-old Jimmy Jo's rise to stardom, and the problem of coping with fame.